A NEW LEASH ON LIFE

CHELSEA THOMAS

Big +
LITTLe
PRESS

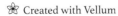 Created with Vellum

1

A DOGGONE SHAME

"Well you heard wrong, Mr. Crimper. I didn't kill anyone in Pine Grove. In fact, I helped catch the killer. There's a big difference." I blinked my big green eyes and straightened my A-line dress.

"That's what they all say." Gerard Crimper ran his tongue over his crooked, yellow teeth. "I know you did it."

I try to live my life guided by joy, optimism, and positivity. But it was my first day in business as the owner of the *Creature Comforts* pet salon in sunny Toluca Lake, CA, and the retired rock and roll guitarist was testing me.

It had been a long journey back to Toluca Lake after my brief time in Pine Grove, New York. My granny, Petunia, and I had taken a big risk on opening the pet grooming shop and I had bet my future on its success. But Gerard Crimper didn't seem to care about any of that. Nonetheless, I remained calm.

"Have you met and spoken with a lot of murderers in your day, Mr. Crimper?" I smiled, like we were having a polite conversation, even though we both knew we were not.

Gerard scoffed. "Of course not. I mean, there was one

guy on my '87 European tour that had a dark energy. But we didn't speak much."

"So what is it about me that makes you think I'm a killer?" I asked.

"Because I've heard all about you," said Gerard. "You've been causing nothing but trouble for years. For one, you married young, to that nice, tall, skinny boy from right here in Toluca Lake. Then you ran off on him in the middle of the night and broke his heart into dozens of minuscule, jagged pieces."

My face flushed red. Gerard was right about one thing: I had gotten married young. But he had the rest of it all wrong. I hadn't left my husband, he had skipped out on me. *Vicey-versey*, as my dad would say.

My ex-husband had been such a terrible stereotype. He'd left one day, saying he was going out for Band Aids, then he never returned. I would tell you his name but he doesn't deserve the dignity, so we'll just call him Beanstalk, 'cuz he was tall and skinny and had zero muscle on his body.

Do I sound bitter? I'm not. It's just true.

I was about to respond to Gerard when my best friend and employee, Betsy, rushed out of the back room, her face redder than mine. Betsy was short and squat. She always kept her hair in a tight top knot and she had fierce eyes that could strike fear into anyone. "Hey, mister! Amy didn't leave her husband, the Beanstalk left her. You're twisting the story and hurling wild, grotesque accusations. Well I know what you're up to. You're just trying to get free grooming for your cat. Despicable, good sir. We told you when you brought Fluffy in here: most cats don't get hair cuts. But you insisted. And now you're complaining about the haircut and spreading rumors about Amy? Unreal!"

Gerard shrugged. "I'm only repeating what everyone in

town has been saying for years. Amy shattered that kid's heart and left him in a pile of dirt. Then, from what I hear, she ruined another great relationship back in Pine Grove."

"Please stop bringing up all my failed relationships." I straightened my dress again. "I'm starting a new chapter here in Toluca Lake."

"But there were so many. It's fun." Gerard made eye contact with me. "Although I'll admit I'm surprised you found the time for dating between all the murders you committed."

I pressed my palms onto the counter and kept the tone of my voice even. "I didn't murder anyone."

Betsy took a step closer to me. "Don't play into this guy's games, Amy. He's trying to pressure you into giving him a discount. Crimper is famous around town for trying to weasel his way into discounts."

"I haven't mentioned a discount," said Gerard. "But since you keep bringing it up, you're absolutely right that I will not be paying full price for what you've done to my cat." Gerard held up a little pet carrier containing his white cat, Fluffy. "His name is Fluffy but you took away his fluff."

I peered in at Fluffy. He was a sweet Persian cat, pretty and white with gorgeous green eyes. And he had been more amenable to grooming than most felines. But it was true that I had cut his hair short. "Mr. Crimper," I said. "As Betsy mentioned, we warned you against Fluffy's haircut. But you said you wanted it short. So I gave him a short haircut. I think he looks beautiful."

"He's the most handsome cat in town," said Betsy.

Gerard's nostrils flared. "I want my money back."

"But—"

"I want a refund!" said Gerard. "You ruined my cat. And you're a murderer. And you take advantage of men and treat them like they're disposable. You're never going to last in Toluca Lake. The people of this town were lucky when you left all those years ago and we don't want you back."

Betsy took a step toward the guy. "You take that back, you washed up loser! Amy is a treasure. Do you know how much I missed her? I haven't had anyone to stay up late with for ten years. You better not scare her away."

Crimper grunted. "I don't need to do any scaring! This town'll do it for me. If I don't get a full refund I'm going to leave a scathing review online that will keep everyone in Southern California away from *Creature Comforts* for life."

My heart sank like that giant blue necklace in the *Titanic*.

Remember that necklace? It was pretty but so impractical. To what kind of event would one wear that? Probably only a party on the *Titanic*. Anyway, my heart sank hard and fast. Gerard was right. If he left a bad review of the pet salon on my first day in business, it would hurt our chances of ever finding success in Toluca Lake. I couldn't afford for that to happen. So I swallowed my pride, punched a few keys on my computer, and issued the unfriendly man his refund.

He slid the cash into his wallet with a sly grin, then looked back up at me. "Don't think this means you're safe in this town. I notified the police of your presence and your checkered past."

With that, Gerard turned and exited. I didn't know it at the time, but he was the one who would not be around for long.

...because Gerard Crimper was murdered that night.

GRANNY KNOWS BEST

*M*y grandma, Petunia, was the smartest, toughest, most determined eighty year-old in all of Toluca Lake. Actually, I think she was the smartest, toughest lady of any age!

Her license said she was 5'1" but she was at least two inches shorter than that. And there's no way she weighed more than ninety five pounds. But she was tough like a bulldog with a bone, she had a gravelly voice, and she never backed down from a fight...ever.

Back in the 80s, Granny had been a train conductor working out of the Amtrak station in Burbank, California. She always says the job toughened her up and taught her how to deal with every type of obnoxious person. After she gave up conducting, she worked as a lunch lady at Toluca High School for a bit. Then she moved to Pine Grove, New York and opened a successful flower shop. Granny says the flower shop was phase one of her retirement, but she worked hard in Pine Grove, and she was a pillar of the community, whether the community liked it or not.

While in New York, Granny also developed a skill for

all varieties of poker games and amassed quite a nice payday from her winnings. Most of that money was earned in the cafeteria of her 'active senior living' community, but Granny had also found success playing online poker and participating in tournaments down on the Jersey Shore.

Granny enjoyed her time in Pine Grove. She didn't even mind when dead bodies started popping up in the cute small town. But it was her idea for the two of us to move back to Toluca Lake to open *Creature Comforts*. She said it would be good for me to get back to my roots, and she wanted the two of us to have some bonding time "like on TV."

Granny entered the shop a few minutes after Gerard left. Her head bounced back and forth like a bobblehead doll as we told her about Gerard's antics. Then, when we were finally done, she let out an annoyed sigh. "I hate that Crimper. He thinks he's so tough. He's been bullying his way through this town for years. He's not very good at guitar, either. He acts like a rock 'n roll legend but his playing is too busy and his solos lack melody."

Betsy's eyes lit up. "How do you know what makes a good guitar solo?"

"Because I'm active listener, that's how. I'm sorry I wasn't here for Crimper's visit. I would have kicked him out just like I used to kick him off my trains. Little weasel used to try to steal rides up and down the California coast. He was a diabolical, despicable, disgrace. You said you gave him a full refund?"

I hung my head and muttered. "Yeah..."

"That was the right thing to do." Granny pointed right at me. "You're an excellent businessperson. That's why I wanted to open this place with you."

I raised my head a little higher. Granny was a tough critic, so her compliments meant a lot.

Betsy bit her bottom lip. "Petunia, do you think I'm great at business too? Are you proud to be working with me?"

Granny wrinkled her nose. "What? I'm not in business with you! You're my employee."

Betsy slumped her shoulders.

Granny rolled her eyes. "Sorry. Yes, Betsy. I'm oh-so-thrilled to be working with you. Hooray."

I shot my grandma a look. "Granny."

Granny rolled her eyes. "Betsy knows I love her. I'm just an aggressive communicator."

Betsy glanced over at me. "I love you too, Gran Gran."

"Don't ever call me that again."

Betsy looked down. "Sorry."

Granny took a step back and looked around the salon. "We've really outdone ourselves in this place. It looks great."

I stepped beside Granny and took in the scene. The shop was emerald green with gold accents. The back wall had a huge mural of a puppy and kitten on it, which we had hired a local artist to paint. And it said "Creature Comforts" in enormous, swirling letters. There were a couple of stainless steel wash basins, also known as 'pet spas,' along the side of the room. And there was a line of kennels nearby where freshly-groomed pets waited to be picked up by their owners.

Quick tangent: 'kennel' is a word that tends to have a negative connotation, like jail for cats and dogs. But at *Creature Comforts*, I pampered every pet and each kennel was decked out like a penthouse suite at the Four Seasons. There were big, plush cushions for napping, bowls of spring water and top-of-the-line snacks, free of charge. Plus, every animal got played with on a regular schedule between grooming and pick up, and each kennel was decorated in my trademark green and gold color scheme.

Granny let out a satisfied sigh as she admired the décor. Then she walked toward the kennels and knit her brow. "Why is Mr. Buttons still here?" Granny asked. "Megan wanted him back by now."

Mr. Buttons was my sister Megan's pretty but snobby Pomeranian. And Granny was right, he was still in the kennels, looking like a bored prince.

"She hasn't come to get him," I said.

"Megan signed up for home delivery after grooming," Granny said. "Look."

Granny hurried over to the computer and typed a few commands with incredible speed. All her time playing online poker had made her a technology wizard. A screen popped up after a few seconds, showing Megan's reservation details. Granny was right. My sister had requested home delivery. To be honest, it was a service I had not been sure about offering. Home delivery takes a lot of time and therefore costs money. But my business was new and I needed to show people how much I cared. I glanced down the rest of my schedule for the day. I had five more pets to groom. Now I also had to make a home delivery?

"I can take care of it, boss," said Betsy. "Megan hates my guts and thinks I'm weird but that doesn't bother me. I still think she's gonna warm up. Maybe after twenty more years."

I chuckled. "It's fine. Thank you, Betsy. But I'll deliver Mr. Buttons right now. I need to see more of my sister, anyway."

Seconds later, I stepped outside and let the southern sun drench my cheeks. A cool breeze swept the heat of the sun away just when my face got hot and I looked around and took in the sights of Toluca Lake.

Creature Comforts was at the far end of Main Street in a French style building from the 1920's. When I was growing up in the area, the building had housed a charming little coffee shop called *Priscilla's Cafe*. I'd always loved going to *Priscilla's* for hot chocolate and a croissant, so I was excited to grab the space for the pet salon. It had a good energy, and the location couldn't be beat.

My favorite grocery store, *Trader John's*, was a few blocks down the road. There was also a juice bar called *Johnny's Juice*, next door. And my favorite restaurant, the *Big Baby Diner,* was a short walk down the road. The *Big Baby* had been in the same spot since the 50's, it had great food and, best of all, it was open 24 hours.

Palm trees lined the street. There were big, wide sidewalks on both sides. And on either side of the main drag were sprawling neighborhoods of adorable houses stretching in every direction. My favorite homes in Toluca Lake were little storybook houses, with sloping roofs, turrets, and ivy winding up the walls. But the neighborhood had houses in every architectural style, which I had always found charming and unique.

The little town of Toluca Lake felt like a secluded enclave, but it was only twenty minutes from downtown Los Angeles and less than an hour from LA's famous beaches.

Although the area was jammed with beautiful homes, my sister and I were raised by our single father in a small Toluca Lake apartment. We didn't have much growing up, at least not by SoCal standards. But our dad had always taught us to appreciate the small things in life. As kids, for instance, he regularly took us on trips to the desert to expand our minds and teach us how to survive in nature and appreciate natural beauty. Toluca Lake had never required a lot of rugged living, but nonetheless my survival skills had proven useful many times. Back in New York, I spent many nights camping under the stars after my ex stole my RV and disappeared with another woman. But that's a story for another time...

As I stood there that afternoon, appreciating my quaint little town, I wondered if I would ever need my skills again. I had no idea how much I would or how quickly...

I loaded Mr. Buttons into my green and gold *Creature Comforts* van and got behind the wheel. "OK, Mr. Buttons. Time to go see Megan. Are you excited?"

Mr. Buttons looked at me from inside his crate. I laughed. "You don't get excited about much, do you? You're not a typical Pomeranian. In fact, you kind of remind me of a poodle."

Mr. Buttons barked once, loud. I laughed. "OK, I get it," I said. "I'm sorry for comparing you to a poodle."

Three minutes later, I was parked out in front of Megan's two-story, Tudor home. The lawn was immaculate. Beautiful lilies lined the front walk. A crisp American flag blew in the wind. I rang the doorbell. Seconds later, my phone buzzed with a text message. It was from Megan. "Bring Mr. Buttons inside. Back door open."

Isn't my sister fun? Such an efficient communicator.

I strapped a leash onto Mr. Buttons and led him toward the back of the house. He walked slowly, as if he was strolling through the Los Angeles *Museum of Modern Art.* I tugged on the leash a little. "Come on, Mr. Buttons. Aunt Amy has a lot of other dogs to groom today. Maybe you can stop and contemplate the existential value of life on your own time."

I'll be honest. When I saw Megan's in-ground pool dotted with relaxing, neon pool toys, jealousy buzzed around my head like a swarm of gnats. But I quickly reminded myself that everyone has their own path in life. Some people do great in school and become lawyers with happy families who work from home. Other people get their hearts stomped on hundreds of times, move in with their Granny and try to open a dog salon in their hometown. Deep down, I knew I was the lucky one. I got to work with animals all day. But that pool sure looked nice.

My phone buzzed with another text. "What are you doing? Come inside." I looked up at the house. Megan waved at me from a second story window and flashed me a thumbs up.

I tugged on Mr. Buttons' leash, slid open the back door, and went inside. The home was cool and shadowy and it smelled like lavender. It was decorated in a midcentury modern style with perfect, angular furniture. There was an expressionist portrait of Megan with her husband and their daughter, Haley, above the mantle. I gave the people in the photo a little wave and led Mr. Buttons upstairs. I wondered if their expressionist eyes followed me as I went.

I found Megan working at her treadmill desk in her office. If you're not sure what a treadmill desk is, it's exactly what it sounds like. It's a treadmill with a desk attached for working. Megan was typing at a laptop when I entered. I walked over and she held up her pointer finger to indicate that I should give her a minute. Then she spoke into the microphone headset. "Barry, Barry. I'm going to need you to shut up. Can you stop talking? My sister is here and she's more important than you." Megan winked at me. "OK. We'll talk later, we'll get the deal done. You know I always get the deal done, Barry. Are you still talking?"

Megan removed her headset and looked over at me. "Amy. You're here. Thank you so much for bringing Mr.

Buttons over. I'm so busy I haven't had a chance to stop walking all day."

I smiled. My sister had a specific personality that some found, uh, grating. But she was honest and always straightforward and she made me laugh.

"Did your eyes get greener?" Megan asked. "They look greener. So, so gorgeous."

I laughed. "I saw you last week when I got into town. My eyes are the same now as they were then."

"Well they've always been gorgeous," said Megan. "And you got those great eyelashes. Not like me. Mine are short and stumpy."

I shrugged. "But the rest of my body is short and stumpy. So you beat me there."

"You're four feet and eleven inches of pure beauty, sister," said Megan. "Blonde hair, green eyes, built like a Russian gymnast. What girl doesn't dream of that growing up?"

In case you were wondering, my sister is built like a supermodel. She's at least a full foot taller than me and her eyelashes are just as long. But she's always been jealous of mine. Maybe 'cuz they seem proportionally longer in comparison to the rest of me.

"How was my Mr. Buttons?" Megan asked, changing speeds in conversation and on her treadmill.

"He was good."

"Contemplative?" Megan asked.

"That's a good word for it. You've got a deep dog here, Meg."

Megan laughed. "I've been teaching him to meditate. But I think he's using his new focused energy to try and trick me into buying fancier dog food."

"Do you maybe want to stop walking for a second?" I said. "You're making me tired just looking at you."

"I forgot I was walking," said Megan, pausing the treadmill. She stepped off the device and wiped a tiny bead of sweat from her forehead. "How are you holding up, anyway? I've been meaning to call you after what happened."

I narrowed my eyes. "I wasn't aware anything happened."

Megan winced. "Oh sweetheart. You haven't seen Gerard Crimper's review."

ALL PRESS IS GOOD PRESS

*M*egan did a quick search of my business name on Google, opened to my only review, and handed me the computer. She was right. Gerard Crimper had reviewed *Creature Comforts*. And here's what he had to say:

"Look, everybody around Toluca Lake knows who I am, right? I've been a staple in this community since I was a kid. Some know me as a guitar prodigy. Some are fans of my work with *Liquid Staple*. To some of you, I'm just a cool dude, a friendly face, someone to down a little whiskey with on a hot summer night. Hey man, we all know the neighborhood has changed over the past two decades. We didn't used to have all of these annoying businesses popping up, trying to sell us things. Toluca Lake used to be total farm country and it was all quaint shops and little tea rooms and cafés. Look, people, I'm a raw guy. I'm truthful and honest. And it's not like I'm against all that stuff. But we need businesses in Toluca Lake that are honest and reputable and staffed by good people.

Creature Comforts, the new pet salon that opened up at

the end of Main Street, does not meet that standard. If you haven't heard already, the woman who runs this place committed a murder in a town called Pine Grove, New York. Somehow she got away with it but mark my words, she's a killer. Don't believe her happy face and her calm demeanor or any of that. I found out about all of this murder scandal after I dropped my cat, Fluffy, off in that murder den. I rushed back to pick Fluffy up but this homicidal woman had already groomed him.

You all know Fluffy. You know him because his name fits his aesthetic. Fluffy is a fluffy cat. He's the fluffiest cat in Toluca Lake. If there were awards for fluffiest cat, which there should be but that's another topic for another time, Fluffy would win that award every year. Well, I went into *Creature Comforts* and asked if they could give Fluffy a trim. I specifically remember that I used the word trim. And that killer did a hack job like I've never seen before. Used a razor and shaved Fluffy down. Fluffy looks sick now. He looks like one of those creepy cats with no hair at all. I barely recognize him!

You know, I spent so many years on the road with my band, *Liquid Staple*, and I met plenty of broads like this Amy chick. She just wants to meet men, chew them up, and spit them out. She's a liar and a cheater. She shouldn't be in our community and she shouldn't be allowed anywhere near our precious loved ones, not Fluffy or any other pet.

All those years on the road, I had to live without an animal companion. It's just weird to have a kitty when you're in a legendary rock and roll band. And a lot of the other guys don't want to have kitty litter on the tour bus. I spent all my spare time during those touring years dreaming of the day I could finally get a cat. Fluffy is the cat I dreamed of. At least he was. Now he's been shaved down so deep I'm not sure if his fur will ever grow back.

Boycott *Creature Comforts* pet salon. Do it for your community. Do it for your pets.

Gerard Crimper, out.

P.S. Check out my solo album, *Metallic Aftertaste*, streaming all over the Internet now. This album is my masterwork and I reached deep into my soul for it.

P.P.S. Say no to *Creature Comforts*. Protect this community."

THE REVIEWS ARE IN

*G*ranny and I lived in a cute little apartment complex about a mile from *Creature Comforts*. The apartment complex, designated for residents 55 and older, was called *Toluca Gardens*. The board had approved me living with Granny on the condition that I actively seek housing of my own. I didn't have a problem with that because I was only thirty... Nowhere near ready for retirement living. But the Gardens were a nice place to settle for a bit, and the slow pace of life calmed me.

The apartments at *Toluca Gardens* all faced a pool in the courtyard, which was surrounded by big, beautiful palms. The place was Southern California living at its finest. Granny told me she had been lucky to grab a spot in the building when it had opened up and her apartment there was adorable. She had floral wallpaper, floral art on the walls, flowers on all the kitchen towels. Although Granny had a tough personality, she loved flowers. What can I say?

That evening I arrived home to find Granny watching *Jeopardy!* at top volume with her feet up on an ottoman.

"Amy. You're finally home. Perfect. Let's gamble on the next *Jeopardy!* question. Ten bucks says I get it right."

"I know this trick, Granny. You're watching a rerun."

Granny widened her eyes. "I'm not watching a rerun. That scam is old! And I don't run scams, anyway." She paused the TV and words popped up on screen confirming that the episode was airing live. "See. This is a live broadcast."

I sat on the couch next to Granny and grabbed a butter cookie off a plate on the coffee table. "OK. But I'll only bet five dollars."

"Your loss," said Granny.

I looked around the little, floral apartment. The furniture was plush and comfy. The wallpaper was busy and bright. Every spare surface was covered in real, blooming flowers. The place might've been overwhelming to some people, but to the granddaughter of a florist, it felt like home.

"We ready to rumble with this?" Granny asked, tapping her foot. "I'm touched by your observation of my stylish home, but I haven't been able to find a good poker game out here yet and it's killing me."

"What happened to all your old poker buddies?" I asked.

"Moved, dead, dying, or broke. I haven't managed to track down all of them yet so I've still got my fingers crossed that I'll find a few that still know how to play."

I laughed.

"Are you ready?" said Granny.

"I'm ready."

Granny pressed play and *Jeopardy!* sprung to life. The question required an intimate knowledge of global currencies. Alex had barely uttered the word currency when I removed a five dollar bill from my wallet and handed it to

Granny. "You win. The only thing I know about currency is that I need more of it. You see Gerard Crimper's review, by the way?"

Granny paused the TV and looked over at me. "It's no fun when you give me the money before we're done with the question."

"Do you want to give the money back?"

Granny tucked the five dollar bill into her pocket with a little smirk. "What review?"

I read Granny the review out loud. It wasn't any easier to swallow the second time around and by the time I finished, she was pacing across the room in anger. "That guy is unbelievable. I hate the way he writes like he's some kind of rock star. *Liquid Staple* was never a popular band. They only went to Europe that one time because Crimper's parents knew the tour promoter."

"Really? He acts like it was a big success."

Granny waved me away. "He talks and talks and talks but he says nothing. And what's with that ridiculous P.S.? I'm not going to listen to his solo project. *Metallic Aftertaste!?* Why would I ever put metal in my mouth? What's wrong with this guy? He can't go around defecating on your good reputation like that."

I chuckled in spite of myself at Granny's florid language. "Do you think people will believe him?"

"No one in Toluca Lake believes anything that guy says."

My shoulders relaxed a bit. "OK, good. So we don't need to take action. I can trust that people around here won't boycott my business based off one bad review."

"I didn't say that," said Granny. "People who know you will trust you, of course. But you've been gone for ten years. And I've been gone for a while too. There are plenty of new people in town. They may not know how stupid Crimper is or what a wonderful kid you are. No, we need to do something."

"What do you have in mind?" I said. "Megan said I could sue the guy but I'm not a litigious person. I like to face my problems head-on and not leave anything up to the court. I think if I take action—"

"Spare me the speech, Amy. I'm trying to think."

I slid to the edge of my seat. "You think I should sue?"

"No way. Your sister only said that because she wants you to hire her. Besides, Crimper's broke, as far as I know. There's nothing to sue for unless you want an old guitar worth less than it was ten years ago."

"I can't play guitar."

"I know."

"Megan also said it's sad that I'm living with you," I said.

"Well, you know it's pathetic," said Granny. "You're a grown woman living with your grandmother. But neither of us think this is long-term. You're going to find a place to live that's closer to *Creature Comforts*. Your sister is also my granddaughter, and I love that girl, but sometimes she stirs the pot when it doesn't need stirring. She just puts too much salt in the soup."

"Too much salt in the soup? Is that an expression?"

"No. Whenever she makes me soup, I end up dreaming I'm dying of thirst for hours at night. I drink the entire cup of water I put next to the bed and I still feel thirsty. You need to tell her to change her recipe."

I held up my hands. "That's not my battle. She never made me soup."

"Weren't we talking about something completely different?" said Granny. "Right. Crimper."

I nodded. "Maybe we can make him a pie and go over and give it to him and treat him nice and he'll take it down."

Granny shook her head. "That may be how they did things over in Pine Grove. But I like to take a more forceful approach."

I furrowed my brow. "What do you mean by that?"

Granny smirked. "You'll see. First thing in the morning."

5

LIQUID STAPLE GUN

*T*he next morning, I shuffled into the kitchen to find Granny sitting at the breakfast bar, drinking coffee and flipping through a copy of *PEOPLE* magazine.

"Morning, Granny."

She flipped the page. "These celebrities have ridiculous lives. You'd think with all that money they'd find a way to be happy. But all they do is argue and sleep with each other."

"Maybe there's such a thing as too much money," I said. "Or maybe they're all secretly broke."

I went to the coffee machine and poured myself a cup. Like Granny, I preferred my coffee strong, black, and served in a mug shaped like the face of a dog. That morning, I chose a pug. When the hot liquid touched my lips, they curled up in a smile. Forget diamonds. Coffee is a girl's best friend.

I grabbed a seat next to Granny at the breakfast bar and peered over at her magazine. "You hardly watch movies or TV. What do you care about celebrities?"

"Just cuz I don't watch TV shows doesn't mean I can't appreciate gossip about strangers' lives. In fact, it's better this way. I don't know these people from anything other than these magazines. Feels like I'm reading about my own neighbors."

"You gossip plenty about your neighbors, too."

"You say that like it's a bad thing," said Granny. "All those years living in an RV with Zach warped your mind. You forgot what it's like to live in a community."

Wince. Zach. Gross. "It wasn't years, it was a few months. And can we not say his name?"

Granny groaned. "You already have me calling the other guy Beanstalk. What do you want to call this one? He was hairy. Should I call him Furball?"

I giggled. "Furball. Perfect. Beanstalk and Furball from here on out."

Granny snorted. "You need to start dealing with your past."

I shuddered. My past was something no one should ever have to deal with. A dead mom, a complicated dad. Two boyfriends who might as well be dead. Years wasted with both of them. No. No way I was trying to deal with any of that. "I'm not concerned about the past. The future is my time to shine. And the present. Speaking of which, I thought you had a plan for how we were going to deal with Gerard Crimper."

"Relax," said Granny. "The bakery doesn't open until eight."

I scrunched up my nose. "Bakery?"

Forty-five minutes later, Granny and I stood at the foot of *Eleanor's Bakery*, one of my favorite little shops in Toluca Lake. *Eleanor's* was in a two-story brick building right in the center of town. It had a big front window with the name of the shop written in beautiful maroon lettering. The inside was packed with oversized arm chairs. And Eleanor made the best baked goods in all of California.

"OK," I said. "Why are we here and what does it have to do with Gerard Crimper?"

Granny pointed to the second story of the building. "He lives right up there."

I chuckled. "You really needed to surprise me like this?"

"What can I say, I have a flair for the dramatic. I owe it to the three months I spent in drama club in high school. But that was only because I had a crush on the drama boy, Theodore. I know, I'm not one for romance typically. But Theodore was seven feet tall and built like an oak tree. And boy did he have—"

"Alright, Granny. I'm sure Theo was great, but I don't wanna know." I motioned to a side door beside the bake shop entrance. "Does that door lead up to Gerard's apartment?"

"Sure. But I can't pick a fight with a failed musician until I've had my morning nourishment." Granny pushed open the door to the bakeshop and I followed two steps behind.

Eleanor of *Eleanor's Bakeshop* looked like a cardboard cutout of Mrs. Claus. She was short with curly gray hair. Bifocals perched at the end of her nose. And her voice was squeaky and cute as could be. "Petunia and Amy. My favorite new business owners on Main Street. How are you?"

Eleanor hurried out from behind the counter. She gave me a big hug, then she gave Granny a big hug, then she stepped back to look at us. "Petunia, you're looking so good, I'm not sure which of you is which."

That seemed more like an insult to me than a compliment to my grandma, but I took it in stride. "I'm the grand-daughter. I can't believe you remember me."

"Amy! How could I forget? Do you still love chocolate chip muffins?"

I blinked a few times in surprise. "That's right. Do you still make them?"

Eleanor hurried behind the counter and pulled two big, beautiful chocolate chip muffins from the display. I looked around at the other customers to see if they were processing the magnitude and beauty of Eleanor's hospitality. A bald man was reading a book, distracted. A mother was feeding her baby a bottle. So only Granny and I witnessed Eleanor's wonderful reveal.

"You better believe we're paying for those muffins, Eleanor," said Granny.

Eleanor let out a twinkly laugh. "Not a chance, Petunia. Don't make me get out my boxing gloves because I will take you down."

"You think you can take me, old lady? I'll get you square in the jaw and then I'll mop the floors with your curly gray hair."

I looked between Eleanor and Granny. I hadn't expected this conversation to turn violent so quick. But the two of them were having a great time. Verbally sparring, thankfully.

After a few more minutes of strangely aggressive banter, Granny got down to business. "By the way... Is the *Liquid Staple* gun home?"

Eleanor rolled her eyes. "He stays up until three in the morning every night and he doesn't wake up till noon. The guy still thinks he's a teenage rock star. Was he ever a rock star at any age?"

"Not sure," said Granny. "But he's dumb as a sack of rocks."

"You're bad," said Eleanor.

"You know it."

Granny and I thanked Eleanor for our muffins, then we marched outside and reentered the building through Gerard's side door. Granny hopped up the steps like a woman fifty years her junior. Then she pounded on the door like an angry cop. "Crimper. Open up. I have several bones to pick with you. And these are not dog bones. They're the real deal."

"What's happening?" I said. "What's the plan?"

She shrugged. "Not sure but it felt right."

Granny knocked on the door three more times. Then she tried the handle and the door opened with a quiet creak. Granny looked at me. "This guy sleeps with his door unlocked? I thought he was suspicious there was a murderer in Toluca Lake."

I shook my head. "Clearly that was all a lie. What should we do?"

Granny pushed the door open all the way. "I say an open door is an invitation to enter."

I entered Gerard Crimper's apartment and the hairs on my arms stood on end. The place looked like it had been burglarized. The coffee table was flipped upside down and shattered. Papers were strewn everywhere. And the television set was toppled over, a giant crack splintering across the screen.

Granny and I exchanged a nervous look. "This isn't good," I said.

Granny shook her head. "Not at all. Do you think…"

"No way," I said. "We left that kind of thing behind in Pine Grove."

Granny took a step into the room. "Gerard? Are you in here you stinker? Hello? Stinky!"

"Maybe we shouldn't shouldn't call him stinky, just in case he is..." I swallowed hard. "Gerard?"

No response. I spotted a door across the living room, presumably leading into the bedroom. I gestured toward the door. "I'm going to look in there. Do you want to come?"

"I'm right behind you, kid. Careful now."

I crept toward what I presumed to be the bedroom door with gentle steps. I tiptoed over the broken coffee table and noticed an old pizza box nearby with the crust still in it. My eyes scanned the room. There were empty beer bottles and fast food wrappers everywhere. I pointed out a few of the empty bottles to Granny. "Either this guy had a party in the past few days or he does not have a healthy lifestyle."

"Just open the door," said Granny. "Don't judge."

I reached out to open the door, holding my breath. Then I grabbed the handle and turned, preparing myself for anything...

6

MUSIC TO MY EARS

*G*erard Crimper was dead. Face down on his bedroom floor with blood pooled around his head.

I opened my mouth to speak but it was suddenly dry as Death Valley. My heartbeat drummed in my temples at a hundred beats per minute.

"This...might have been an accident," Granny said.

I turned back to Granny. "This was a murder, Granny. Gerard Crimper was reviled throughout town. And who knows how many enemies he made during his touring days. This place was ransacked. Maybe the killer was looking for something or maybe there was a scuffle. But it's clear to me this was no accident."

Granny held onto the wall to steady herself. She blinked rapidly, like a malfunctioning doll. "Dead body... Blood... Not what I expected..."

"I think you're in shock, Granny. You don't need to stand here looking at this body for any longer. Let's go back out to the other room."

I took Granny by the hand and led her into the living room. Then I pulled out a bottle of water from my purse and handed it to her. Granny took a sip and the color returned to her face.

"That was a lot to process," Granny said. "Still, I'm surprised I freaked out like that. I'm normally such a poker-faced stoic. I'm better now."

I put my hand on Granny's shoulder. "Are you sure? It makes sense that you had a strong reaction. That was a strong image in there."

"I'm fine." Granny waved away my concerns. "I was just surprised, that's all. You know me, Amy. I don't scare easy. Now let's get back in there so we can start to solve this crime."

"Hold on a second. I think you spent a little too long in Pine Grove. We don't need to solve this mystery. We need to report it to the cops."

"The cops in Toluca Lake are worse than the police in Pine Grove. They're not going to solve this thing."

"Granny," I said with caution in my voice, "I really don't think we should go back in there. You almost fainted."

Granny scoffed. "I did not almost faint. I've never seen a dead body before that wasn't already on a stretcher. That's all. You're exaggerating, anyway. I was fine the whole time."

"Well we just got back into town and we're launching a business. We shouldn't throw ourselves into some crazy murder investigation." I pulled out my smart phone. "I'm calling the police and you can't stop me."

"Do whatever you want, sweetheart, but I'm going to be looking for clues."

I stepped into the kitchen and placed a call to the Toluca Lake Police Department. The phone rang fifteen times before someone answered. Whoever picked up sounded like a 200-year-old man. He was confused and slow-talking and complained several times that I had woken him from a nap.

But I was persistent and I didn't hang up until the ancient sloth man promised to send someone over to Gerard's apartment. I hung up the phone and walked back into the living room. Granny was nowhere to be found.

Then she called to me from Gerard's bedroom. "Amy. Come here. You need to see this."

I entered the bedroom. Granny was standing on the far side of the bed pointing at a little tray table that held a bottle of champagne, a bucket of melted ice, and a dozen red roses.

"Crimper was trying to romance some unlucky woman last night," Granny said. "Thank goodness she made it out alive."

I stepped closer to get a better look at the romantic display. "I don't think the unlucky woman showed up in the first place," I said, pointing at the champagne. "The champagne wasn't opened."

Granny smirked. "You picked up a thing or two from those ladies in Pine Grove."

I shrugged. "All I did was observe that the cork is still in the bottle. I don't think that requires any expert skills of detection."

Granny scooted her way around the bed, back over to the main part of the bedroom. I took the opportunity to look more closely at my surroundings. I mean, why not? I was in there, waiting for the police. Might as well look around.

The bedroom walls were covered in posters of Gerard's band, *Liquid Staple*. The posters were all dark black with red writing and Gerard's face was visible in a few of them. There were also a couple of angular, black guitars hung on the wall. It looked like the entire room had been rigged for surround sound, with a speaker in every corner. Except one of the speakers was no longer in its corner and instead lay beside Gerard's limp body. There was blood on the edge of the speaker. I pointed down at it. "Murder weapon?"

Granny nodded. "Murdered by a cheap speaker. That's an ironic way to go."

I let out a deep sigh. "Poor guy. Who knows what could have happened here? Maybe he was just sitting at home when someone broke in and killed him. I know he wasn't everybody's favorite—"

"He was hated by all," said Granny. "That's an important distinction."

"Well I didn't know him enough to hate him," I said. "Sure, he left a nasty review for the salon. And I definitely didn't like him. But maybe he was having a bad day. Maybe he had a hangnail or one of those annoying sores on the inside of his cheek. Those sores are enough to make anyone do almost anything. Whenever I get one it makes me wanna scream so hard I hurt my vocal cords."

Granny chuckled.

"I'm glad that delights you," I said.

"I'm sorry but the thought of you with damaged vocal cords is hysterical. You're so chatty all the time. How do you communicate with people if your voice is broken?"

"I didn't say I stopped talking," I said. "But I did say that I don't want to investigate this murder. I stepped away for one ridiculously long, slow conversation with the old man who answers the emergency line at the police station and when I come back, here you are, snooping around."

"It's almost like I have a mind of my own," said Granny. "You wanna know what took you so long? You got Chief Samuel."

"That guy's the police chief? He sounded like Methuselah!"

"Oh, yeah, he's been chief for years. But he's mostly a figurehead. Like the mermaid on the front of a boat."

"Well, I'm sure the department is capable of figuring this out." I shuffled back out into the living room. Granny followed. I gestured at all of the empty fast food containers. "This guy was living a pretty depressing life before he got killed. Can't you imagine him sitting here, gorging himself on fast food, pining after some woman who doesn't even show up when he invites her over for champagne and roses? Murdered in his own bedroom, his only friend a fluffy Persian cat whose beautiful coat was ruined by an overzealous groomer..." I squatted down to look under the couch. "Hold on a second. Where is Fluffy? He should be here somewhere."

Granny shrugged. "Maybe the cat killed him. Got sick of him blasting his own music from those stupid speakers and bashed him in the head."

"Fluffy is a sweet boy. He wouldn't do something like that."

"I don't think the man was really killed by his cat, Amy."

I stood up and patted my leg with my hand. I clicked my tongue. "Kitty. Here, Fluffy." I whistled and snapped. "Fluffy. Here, kitty. Here kitty, kitty."

That's when I spotted a pair of little green eyes peering out at me from under a pile of trash in the kitchen. "There you are." I pointed over in that direction. "Look, Granny. He's hiding. He must have been there all night. Poor guy was here for the whole thing."

I pulled a few cat treats from my purse and held them out in Fluffy's direction. The once-fluffy feline slowly crept out from underneath the pile of garbage, shedding candy wrappers and soda cans as he got closer to me. I gave him a little smile as I set down a treat and stepped back. "There you go. There's nothing to be scared of. Everything is OK now."

Suddenly, there was a loud knock on the front door and Fluffy scurried away with the treat in his mouth. I turned to the door and there stood a young police officer with a broad chest and big, brown eyes.

I hadn't seen him in years, but I knew the cop was named Mike Fine. How did I know? Because he was the most popular kid my year at Toluca High.

7

FINE AS FROG HAIR

I hate to say it but Mike Fine looked, well, fine. His blue police officer uniform was tight-fitting around his biceps, his caramel skin glistened in the fluorescent overheads of the apartment, and his stubbled jaw was strong and sharp.

"Did someone here call the police department about a dead body?"

I half raised my hand. "That was me. Hi, Mike."

He looked me up and down. "I'm sorry. Do I know you?"

I couldn't believe it. He didn't even remember me?! "It's me, Amy. From high school. We sat next to each other for an entire year of chemistry." That was kind of ironic, considering we never got along, I thought.

Mike broke out into a big smile. "Amy. Of course. Hey! I thought you were over in New York City or something. At least that's what I heard. You're back in town?"

Mike's smile was friendly. Much friendlier than I had expected, and much friendlier than I remembered from high school. Back then, Mike was one of those apathetic jocks who never took the time to be nice to anyone. His new, kind demeanor caught me off guard, so I stammered for a few seconds before I spoke.

"Um...... Yeah. I did some traveling for the past few years but I just opened a pet salon here in town."

Mike pointed at me. "*Creature Comforts*!?"

I smiled. "Yeah. You know it?

"Of course! A new business in town is big news." Mike laughed. "Wow! I can't believe that's you. Makes sense, though. I remember how much you loved animals, even back in high school. All your notebooks were covered with stickers of dogs and cats and parrots and stuff."

I laughed. "You remember my notebooks."

"I remember a lot about you. I mean, I always felt so lucky. I got to sit next to a pretty girl during a boring class."

Blood rushed to my face. I could only imagine I turned the actual color of beets. Back in high school I had been quiet and some might say extremely, insanely nerdy. Mike had been the captain of the football team or the basketball team or maybe all the teams? I had no idea he had ever noticed me, and the fact that he remembered anything about me was a surprise. Plus, he thought I was pretty?

"Now's the part where you say you remember me too," said Mike. "Talk about how I was charming and confident and how you liked sitting next to me, too."

I giggled. Although I think it came out more like a snort. I'm not sure. But before I had a chance to return Mike's banter, Granny stepped forward. "All of this back and forth is so charming it's warming my heart and everything. But you're here about a dead body, remember? That's why the beautiful young woman with the weird notebooks called you."

Mike put his palm to his forehead. "You are so right. I should not be flirting at an open crime scene. That's bad, right? Is that the kind of stuff that cops get fired for? Oh man. This is my first month on the job. I don't want to get fired. If I get fired I'm going to have to go work at the deli and lunch meats freak me out. How do they get so slimy anyway? Turkey is not slimy at Thanksgiving. I think delis have some sort of slime-inducing mechanism. Man, now I'm talking on and on about slimy meat. That's not hot."

"You're not here to be hot, kid," said Granny. "Would you like us to introduce you to the corpse, perhaps? Or maybe you want to ask us a few questions? Dust for fingerprints? I don't know what you people do."

A high-pitched voice rang out from behind us. "Yoo-hoo!"

I looked over toward the front door just as Eleanor from *Eleanor's Bakeshop* entered, carrying a tray of what smelled like fresh baked peanut butter cookies. "Sorry to interrupt. I saw the police arrive at the building and I was wondering what might be going on. I've been standing here for a few minutes waiting for the flirting to stop. But then I figured I better just enter. The cookies are getting cold and I need to get back down to the bakery."

Mike plucked a cookie from off the plate and took a bite. "These cookies are fire, Eleanor. Thanks."

Eleanor scrunched up her nose. "Are fire cookies a good thing or a bad thing?"

"Good thing," said Mike, mouth full.

Granny threw up her hands. "How can you be enjoying cookies at a crime scene? Do your job. Look for clues."

Mike swallowed his bite of cookie. "To be honest, I'm not really allowed to do anything yet. I came over quick to make sure everybody was safe and sound. But I can't get into the scene of the crime too deep. Have to wait for Detective Rotund to arrive."

Granny balled up her fists. "That chubby French buffoon is still the head detective at the Toluca Lake Police Department?"

"Head detective and only detective," said Mike. "I hope to join his ranks one day but like I said I'm just a rookie cop for now. He takes me out on a lot of investigations though. So I'm getting good experience. My mom says—"

"No one cares about your mother but you, Michael." A portly man, around 65, entered. He was wearing what looked to be a detective's Halloween costume. Long trench coat, derby hat, light brown tie with a three-piece suit. The man had a French accent and a thin, French mustache.

"Hey man, that's not true," said Mike. "Lots of people care about my mom. I've got a big family. Plus, her neighbors love her because she's always making treats and sharing them. She's a beloved woman."

Rotund held up his hand and Mike shut his mouth. "Who here found the body?"

I again half raised my hand. "I did. I'm Amy."

"I know who you are. You have opened a new business in my town. It is my business to be aware of all business around these parts."

I kicked my toe into the ground. "It is?"

"Don't talk back to me. Tell me why you killed this man."

I gasped. "I didn't kill anyone."

"Yeah," said Mike. "Amy's cool. We used to sit next to each other in chemistry. She's not a killer."

"Stop talking." Rotund used a sharp tone with Mike. "The person who discovers the body is almost always guilty of something. Write that down."

Mike pulled out his phone and began typing with his thumbs.

"Not in your phone. Write it in a notebook. Remember

that little stack of paper where all the paper was attached by a coil? And do you also remember that long skinny piece of wood with lead at the end? You use the skinny piece of wood to write on the stack of paper. It's amazing technology."

Mike mumbled. "I know what a paper and pencil is."

Granny stepped forward. "Will you come off your high French horse, Rotund? My granddaughter is not a killer. She's a sweet animal lover and she's never hurt anyone. She never will, either. I think it's her biggest flaw."

"Perhaps you're the killer then," said Rotund.

Granny rolled her eyes. Rotund gave her a meaningful look. "It has been too long, Petunia, since I have seen that eye roll."

"I'm not going to let you seduce me, Rotund," said Granny.

"But you already have."

"We went on one date a million years ago and I left early by sneaking out the bathroom window. It wasn't true love."

"You're the most beautiful woman I've ever seen."

"No, I'm not! What's wrong with you?" Granny asked.

Mike looked down at the ground. It was clear to me from his behavior that he also thought Rotund was being inappropriate toward my grandmother. But that was a little hypocritical because Mike had barely stopped flirting with me when Rotund had arrived on the scene.

Rotund winked at Granny. "We shall pick this up later. First, show me to the corpse."

I pointed over toward the bedroom door. "He's in there."

Rotund crossed into the bedroom then immediately uttered what I imagined to be foul, French curses. He sounded disgusted and I also heard him gag. After a few seconds, he reentered the living room. "Officer Michael.

Take these women outside. Get their information. It's time for them to go. Then get back in here. We have work to do."

"Bye," I said to Rotund.

"Yes, yes. Goodbye. Get out."

Granny and I followed Mike toward the front door. Fluffy jumped out from his pile of trash and trotted along beside us. I scooped him up in one quick motion and tucked him under my arm.

"Ladies," said Rotund.

I turned back. "What? I'm taking the cat with me. It's only right."

"That is fine," said Rotund. He set his jaw and glared at me. "But don't either of you go far."

8

MORE PUPPY, MORE PROBLEMS

*G*ranny and I entered *Creature Comforts* to find Betsy in a heated debate with Toluca Lake's youthful mayor, Tommy Flynn. I say youthful but in truth, Tommy was just young. At the ripe age of twenty, he was the youngest mayor in all of California. I had seen pictures of Tommy and his baby face, and I had heard all about him from Granny and her friends, but he and I had never met until that day.

At that moment, Tommy was pacing back and forth, clutching a golden lab puppy to his chest. "Please help me. I don't know what to do. I'm in over my head."

"I already told you I can't. We don't do animal training here at *Creature Comforts*. We can only groom them, not teach them how to behave."

"But you're animal people, right? Can you teach the thing how to go to the bathroom? Or how to stop barking? Or how to stop going to the bathroom? If things continue like this I'm going to lose my sanity. And my security deposit!"

"I'm not convinced you ever had sanity to begin with," Betsy said. "What made you want to be the mayor of Toluca Lake when you were nineteen?"

"I'm twenty. And I have a passion for leadership, diplomacy and—and—"

"Calm down, kid," said Granny, taking a step further into the salon. "I gather you adopted a dog without thinking through the decision first? You've got a classic problem on your hands. And it seems you're not a strong decision-maker. That doesn't bode well for our quaint small town, does it?"

Tommy's phone rang. He silenced it. "My decision to adopt Puppy has nothing to do with my ability to lead this town."

"You named your dog Puppy?" said Granny.

"I can't decide on another name. But I will. Soon."

Betsy walked out from behind the counter. "I'm glad you ladies are here. My mom and I have an appointment and I can't be late."

"Where are you going?" I said.

"We're going to pick out our grave plots over at Heaven's Gate."

Granny and I exchanged a freaked-out look.

"Is that weird?" Betsy said. "Every time I tell someone we're going grave shopping I get the same look. I thought this was normal. If I don't buy the plot now, how am I going to negotiate for a good price when I need it? I'm not going to be around then."

Tommy's phone rang again. Once again, he silenced it. "I'm sorry to interrupt. But this puppy is urinating on me as we speak. As the mayor of this town, I command you to train my dog."

"How about I do you one better," I said, getting an idea. "I would love to adopt Puppy, if that sounds good to you. I've been hoping to get a dog of my own. At the moment, I can only live vicariously through other people's animals. I already picked up a cat today," I held up Fluffy. "I might as well pick up a dog too."

Tommy's eyes widened. "For real? You would seriously take Puppy? Yes. Yes, that's a deal. I've learned my lesson and I'll never get a dog again."

Tommy's phone rang again. He silenced it.

"Who keeps calling you?" Granny said.

"It's just Samuel, the chief of police. I think he wants me to bring in a pastrami sandwich. But I'm not his errand boy. I have a town to run."

"I've got a hunch Samuel is calling you for another reason," said Granny. "Pick it up. You might have a long day ahead of you."

With that, Tommy foisted Puppy into my arms and hurried out onto the street, answering his phone. As soon as he left, Betsy, Granny, and I let out a simultaneous sigh of relief.

"That guy is a bundle of nervous energy," I said. "How did he win the election?"

"He promised free parking everywhere in town," said Betsy. "It was visionary, it was triumphant, it was doomed to fail. People started leaving their cars overnight on Main Street. He had to repeal the free parking promise two months into office. Since then, no one respects him and everybody asks him to bring them sandwiches. It's kind of a fun joke but it's also serious. He brought me bologna on a roll last week. Anyway, I'm off to find my dream grave."

"Go ahead," said Granny. "Amy and I need to discuss what we're going to do about this big mystery, anyway."

Betsy turned around just as she reached the door. "Mystery? Betsy likey herself some mysteries. What happened? Is someone cheating or having an affair or stealing cheese from the fancy cheese section of the grocery store? I can't help it. Sometimes I get confused and think they're free samples. I'm innocent!"

Granny looked over at me. "Should we tell her?"

Betsy took a step toward me and Granny. "You better tell me. My grave can wait a few more years."

I didn't need much prompting. Within seconds, I launched into the story of what had happened at Gerard Crimper's apartment. Betsy followed along with rapt attention as I spoke. Occasionally she had a question like, "Was there cheese in his refrigerator?" Or "What was the square footage in that place?" But for the most part, she just listened and nodded and gasped at all the right moments. Then, when I finally finished the story, Betsy pumped her fist in the air and exclaimed... "You have to solve this mystery."

Granny pointed at Betsy. "That's what I'm trying to say. As far as I'm concerned, we're officially amateur sleuths."

I shook my head. "That's just not a good idea. We're trying to launch a brand-new business in Toluca Lake. We already have a bad reputation thanks to Gerard's review. And people are going to be talking once they find out we discovered the body. We need to stay as far away as possible so we can take care of all these cats and dogs."

"You're wrong," said Granny. "If we don't solve this, the business is doomed. This is our only choice."

Betsy's phone rang and she answered it. "Hello? Oh hi, Mom. Sorry. I'm coming. No, you're not going to have to dig yourself a grave. Very funny though." She hung up and looked back at me and Granny. "I should jet. Amy, come over for coffee and cookies later? I'll tell you all about my plot and you can tell me all about your plan."

"It's not going to be a plan," I said.

Betsy tried to wink but ended up blinking with both eyes at the same time. "Whatever you say."

Just like that, Betsy was gone and it was just me, Granny, Puppy, and Fluffy, alone in the shop. Granny went around the counter and started straightening out the bags of pet food on display. "You know I'm right, Amy. No one is going to come near this place with the cloud of murder hanging over our heads. We need to solve this."

"The police are going to solve it. No need to do anything."

"That young cop is handsome but he struck me as a male bimbo. Did he get good grades in your chemistry course?"

I shook my head. Mike had been a terrible student. "It's possible he's gotten smarter since then."

"Didn't seem like it to me, no offense." Granny continued straightening the dog and cat food. "And Detective Rotund has no idea how to solve a murder. There's barely been any crime in Toluca Lake before now. If we rely on him to solve this, he's going to take the easy way out. You know what that means, don't you? He's going to put the two of us in jail just to make his own life easier. We were the ones who found the body, remember? That's all the proof he's going to need. And it's not going to be hard for him to sell Samuel on our guilt, either. Samuel's just the mermaid on the head of the ship, remember? Rotund runs that department."

My heart fluttered in my chest. "You think Rotund would put us in jail for a crime we didn't commit?"

"I have no doubt Rotund will do whatever it takes to make his own life easier."

I swallowed. My life in Toluca Lake was supposed to be peaceful and safe. But I had a bad feeling things were about to get complicated. And I was suddenly hungry for a sandwich.

9

A HILL TO DIE ON

That day Granny and I spent a few hours trying to train Puppy sit. I wouldn't call it a success, but, he did eventually lie down and stop chewing on my shoe. I decided that was good enough and I headed out to visit Betsy.

Betsy lived in an affluent community in the hills of Toluca Lake, aptly named *Toluca Hills*. The neighborhood was dotted with big, beautiful homes from every era. My favorite, a Spanish style home with a yellow door, had two adorable toddlers playing tag out in the front yard. A young mother watched, perched on the front steps. All three of them were basking in the glow of the setting California sun.

I know, you must be wondering... How did Betsy afford to live in this gorgeous, wealthy hamlet of Toluca Lake? The truth is incredible and it is so Betsy. Apparently, while I was off on my decade of travels, Betsy had inherited a quarter acre lot up in the hills. And she had decided to put a tiny house in the style of a log cabin on the property. It was an unconventional decision but the neighborhood had welcomed her. The people of Southern California love charming little quirks, and Betsy's home was a perfect example of that.

When I spotted Betsy's place, I parked, climbed out of the grooming van and stood back to admire the tiny home. It was twelve feet long and no more than twelve feet deep. Smoke billowed from a black pipe in the roof. And adorable stones led to a cute little front porch that held two rocking chairs. I smiled and knocked on the bright red front door.

"I'm on the phone," Betsy called from inside. "Just come in."

I entered. The little home was plush and teeming with character. The bed was lofted with a bright purple couch beneath it. An accent wall was painted mustard yellow. And the tiny kitchen had elaborate, polka-dotted wallpaper. Somehow, the whole thing worked, and the place felt so cozy I wanted to scream.

Betsy was having a FaceTime call from the couch. She motioned for me to come in and sit beside her. Then she turned back to the FaceTime conversation. "I told you, Adam, I'm not interested. We're not compatible, OK?"

I plopped on the couch beside Betsy and peered over at her screen. She was talking to a twenty-something man with a big smile and even bigger puppy dog eyes. I presumed the man was Adam.

"You say that but you haven't given me a chance to woo you," said Adam. "I can woo with the best of them. Give me a chance. You're gorgeous, Betsy. You're hysterically funny. And you move with the incredible grace of an eagle crossed with a flamingo crossed with a cloud."

"Is the cloud cumulonimbus?" Betsy asked.

"Does it matter?" Adam said. "I'm professing my love to you."

"You profess your love to me all the time. It's getting old. Anyway, I have to go. Amy is here."

"Hey, Amy," said the man with a surprising note of familiarity in his voice. "Big time congratulations on *Creature Comforts*. The place is adorable, Betsy showed me pics. It's gonna be a smash hit. And I heard you adopted a puppy too? So cute! How's training going?"

"Training is going OK, I guess. Puppy can kind of sit now. He's very cute. Worth all the hours of attention and cleaning up pee in weird places. But um..." I leaned over to put my face in the frame of the camera. "Do I know you?"

"Not yet," Adam said. "But you will get to know me, I'm sure. You'll probably be the maid of honor at our wedding. You'll give a great toast. Funny, sensitive, and just the right amount of sweet."

With that, Betsy ended the call. Then she hopped up off the couch and crossed to her kitchen, which held a half-size stove, mini refrigerator, and a minuscule sink. "I promised you coffee and cookies." Betsy opened a little oven and pulled out a tray of fluffy, pink cookies. "And I follow through on my promises."

"Everywhere I go in this town someone offers me a treat," I said. "What kind of cookies did you make?"

"Strawberry Delight. It's a Betsy-trademarked recipe so don't think about stealing it. Seriously, don't. I don't take kindly to those who infringe on my intellectual property."

I laughed. Betsy had such a strange way about her but she and I had always gotten along so well. We met on the playground in first grade and had been inseparable until, well, you know, I made that series of bad choices. "Don't worry. I'm not here to infringe. But I'd be happy to binge on those cookies. I wanna eat so many it makes my stomach hurt."

Betsy crossed back to me in three big steps and held the platter out for me to grab a cookie. I popped one in my mouth. It was sweet and a little salty and somehow tasted... pink. "Amazing! I understand why you're so protective of the rights to this recipe."

Betsy grinned. "Thank you. May I join you on the couch?"

"It's your couch, remember?" I glanced around as Betsy got settled. "I love your place, by the way. The pictures you've sent haven't done it justice. The colors are so vibrant. Everything is completely...Betsy. That's what I like about it the most."

"There's no point doing anything unless you're going to do it your own way," said Betsy.

"What's with the guy, by the way?" I said.

"Adam's a puppy dog," Betsy said with a dismissive wave of the hand. "He's not ready for all this woman. Not even close."

"Seems to me all the men in Toluca Lake love to profess their devotion. Did I tell you about Mike Fine? He was definitely flirting with me at the murder scene."

"There's a sentence I never thought I'd hear," said Betsy. "Hot though."

"And Detective Rotund was drooling over Granny."

"The woman has an incredible allure. We all do. We're all busy, professional, high achieving ladies. We don't define ourselves by the men in our lives. We've got far too much going on for that. Like me and my cookies. And you with *Creature Comforts*. And your grandma with her aggressive poker playing, entrepreneurship, and hostile demeanor unrivaled by anyone else in town. That's not to mention that the two of you are about to become big time amateur sleuths in Toluca Lake."

I hung my head. "I don't think I want to do that, Betsy. You said it yourself. I'm trying to open a business. It's not easy in any economy, let alone this one, and this whole area is so competitive. I need to be on top of my game if I'm going to show the customers I deserve their business, so I can't be distracted by a crazy murder investigation."

"No offense, Amy, I love you... But that is a big load of you-know-what in the baby's diaper. This murder is the catalyst in your hero's journey. Don't you recognize that? This is your call to action. Of course, as Joseph Campbell predicted, you're resisting the call. But there's no point resisting any further. You're meant to solve this murder and perhaps many others. The dog grooming business will thrive despite your intense investigation because it's destined to be! But whatever you do, you can't turn away from the call."

"Joseph Campbell? Hero's journey? What are you talking about?"

"Joseph Campbell is a preeminent scholar on writing and he's the author of all the best theory on story telling."

"OK." I grabbed another cookie off the plate and took a bite. "But why do you know that and why are you telling me?"

"We're right around the corner from Hollywood, baby. I've written fifteen screenplays over the past decade. I haven't show them to anyone but it's a prerequisite for anyone living here to understand story theory and the hero's journey."

"I didn't know you were a writer."

"I'm not. You don't have to be a writer to author a screenplay. Every page has more white space than words. It's just something I tried, like playing my numbers in the lottery. Anyway, now you're just keeping this conversation from its inevitable conclusion. Tell me you're going to solve that mystery."

"I don't think I am."

Betsy shoved the entire cookie in her mouth then grabbed her phone and stood up to make a call. "You need more convincing. Fine."

Betsy dialed a number and put her phone on speaker. It rang once and then a familiar voice picked up. "Hullo?" I recognized the voice as belonging to Toluca Lake's young mayor, Tommy Flynn.

"Hello Tommy," said Betsy.

"What's up? Are you calling about official Toluca Lake business or do you want to place a sandwich order for tomorrow?"

"Official Toluca Lake business."

Tommy responded with a hint of pride in his voice. "Great. You want to pick the mayor's brain on an important civic issue. Fire away."

"Yeah, I was wondering... How did your conversation with Samuel go earlier? What's going on with Crimper's death?"

"Well, it was a murder. They're sure of that because of the way the guy died."

Betsy made eye contact with me. "And do they have any suspects?"

"I don't know if I should disclose that—"

"Just come out with it, Tommy," said Betsy. "I don't have time for your impotent posturing."

"OK," said Tommy. "Apparently Amy and her grandmother are the two top suspects. Samuel mentioned something about a nasty online review, I don't know. It's sad, I was excited to have a new business in the old *Priscilla's* location.

But now Amy had to go and kill someone, and that ruins everything."

"Amy didn't kill anyone!" said Betsy. "But thank you for the information. That's all I needed to know. Oh! And I'll have a pastrami on rye tomorrow for lunch. You can deliver to *Creature Comforts*."

Betsy hung up, crammed the phone in her pocket, and looked over at me. "Solve the murder or go to jail. It's your choice."

10

FLUFFY'S TAIL, PART ONE

*T*hat's cute. You thought this was Amy's story. Well, cats have their own lives. Nine, to be exact. And what goes on with us is far more interesting than what happens with silly humans.

My name is Fluffy, and I am a detective in my own right. This is my story.

It was around 9 PM on Tuesday night when I realized someone or something had been eating my tuna. How did I know? I hadn't taken a single bite but when I trotted over to the open can, a little chunk was missing. Some cats might not have noticed. But I have eyes like a hawk. Uch, hawks. I hate 'em.

I looked over at the old lady, Petunia, sleeping in her armchair. I imagined her down on all fours eating out of my bowl. Something about that didn't make any sense. The lady didn't have enough hip mobility to get that low.

Besides, she and Amy had spent countless hours fawning over the dog they call "Puppy" that day. They had tried to get him to sit. They had rewarded him with treats.

They had exploded with happiness at every minute action he took.

It was pathetic. But it was a strong alibi. Neither of them could have been sneaking bites of my tuna.

You're probably wondering about my last owner, Gerard Crimper. Yeah, I know what happened to the guy. It was intense. I'm a tough cat and Gerard's demise sent even me into hiding underneath a pile of trash. But that guy was a bad owner, I'll say it. So I'm not going to spend any time on him or his story. I'm sure someone will find the truth about his death eventually. As far as I'm concerned he's the past and I'm the future. And I had a bigger mystery to solve.

The tuna.

The thing is, I don't like to share my food. More important, I don't like when others steal from me and think they can get away with it. You let something like that slip, the whole world starts to crumble. Before you know it, gangs of thieves are roving everywhere, and your life is turned upside down.

After seeing what happened to Crimper, I knew how cutthroat the streets of Toluca Lake could be. And I wouldn't allow that undercurrent of crime to permeate the walls of my own home, no matter how floral those walls might have been.

I walked slowly from my partially nibbled tuna over to the dog. He was secured by a puppy gate into a small area, maybe 3 feet wide and 3 feet deep. The vile creature had urinated on a pad like a wild animal. He was eating with such fervor that his own kibble was all over the floor. And he was jumping up and down like he was hopped up on something, probably street narcotics.

"Did you eat my food?" I said. "Did you escape the confines of your pen and dare to steal my tuna?"

The critter rolled over three times, then sprung to his feet and began running in circles. I made a mental note to question him after he came down from whatever drug he was on. My new home was nicer than the last place by a mile. But now I was living side-by-side with someone who was clearly out of his mind. I'd have to deal with that later.

Petunia stirred in her armchair. She looked in my direction. "Fluffy. What are you doing over there? Don't bother the puppy."

I spun and looked at her. How could this woman think I was the one bothering that dog? It was the dog who bothered me.

Petunia snapped her fingers a few times. Somehow that sound pulled me closer to her. I took one step toward the woman, then another. Although I remained suspicious of her motives, I couldn't resist those snaps. Then she began patting the seat beside her and I had the overwhelming urge to join her up on that armchair. Before I knew it, I had jumped up onto the chair and found a comfortable position on Petunia's lap. The old broad was warm and I liked the way she rubbed my back. I looked up at her. She smiled. "Oh, yes. You're such a beautiful boy. So sorry you had to see whatever happened to Gerard Crimper. That must have been terrible."

I didn't want to talk about Crimper. Why couldn't she understand that? I stood to go but she petted me with both hands. I couldn't help it. I settled back onto the woman's lap.

Across the room, the puppy stopped spinning in circles long enough for the two of us to make eye contact. I wondered... Could that beast have eaten my tuna? If he didn't, who did? And how could I catch the culprit in the act?"

11

DREAMING UP A PLAN

I came home from Betsy's house that night drunk on pink strawberry cookies. Betsy had passionately encouraged me to solve the murder of Gerard Crimper. She had been so impassioned, in fact, I had forgotten to ask her about her afternoon shopping for graves with her mother. Yet I still hadn't made up my mind…

Did I have what it took to solve a murder? And did I want the job of amateur sleuth just as the pet salon was launching?

I thought of Betsy and her grave sites as I washed my face before bed. I dried myself off and looked at my reflection in the mirror. Exhaustion carved deep circles under my eyes and caused my mouth to sag in a tired pout. Maybe I should be shopping for graves too, I thought. But no sooner than I had the depressing thought than I shook it off with a wiggle of my shoulders.

I spoke directly to my reflection in the mirror. "You don't look dead. You're just tired, Amy. You're tired and you got wasted on cookies because of peer pressure. One cookie is nice. Two or three cookies is fine. No one needs eleven, no matter how stressed they may be. Just brush your teeth and get in bed, girl. You've got to wake up in the morning and run a business."

The pep talk worked. I brushed my teeth like a U.S. Army soldier with quick, diligent, and focused movements. Then I spat into the sink, rinsed my mouth, changed into my kitty cat onesie and climbed into bed. As I closed my eyes, I spotted Fluffy perched on the windowsill, staring off into the darkened distance. The cat had an odd look of determination on his face. But I was too tired to focus much on that. I faded into sleep seconds after my head hit the pillow.

That night, I dreamt that I was walking through Toluca Lake wearing my favorite A-line dress. The dress was bright red, covered in illustrations of little Persian cats. Super cute, maybe not so fashionable, but who cares?

Anyway, I was walking down the street in this dream and I kept seeing familiar faces of people I grew up with or other people I knew from town. I would wave at the townspeople but time and time again, when they saw me they turned away in disgust. As I walked, nervousness filled my arms and legs with a warm, anxious energy. Then I got to *Creature Comforts* and my heart sank. Hundreds of people had gathered in front of my little shop and they were protesting me.

An old man held a sign that said "Go Away, Murderer." A little girl held up another sign that had a picture of my face with an X through it. Everyone in town seemed to think I was guilty of murder. And when they spotted me approaching the shop, they turned and charged at me like a zombie horde. I ran away from the horde only to find another, larger group approaching from the opposite direction. In what felt like seconds, I was surrounded on every side by angry friends and neighbors who thought I was a murderer and who wanted me to leave town. The horde was about to close in on me when my eyes snapped open and I sat upright in bed.

My hand flew to my chest and I let out a few shaky breaths. When I looked around my bedroom, for a few seconds I didn't know where I was. The dream had felt so real and so scary. Then Fluffy walked across my lap and I remembered where I was. I let out a sigh of relief. "It was just a dream."

I crossed to my window and parted the blinds. It was daylight. Granny was sitting at a small table beside the pool, drinking her coffee. When I saw her sitting there I realized I had something important to tell her. So I slipped my feet into my slippers, which were shaped like cute little beavers, and I shuffled outside.

When I got outside, Granny set down her coffee cup and looked over at me, blocking the sun from her eyes with her forearm. "I forgot how much I hated this Southern California sun. It's only 65 degrees out here but the sun is scorching the skin on my neck. I feel myself turning into a lizard. I hate lizards. They're disgusting."

I put my hands on my hips. "I have to tell you something. No more lizard talk."

"I can't make any promises," said Granny. "But go ahead. You're acting weird. What's up?"

"I've made a decision."

Granny turned up her hands. "Don't tell me you're going on a low-carb diet. You don't wanna live with a crazy person and I need pancakes to keep me sane."

"I want to solve the mystery. I think the two of us should figure out who killed Gerard Crimper. If we don't, everyone in town is going to start talking. They'll begin to see the two of us as murderers and the business will never survive."

Granny kicked her feet up on the table. "I knew you'd come to your adorable senses. This is going to be good. With my natural suspicion of people and your optimistic determination there's no killer the two of us can't catch."

"Betsy seems to think it's our destiny," I said.

Granny threw back her head. "That girl wears me out. Who goes shopping for graves with their mother? It's creepy, Amy. I know the two of you are friends but I have to say it."

I laughed. "Betsy is unique but you're going to get used to her. And you're going to love her."

"I'll take your word for it." Granny sipped her coffee. "So how do we start a murder investigation? I've never done this before, I've only admired from afar as Chelsea and Miss May do it."

"First I need to get a little caffeine in me. Can I have some of your coffee?"

Granny slid her mug toward me. I took a sip. Nice and burned, just how I like it. Then I slid the cup back to Granny. She slid it back to me. "You keep it. If I have any more caffeine this morning I'm going to end up in a boxing ring with Mike Tyson. I'm not trying to hurt anyone out here."

I took another sip. "Alright. I think we need to start off by thinking back to the scene of the crime. Was there anything there, in retrospect, that seems like it could have been a clue?"

"Everything seems like a clue to me," said Granny. "Let's talk about the living room, for instance. The place had been turned upside down. So maybe the killer was at Gerard's apartment looking for something valuable. Maybe old rock 'n roll collectibles, something like that."

I nodded. "That's a good point. I have been thinking that Gerard's murder could have been the result of a robbery gone wrong. But I was confused as to why nothing valuable had been taken from Gerard's place. The TV was there, the guitars were still there... Anything that could have been sold or pawned, it was left behind."

"That's why I think it might have been something specific," said Granny. "If somebody broke into that house, maybe they were after something you and I don't even know existed."

A bird swooped down over the pool with a tiny splash, then landed on the water's edge. A laugh escaped my lips as I looked over. The bird was red and green and blue with a beautiful beak. "I'm sorry. Is that a parrot?"

"Looks like a parrot to me," said Petunia. "Unless the local kids have been spray painting pigeons again."

"But that doesn't make any sense." I blocked the sun from my eyes so I could get a better look at the parrot in the pool. "Southern California is hot but we're not a tropical rainforest down here. We don't have parrots."

"Oh yes we do," said Granny.

I furrowed my eyebrows. "We do?"

"I can't believe you never noticed them before. There was a huge fire at a pet store in Burbank in the 70's. None of the animals got injured, thank goodness. But plenty escaped. The most notable escapees were about thirty parrots. Over the years, those parrots got friendly with each other. So then there were more parrots. And more. And more. Today this little area has the largest wild parrot population in the entire country and it's still growing. Burbank's only a few miles from here, so we get parrots in Toluca Lake all the time."

The parrot flapped its wings and took to the sky. I watched as it exited the courtyard and disappeared into the distance. Then I remembered another detail from the crime scene. "What about the flowers and the champagne in Gerard's bedroom? Those items, more than anything, strike me as potential clues. They looked so out of place in the bedroom there. The champagne wasn't even open, remember?"

"Maybe that stuff was for Gerard's wife."

"Was he married? That apartment looked more like a bachelor pad then the home of a happy couple."

"I have no idea what his love life was like," said Granny. "I think he used to be married to a girl named Sandra. But I didn't keep up to date on the Toluca Lake gossip while I was in Pine Grove."

"Maybe he was married." I stood up and paced. "But what if he was cheating on his wife? What if he kept that apartment as a bachelor pad? What if his wife found him up there with another woman and then freaked out and destroyed the apartment?"

Granny shrugged. "Sounds like a theory worth investigating."

12

CHAMPAGNE PROBLEMS

"We don't have any grooming appointments this morning so let's start the investigation right now." I climbed into the *Creature Comforts* van. Granny was already in the passenger seat, waiting. "We need to find this Sandra lady somehow. If she killed Crimper, she could be on the run. Back in Pine Grove, I used some of the animal tracking skills dad taught me out in the desert in an investigation. I might be able to do that again on this investigation. But the terrain is so much different. I've never tracked anything, animal or person, in a little town like Toluca Lake."

"You're getting ahead of yourself, Amy. I might have been away from Toluca Lake for awhile, but my roots here run deep. And so does my well of knowledge. Sandra Crimper used to own a salon over in the *Burbank Town Center*."

"As in like, a town hall or something? Why would there be a salon there?"

Granny shook her head. "It's not a literal town center. It's a mall. I used to take you there when you were a little girl.

We would go to the movies and then we would get Mongolian barbecue from the food court. That was until the owners of the barbecue banned me for piling my plate too high. There was nothing in the rules that said I couldn't expand the size of my bowl by using broccoli to fortify the edges. It's ridiculous!"

"You're getting really passionate about broccoli right now. I support that because you're a strong woman. But maybe we can stay focused on the whole murder thing."

"I'll focus on broccoli if I want to focus on broccoli. The barbecue ban has stayed with me, that's all I'm saying. There was nothing in the rules, Amy."

"OK. So are you thinking Sandra might still have her salon at the mall?"

"Yes." Granny pointed out toward the road. "Take Burbank Boulevard all the way down to San Fernando. The mall is where San Fernando and Burbank meet. You'll remember it when we get there."

Granny was right. As soon as I pulled into the parking garage at the *Burbank Town Center* my body flooded with sense memories. And when we stepped into the mall through a side door connected to the parking lot, a big smile crossed my face. "We came to the arcade here. We played air hockey."

Granny pointed at me. "I knew you would remember. You almost disappointed me big time, Amy. I let you win that air hockey."

"You did not. I beat you fair and square every time. That I remember!"

Granny waved me off and walked further into the mall. I followed her and a big smile broke out across my face. Although mall culture had dwindled in much of America, Southern California never seemed to get the message. The

Burbank Town Center teemed with people. I saw a happy Hispanic family hurrying into the movie theater. An old man rolled past me on a motorized wheelchair, licking an ice cream cone. And a young mother hurried past, pushing twins in a stroller, making a beeline to a little daycare center.

The mall had bright white walls, massive skylights and big, long corridors lined with my favorite shops. The whole place felt like being a kid and I loved it.

Granny looked back at me with an impatient glare. "Pick up the pace, kiddo. There's a murderer on the loose, and we're not gonna catch 'em strolling down Memory Lane. Get your head out of the clouds. We'll hit the arcade after the investigation, if we solve it. But first we need to solve it."

I nodded. "Coming, Granny."

Granny and I turned a corner and came face to face with *Sandra's Salon*, a big storefront with neon writing and busy hairstylists bustling back and forth inside.

"I think we might have found the salon," I said. "This place looks like it never left the 90s. I love it!"

"Let's see how much you love it after we find out the owner is a murderous vixen with a thirst for blood," said Granny.

"Let's just get inside already." I walked up to the welcome desk at the salon and I was greeted by a sixty-something woman with short gray hair and glasses. The woman had a thick New York accent, which reminded me of some of the people from Pine Grove, and her kind eyes comforted me.

"Welcome to *Sandra's*. You have an appointment?"

"Actually, we're here to see Sandra. Is she around?" I leaned forward. "It's a little personal."

"She's not in today, sorry. But I love talking about other

people's personal business. What's going on? I'm Kitty Kat, by the way."

Granny scoffed. "What kind of name is Kitty Kat?"

"It's my name. I chose it and had it legally changed a few years ago! If it were up to me, I would choose to have the powers of a cat too. That's my dream. I want to be able to see in the dark and prowl around and always land on my feet."

Granny gave me a look as if to say, "this lady is crazy."

"Great to meet you, Kitty Kat. I'm Amy and this is my granny, Petunia. Do you think maybe we could talk to you for a few minutes?"

Kitty Kat looked back at the bustling salon. Then she craned her neck to get a look at a long line of customers waiting to talk to her. Then she shrugged. "Sure. I can talk for a few."

Kitty Kat stepped out of the salon and crossed over to a bank of large leather massage chairs nearby. "Let's get a massage while we talk. These chairs are amazing. Have you tried them?"

"If I get a massage on one of those chairs, they're going to have to take me out of here in a stretcher," said Granny. "You girls go. I'll pay."

Kitty Kat and I took adjacent seats, Granny fed a couple dollars into the little mechanism, and the seats began rumbling. Kitty Kat tossed her head back and closed her eyes. "You two know Sandra's husband was just murdered, right? Is that why you're here? Looking to pay your condolences?"

"That's right," I said, a little too quickly. I should've thought of an excuse earlier but condolences were perfect. "We're here to pay our respects. That's all."

"So you don't know what was going on between them." Kitty Kat had a frank manner of speaking. And she didn't open her eyes once the whole time her massage chair was running. "The two of them have been separated for a while."

Granny leaned forward. "Really? They were on the rocks?"

"Oh yeah. And they were big rocks. The whole beach was made out of rocks. Sandra had been staying with her mother for awhile by the time Gerard got killed."

Granny stroked her chin. "Interesting. I had no idea."

"Yeah. I couldn't believe it when I first heard. They seemed so happy. And it's so sad, Sandra was still holding onto a little hope, I guess. But I've known for a while the two of them had no chance, whether or not the guy got himself murdered. He was a player. He loved women and he couldn't stay away. They didn't have a chance."

"Did Sandra hate Gerard?" I asked, my voice vibrating as the chair punched my back.

"Maybe. I don't know. All I know is, the rocks were spiky and they stretched as far as the eye could see. The whole relationship stressed Sandra out. Made work very unpleasant for all us other girls."

"So why do you still work here? Surely there other salons around."

"I'm going to be getting out of here first chance I get. I want to open an ice cream shop or a restaurant, something like that. Don't you think a cute little ice cream shop or restaurant would do good around here?"

Granny shrugged. "If you're good at running an ice cream shop or restaurant, I suppose it would do good."

"My establishment is going to draw people from up and down the coast. I can just see it now. Will you two come?"

I shrugged. "Sure. We'll come to your grand opening."

Someone cleared her throat behind us. I turned around.

It was a middle-aged woman with tinfoil in her hair. "Kitty Kat. Excuse me?"

"Who's there? I'm getting my massage. I need five minutes."

"You were in the middle of coloring my hair. You said you were just going to get a drink of water."

Kitty Kat sat up. "Oh! Oh, I forgot. I'm so, so sorry. Your coloring is on me."

"I wanted a little streak of blonde. It's been on there so long, the streaks are going to be pure white."

Kitty Kat gave us a nervous little smile. "Nice talking to you ladies." Then she hurried away, dragging her customer by the hand. As Kitty Kat hurried away, I wondered... Could the owner of that salon have murdered her own husband? And if so, would she ever return to work again?

13

A CUT ABOVE

*T*he *Burbank Town Center* food court was a sight to behold. The place was laid out like a shoehorn with classic fast food restaurants every ten feet or so. There was a *McDonald's*, of course. And there was a local Southern California place that only sold fish tacos, not as much my thing. And there was a little cinnamon bun stand and the aforementioned Mongolian barbecue spot. But my favorite place, above all, was the pizza joint. As Granny and I strolled into the food court, I pointed right at the giant pizza slice logo and smiled. "We have to have that for lunch."

Granny groaned. "If you still think that's good pizza, you didn't live in New York for long enough. The crust is so thick and chewy. There's a pound of cheese on every slice. And don't get me started on that sauce they serve." Granny made a gagging sound. "No thank you. I'm having a cinnamon bun for lunch."

I laughed. "Come on. We always used to get *Patty's Pizza* when I was little. And look, the prices haven't even changed. Two slices and a soda for $4.99."

"The fact that the prices haven't changed should alarm

you, Amy. At that rate, this place hasn't even kept up with inflation. How can they still afford to sell their slices for so cheap? There's only one answer... Inferior ingredients. I bet the cheese comes from powder in a bag."

I charged up to the counter at *Patty's* with my chin held high. "Two slices and a soda please. And make one slice pepperoni for my Granny. I'll have mine plain. Thank you very much."

The teenage employee gave me a thumbs up and then went to the glass display case to select our slices and throw them in the oven. I looked over at Granny with a satisfied smile but she was no longer by my side. Instead, she was already over at the cinnamon bun place, accepting her over-sized bun from the employee. Granny caught my eye from across the food court and took a big bite of cinnamon bun, as if to make a point. Then the worker at *Patty's* placed my slices and soda on the glass countertop, so I grabbed them and met Granny at a table by the window.

Granny looked down at my pizza and wrinkled her nose. "I'm telling you that is not a naturally occurring cheese. I don't think there was a cow involved anywhere in that process."

I followed Granny's gaze down to my slices. They looked delicious to me. The cheese bubbled. The sauce was bright red. And the crust looked fluffy and delicious with little crumbs of Parmesan baked right on top. When I took a bite, that warm, familiar flavor traveled right to the pit of my stomach. "So good. You need to have a slice."

"I'll get pizza next time I visit Pine Grove. Besides, you know I like my sweets in the middle of the day. They're the secret to my longevity."

"Somehow I don't think that's true."

Granny set her cinnamon bun down. "Speaking of

longevity, or the lack thereof, let's talk about Gerard. That weird hairdresser seems to think he had been having problems with Sandra. Doesn't surprise me considering his general demeanor and borderline hideous face."

"His face was over the border," I said. "I don't like to gossip about people, especially not after they've been murdered... But he was ugly."

"So you think the wife did it?" Granny ripped off a piece of her cinnamon bun and popped it in her mouth. I'll admit, it looked good.

I shrugged. "It could have been her. But it also could have been one of his many other lovers. Not sure how that guy attracted so many women but someone had to be jealous."

Granny wiped her mouth. "I guess you're right about that. But let's not go too far down this rabbit hole. Remember, we're utilizing information provided by a hairdresser who admits that she one day would like to have 'powers like a cat.' Not sure she is of sound or stable mind."

"I think she just thought that was funny. Maybe she wasn't being serious. I trust the information."

"Fine," said Granny. "But you can still admit, it didn't help much in either direction."

"That's not true. We learned that Sandra and Gerard were technically still married but hadn't been getting along. We learned Gerard was a cheater. So now we know that Sandra had motive to kill Gerard. Prior to this, it was only speculation."

"That's true." Granny removed her glasses and cleaned a spot on the lens. "But it's equally likely that one of the other lovers is guilty. That's all I'm saying."

"We need to find out who was the intended recipient of the champagne and flowers, I think. If all that nice stuff was

Sandra's, then I doubt she's the one who killed Gerard. But if Sandra discovered that spread and it wasn't for her...seems to me she might be the guilty party."

"So we're still on the hunt for Sandra Crimper," said Granny. "Good thing I know where her mother lives."

I laughed. "Wait, what?"

14

A CRIMPER IN THE PLAN

"*I* lived here for a long time, Amy. I know where most people grew up, including Sandra Crimper. Although back then she was Sandra Kirsch. Neither last name is beautiful, if you ask me."

"I suppose neither name rolls right off the tongue," I said.

Granny pointed at a freeway on ramp up ahead. "Jump on the 134. We're going to North Toluca."

I looked over at Granny. "North Toluca? I never knew anyone who grew up there."

"You made all your friends in Toluca Lake. But North Toluca is technically part of this town as well. It's where all the aspiring actors, writers, and directors live before they can afford to move to Los Angeles proper."

"I guess that's why I never went there. It's mostly twenty-somethings, right? Aren't there a lot of bars over there, stuff like that?"

"Bingo is my name oh," said Granny. "Sandra's mother wanted to be an actor back in the day. That's probably how they ended up in North Toluca."

"Did she ever succeed?"

"Her arm appeared in some sort of commercial in the 80's. I think she lived off the arm money for a few years. Then she gave up and became a receptionist or something. Maybe there's a sister or brother, too. Don't know anything about the dad in that family. Not sure he was around. Lack of a male role model, that's probably how Sandra ended up with someone crummy like Gerard."

"How have I ended up with so many crummy guys?" I said, looking over at Granny. "My dad is your son. He's not crummy."

"He's scattered. One of those paranoid desert people. I don't know how I raised him. The guy has plenty of great qualities, but I wouldn't say he was an ideal dad in any way."

I chuckled. "Granny you can be so harsh."

"Some people love me for my harshness other people despise me. You have to love me because you're my grand-daughter. And you know I'm right."

I thought about my dad. He had been living the nomad lifestyle, traveling across the world, for years. The last time I had seen him, his beard was at least a foot long, but other than that he had looked just like he had when I was a kid. Tall, skinny and scrawny, with a mischievous glint in his eyes. Granny was right. He was more than scattered. But he had taught me so many valuable skills out on our desert trips and I remembered those days with fondness.

Granny and I drove down the 134 in silence for a few minutes. A lot of people complain about California highways and traffic but if you catch a freeway at the perfect moment... There's no better way to travel. That day we stumbled upon just such a moment. There was no traffic and my van sailed past palm tree after palm tree like I was in paradise.

Granny snapped me out of my paradise with a panicked direction. "Take that exit, take that exit!"

I crossed four lanes of highway in fifteen seconds. "Thank goodness there's no traffic right now." Then I sailed down the exit ramp and found myself in the heart of North Toluca. The little neighborhood was just as I'd thought, with bars and sushi restaurants donning a busy main street. Twenty-somethings strolled from one business to the next, laughing and chatting, wearing what looked like the inexpensive version of the most modern trends. Everyone was so fit and beautiful. A pair of shirtless guys passed by, running faster than I was driving. They were quickly followed by a girl running even faster than they were.

"It's so weird that Toluca Lake is this close to all these aspiring Hollywood people," I said, slowing to a stop at a red light. "I never felt any of that Hollywood stuff growing up in Toluca Lake."

"Plenty of your classmates did." Granny rolled down her window and perched her elbow on the door. "Remember that one girl who got to play a dead body on *Law & Order*? She won prom queen after that episode aired."

I laughed. "She won prom queen because she was beautiful and popular."

Granny shrugged and looked over at me. "She got the part because she was beautiful and popular, too. Chicken or the egg, Amy." The light turned from red to green and Granny nudged me. "Go straight for three blocks. You'll see an old cottage on the left. It's the only house in this business district. Sandra grew up there, so let's hope her mom never moved."

Thirty seconds later, I pulled up in front of the house. It was blue with red shutters, one-story with a tiny front yard and a white picket fence. "This house is so cute," I said. "But there's one significant problem. No driveway. Where do I park?"

"You need to get used to this Southern California living," said Granny. "Park here on the street."

I'll admit it. It took me fifteen minutes to park my van. Although I want to tell you that I had to maneuver into a tiny parallel parking spot, I had all the space in the world. Granny was watching me, and I felt like I was under a microscope. I'm a nervous parker, despite my abundance of natural confidence. And Granny also kept saying things like, "You're going slow. Turning the wheel the wrong direction. Not sure what's happening now. Maybe we should leave."

I felt accomplished when I finally had the van parked, so I climbed out of the van with my head held high. Then I approached the little house and knocked on the door. Out came an older woman with bleached blonde hair and a curious glimmer in her eye. She took a few seconds to shove dentures in her mouth, then she gave us a picture-perfect smile. "Hello. How can I help you?" The woman was dressed in a long, flowing sarong. Her fake teeth were a perfect shade of white. And she looked to be in better shape than some of those joggers outside. I assumed she was Sandra's mother, the once and perhaps still aspiring actress. She looked like she was hungry for her big break, despite her advanced age.

"Hello! Good to meet you. I'm Petunia and this is my granddaughter, Amy. We're here to offer condolences about your son-in-law."

Mrs. Kirsch's face fell and she responded with a dramatic flourish. "It was so terrible what happened to that boy. Night fell over Toluca Lake, and the depth of that darkness couldn't be anticipated. He sleeps now, with the angels. He is no longer on earth with the suffering and is now in the celestial heavens, where he belongs."

I wrinkled my nose. Was it just me or was a lady speaking with a hint of a British accent? Once an actor, always an actor, I guess.

"Is your daughter home?"

"They both are," Mrs. Kirsch said. "Who are you after?"

"Sandra." I pulled up my pants half an inch. "Is Sandra here?"

A second woman appeared in the doorway. She looked just like Mrs. Kirsch but about thirty years younger. She too was wearing a long, flowing sarong. Hers was completely black. Unlike her mother, Sandra's grief seemed genuine. "Do I know you?" Sandra asked.

"Uh, we were friends of Gerard. My granny here used to go to all the *Liquid Staple* shows. For a few years, she worked behind the scenes, managing the pyrotechnics. Naturally, I grew up a fan as well. Then the two of us moved to Toluca Lake and the three of us became friends. We're Amy and Petunia. He never mentioned us?" Did I mention I have a natural talent for lying? I don't use my powers for evil. Usually. But I'm capable of speaking with immense confidence, no matter the situation. I could tell from the increasingly relaxed look on Sandra's face that my lies had worked.

"So you two are fans and friends. So beautiful. His music brought so many of us together." Sandra looked right at Granny. "Did you have a favorite song?"

"Of course," said Granny, with even more confidence than I had mustered. "'Steel Collapse' had to be my top track. It was on a B side. Didn't play it live very often. But I always enjoyed the deeper cuts."

Sandra nodded, once again buying the lie.

"Gerard was a beautiful person," said Granny. "I'm sure

you're more aware of that than anyone. He was free-flowing and open. It came through in his music and it came through in his personality, as well."

"He was certainly open," said Sandra, with a hint of jealousy in her voice.

"I hope you two had a chance to make some sort of amends before he left the mortal coil," Granny said.

"You knew about our...troubles?"

"He never said so explicitly, but it was easy to tell," said Granny.

Sandra bit her lip. "It's true, we'd had challenges of late. But things had been looking up, until..." Tears streamed down her cheek. "We had started having dinners together again. Those dinners were filled with conversation and laughter. They felt good. They felt like things had always felt when things were good."

I hung my head. "That sounds beautiful." Then I looked up and decided to take a little gamble. "Were you able to see him the night he died?"

15

FLUFFY'S TAIL, PART 2

*B*ack before I started living with Gerard, I was a street cat. Life for me was spent bouncing between Toluca North and Toluca Lake, living the life of a typical Southern California transient. I was all about the sunshine back then. Every grocery store left food out for me in a little bowl out back. Every little old lady had a street handout. Life was easy. Maybe a little too easy. Because back then, I had no routine and I had few expectations. But I grew accustomed to my own food on my own terms, not shared with anyone.

I know what you're thinking. You were a street cat. Didn't you have to share your food with the other street cats in those alleyways?

I guess I was lucky, but yes, I had my own food in those alleyways. I felt like a prince for every meal, and I loved all the special attention I got from the shop keeps. That was why I couldn't tolerate the situation at Granny's apartment. The thought of my missing tuna kept me up nights and haunted my days. The desire to solve the mystery consumed me. The weight of my suspicions dragged me down and I knew I needed to act or suffer the consequences of inaction.

As far as I could tell, Petunia's home would be difficult for an outsider to permeate. So it was unreasonable for me to think another cat was entering the house and stealing my food. The only real suspect was that tweaked out puppy dog, chasing his own tail in his enclosure. Maybe that whole thing was an act. And if so, the guy was diabolical. So I set out to prove it.

Every mission starts with reconnaissance. So in order to prove that Puppy was guilty, I began to study him with all my energy, every waking moment. As soon as I had the house to myself, I approached the enclosure. Puppy stopped chasing his tail, turned and looked at me. I'll admit there was an adorable glow in his big, brown eyes. But I knew not to trust it.

"I'm not the old lady," I said, trying to puncture the dog's soul with my gaze. "You can't distract me with your puppy dog eyes or your wagging tail. You've been stealing my tuna and it ends today. Tell me how you're doing it. I already know it's you. Now I need to know how."

The dog sat down and scratched at his ear with a free paw. I let out a dark laugh. "You're going to play dumb. Fine. If you won't talk, I'll find out for myself."

With slow and careful steps, I inspected every inch of the plastic enclosure. It was at least three feet high. The plastic was firm and there were no unbroken links in the lattice. As I conducted my inspection, I caught sight of my reflection in the dog's ball. Gerard hadn't liked how I looked all shaved clean. But I thought it gave me an intimidating presence and better reflected my inner ferocity than my previous fluffiness had. I didn't hate being fluffy. It was an identity. But perhaps I needed to shed that identity to embrace my new mission to defend my tuna with the guts and determination required of a hero. Once I completed my inspection of the enclosure, I was once again face-to-face with Puppy. He looked at me through the gate with those eyes. For a second, I thought I saw innocence flicker through them. And then the dog started doing that thing where he rolls over again and again and can't be stopped. The incessant rolling reminded me that this beast was nothing more than a tweaker at best, or, at worst, a mastermind who was dealing in pet narcotics.

"Where do you get the drugs?" I said. "Where are you hiding them?"

The dog kept on rolling. And rolling. And rolling. It was clear to me that moment that my intimidation tactics were lost on the creature. The dog seemed so hopped up on drugs that he had no fear. The thing probably didn't even know where he was. Yet there I stood, trying to coax the truth out of the beast? I laughed to myself. I had been going about my investigation all wrong. If I wanted to catch the puppy, I couldn't use the standard interrogation tactics. I would have to set a trap.

The dog stopped rolling over, put his front legs up on the gate and looked at me with his tail wagging. I did my best to snarl. But I'll concede, I almost laughed at that wagging tail. It was silly, OK? The dog had so much energy. I'm not saying I wanted to hug him, but I understand how humans are duped by puppy dogs. "I'm not done with you," I said.

The puppy barked and I walked away. Seconds later, I found myself staring down into my bowlful of tuna. When I had begun to question the dog, the bowl had been full. No bites had been stolen. But, paw to my heart, when I returned to the bowl... several bites had been taken. I looked back at the dog. "It couldn't have been you. I had eyes on you this whole time." I looked back at the bowl of food and let out a deep sigh. "But if it wasn't the dog, who was it?"

16

FURRY ROAD

*S*andra clenched her fists in tight, angry balls and her voice shook when she spoke. "No, I didn't get to see Gerard the night he died!"

I took a step back. "Oh. OK. Sorry. I just—"

"I'm so mad at myself," she continued. "I was at work cutting hair instead of spending time with my husband. I had a bad feeling that night. There was a little voice in my head that said I needed to keep working on the relationship and that I shouldn't be such a workaholic. But I went to the salon anyway. And I'll pay the price for the rest of my life. No money is worth that. No client is worth that."

Granny and I exchanged a look. If Sandra had spent the night cutting hair it was less likely that she had killed Gerard. It was a strong alibi but a little convenient. At that point we had no way of knowing if it was true.

After Sandra provided the alibi, there wasn't much more of a reason for Granny and I to stay in Toluca North. So I made up an excuse, uttered a few more condolences, and Granny and I hurried back to the *Creature Comforts* van parked on the street.

I put the car in gear, then headed back to Toluca Lake as Granny checked the *Creature Comforts* voicemail and returned phone calls we had gotten, booking appointments with new clients as I drove. She was great with the customers. She took careful notes on a little notepad and was shockingly polite considering her general personality. Granny was a wonderful business partner and a warm feeling of gratitude flooded my chest. When she hung up the phone I put my hand on her arm. "Thank you for helping me get this business running and for working so hard to make it a success. I'm lucky to have you."

Granny pulled her arm away. "Don't get all mushy and squishy with me, Amy. I'm just doing my job. And of course you're lucky to have me. The entire world is lucky to have me."

Granny and I stopped by *Creature Comforts* to groom a few pets and to check on Betsy. Betsy smiled big when we entered. "So glad you two are here. I've had to go to the bathroom for hours."

"You can go to the bathroom when you're alone at the shop," I said. "As long as the pets are in their kennels it's not an issue."

"I know. But I felt rude leaving them out here by themselves. By the way, is there such a thing as too much gentle shampoo? We got a golden retriever in here today, Skippy is the name, I think it's possible I got the poor guy too clean. He just looks... Well, like I used too much shampoo."

I looked over toward the kennels. It wasn't hard to spot Skippy. His golden hair was all frizzy and brushed to the side. But he looked cute. "You might have over-brushed him a little. But did he like it?"

"Oh yeah. He laid at my feet the whole time. All that brushing put him to sleep. Maybe I should've stopped after twenty minutes or so. But the guy suckered me in with his calming energy. Brushed him for the better part of five hours."

I laughed. "Skippy looks good. You did a great job. By the way, I meant to ask how grave shopping went with your mom yesterday."

Betsy gave me two thumbs up. "Amazing. We got the best plots in the cemetery. Side by side. We're going to be so happy once we're dead."

"You are so strange," said Granny.

"And you love me for it," said Betsy, hurrying off toward the ladies room.

Granny shuffled over to the computer to input all of the new reservations she had booked over the phone. Then, once Betsy got back, she and I teamed up to groom the rest of the pets. By 6 PM, all the animals had been picked up by their owners and it was just me, Granny, and Betsy in the shop.

Granny turned the "Open" sign on the front door to "Closed," then she locked the door and leaned against it with a sigh. "Wow, that was a long day. It's hard squeezing murder investigations into the workday."

Betsy smiled big. "You started the investigation! Huzzah, I convinced you!"

"You both convinced me," I said. "But yeah, talking to you helped. Thanks."

Betsy pulled out a stool from under the counter and pointed at it. "Sit down and tell me everything that happened."

I did as I was told and spent the next fifteen minutes reviewing the conversation Granny and I'd had with Sandra. Betsy devoured an entire chocolate bar as I spoke and she hung on all my words. After I finished speaking, she tossed the candy wrapper in the trash and crossed back over to me. "So Sandra had an alibi. What does that mean for the investigation? Who are you going to go after next?"

"Not so fast, Betsy." Granny pulled up a stool and sat next to me. "Sandra's alibi was far from airtight. The woman claims she was working at her hair salon but we haven't confirmed that. And she gave me a weird vibe. I'm not sure she was even upset that Gerard was dead."

"Really?" I turned to Granny. "I thought the grief seemed real."

"Did she sob real loud?" said Betsy. "Was there snot coming from her nostrils? Did she use more than one tissue? Did her face go red like a tomato that's almost rotten?"

"Who thinks of these questions?" Granny said. "I don't know every stage in the ripeness of a tomato. And I didn't count how many tissues she used."

"So she did use tissues," said Betsy. "That's important. Tissues equal real grief, in my experience."

I spun around on my stool so I was facing Granny. "Maybe you're right. Maybe Sandra was a touch insincere. It wouldn't be shocking, considering her mom's theatrics. Maybe the acting bug didn't fall far from the tree."

"Sandra Crimper's mom is an actor?" Betsy asked. "Maybe she can star in one of my screenplays."

"Her hand is an actor," said Petunia. "Save your script for someone who's face has been on TV."

Betsy pointed at Petunia. "Great suggestion. You can be the producer. I can offer you 2% of the backend but no money up front."

"I'm not interested," said Granny.

"I think she might have used a few too many tissues," I

said. "And now that I'm thinking about it, what Sandra said about having dinner with Gerard doesn't quite match up."

"What do you mean?" Granny said.

I grabbed a rag and cleaned the front counter to make it shine. Cleaning has always helped me think and that evening was no different. "Well, Sandra said that she and Gerard had been having a lot of dinners together lately. She claimed the two of them had begun rebuilding their relationship."

"So what?" Betsy said.

"So there were a lot of fast food wrappers in Gerard's apartment. Like...a ton. Like...it looked like he'd eaten fast food for every meal for weeks on end."

"Were there roaches on the wrappers?" Betsy asked.

"I didn't see any roaches," I said.

"OK, thanks. I was just trying to imagine the scene."

"You make a good point," said Granny. "Maybe Sandra and Gerard were still angry at each other. Perhaps they hadn't been rebuilding the relationship at all. And maybe Sandra lied about working at the salon that night. Thinking back on it, Sandra didn't give us a single reason to trust her. I don't believe any of the details from her story. And I don't think she and Gerard were on the mend."

I looked up from scrubbing the countertop. "I don't think so either. But how can we confirm that?"

17

HOUSE HUNTING

*T*he next morning, Granny woke me up by poking me with an old walker. "Wake up. We're going to Gerard's apartment. And we're late."

I rubbed my eyes. "We can't be late for our own investigation. And why do you have that walker? You can walk fine."

"I walk fine now but nothing in this life is promised forever. I'm prepared for limited mobility at some point in the future. Sometimes I take this thing out for a spin in town to get my sea legs about me. Walkers are actually kind of nice."

"So you're going to take a walker out today even though you don't need one."

"No. Today the walker is just for waking my lazy granddaughter."

I looked over at the clock. "It's not even 8 AM."

Granny poked me once more with a walker. "Rise and shine, ladybug. You're lucky I didn't wake you up sooner. I thought about coming in here at six."

As I climbed out of bed, Fluffy stalked past my open doorway, eyes darting from side to side. He took careful steps and seemed to be looking for something. "Has Fluffy seemed weird to you lately?"

"He's not fluffy, if that's what you mean. But I blame the groomer for that."

"Gerard said he wanted a standard cut." I pulled my slippers onto my feet. "And that's not what I mean, anyway. The cat just seems off to me the past couple days."

"He witnessed a murder. Plus, he spent goodness knows how many years living with his previous owner. Wouldn't you be spooked if you had to be roommates with Gerard Crimper? All that mediocre guitar music is enough to make any person or feline sick."

Fluffy stalked past the door once more. I shrugged. "I guess he's getting used to a new house. Cats can be so strange."

Granny pulled a bright orange dress from my closet and threw it at me. "So can people. Get dressed. I've got the van warming up outside."

"You don't need to warm it up, Granny. We're back in Southern California."

Granny ignored me and charged out of the room with the walker slung over her shoulder like a baseball bat.

"I can't let you up there." Eleanor slid a tray of tarts into her display counter and looked up at us. "The police said the place needed to be locked down during their investigation."

I sighed. "That's disappointing."

"Did you forget something in Gerard's apartment the

other day?" Eleanor crossed to a coffee machine and poured us both a cup. "Maybe you should call Officer Fine or Detective Rotund and let them know you need to get back in. Those men are such sweethearts, I'm sure one of them will come right over."

Granny wrinkled her nose. "Do you like everyone you meet?"

Eleanor smiled. "Pretty much."

Granny chuckled. "And now I understand why you like me."

Eleanor handed me one of the cups of coffee and then handed another to Granny. "Don't be silly. I like you because you're a great lady. I admire your sense of spirit and adventure. You lived all those years in New York in that dangerous town. Every time a new dead body showed up, I thought to myself... Petunia is going to come back to Toluca Lake now. I know it. But you stayed. And I read in the *Pine Grove Gazette* that you were helpful in those investigations. So convenient the paper is available online."

"I guess I helped the investigations a little." Granny sipped her coffee. "Weird. Moving never crossed my mind. It didn't matter who died or how many bodies turned up in that town."

"It really is super cute, other than the murders," I said. "Towns like that are hard to find. And the killer always got caught. I felt safe. Usually."

Eleanor shuddered. "And now we have a murder right here in Toluca Lake. I never thought I'd utter those words. We're lucky Officer Fine and Detective Rotund are on the case."

"Rotund is worthless and Fine is a mimbo," said Granny.

Eleanor scratched her head. "Mimbo?"

I sighed. "She's calling him a male bimbo." I glared at Granny. "It's not a nice term and she should stop using it."

"She's standing right here and she thinks it's funny and accurate. Stop censoring me, Amy."

Eleanor threw back her head and laughed. "You two crack me up. On the one hand, you've got a grumpy granny who insults everyone she meets. On the other hand you've got this sweet girl and all she wants to do is shampoo dogs and cats."

Eleanor's fondness for us gave me an idea. "I don't only want to groom people's pets, you know..." I gave Eleanor my biggest, cutest eyes. "I'm also looking for a place of my own to live. Granny's apartment in *Toluca Gardens* is nice and all but I can only stay there so long. I don't know if you noticed, but I'm not 55 or over. So I'm a little young for that neighborhood."

"A little young and a little too much in my space," said Granny. "She keeps moving my clicker, Eleanor. It's a nightmare."

"Poor kid. Hey, I understand your problem more than most. I lived with my parents into my 40s. The last ten years or so were tough. I needed my independence. And they wanted their kitchen back. I baked more than any family of three could possibly eat."

Eleanor was falling right into my clever little trap. I almost smiled, pleased with myself. But I managed to keep it inside and I kicked the floor, trying to look shy. "That's why we're here this morning, actually. There are so few apartments available here in Toluca Lake... I was thinking maybe you could give me a tour of Gerard's place. You own it, right? You probably want to rent it as soon as you can."

Eleanor bit her lower lip. "I do need that rental income.

But the police were stern. And I've got a bakery full of customers here."

Granny took a small step forward. "Let us borrow the key for a few minutes. We won't touch anything and we'll have it back to you before you know it..."

18

CREAKY BLINDERS

*T*he door to Gerard's apartment opened with a long, loud creak.

Before I stepped inside, the stench hit me like a ton of decomposing bricks. It was the same smell that welcomes you home from vacation if you forget to take the trash out before you leave. It made sense considering Gerard probably hadn't had the chance to take his trash out after he was murdered, and house cleaning wasn't quite under the purview of the police. For some reason at that moment the smell of forgotten trash saddened me. We all leave so much behind when we pass, of course. But I hated the thought that someone might one day need to deal with trash I had forgotten to take out.

I stood by the doorway with my hands on my hips. Granny struck the same pose beside me. Then Eleanor inched her way between us, stepped into the living room, and gestured around. Although Granny and I had done our best to dissuade Eleanor from joining us in Gerard's apartment, the kindly baker had insisted. So our task was to investigate potential clues in the apartment all the while keeping up the ruse that I was only there with interest as a prospective renter.

"So this is the place," said Eleanor. "It's not big but it's charming. You've got nice windows, facing west. I replaced the carpet last year after Sandra Crimper spilled a bottle of red wine. Did that free of charge. I'm a good landlord. What else can I say? You already know the man was killed up here. But that doesn't bother you so I'm not going to focus on it. Just...don't touch anything. The police said they might be back for more clues."

I looked over at Granny. She raised her eyebrows. We both knew we had to get to the clues before the cops, but it was going to be difficult with Eleanor breathing her cookie-breath down our necks.

"I was hoping you might be able to reduce the rent considering that this was the scene of a tragedy," I said. "You think you have any wiggle room?"

Eleanor pushed in a chair at the kitchen table, apparently unable to resist the urge to tidy. "I can't wiggle. Ever since I was young, I've never been good at wiggling. It's the same now. I'm afraid I can't wiggle much. I need to cover my costs, you see."

"Can't you at least give the girl some free muffins in the morning?" said Granny. "Free muffins for the renter and her grandmother are standard when you're living above a bakeshop."

Eleanor chuckled. "Of course. Free muffins and whatever else you like. Plus, you know if you ever need to borrow a cup of sugar your neighbor has you covered."

"That sounds wonderful." I gave Eleanor a nice smile. "Would you mind if Granny and I spent about fifteen minutes up here? We just want to look around. Test the water pressure. That kind of thing. I don't want to keep you from the bakeshop."

"I'm afraid I just can't leave you up here alone, and fifteen minutes is too long anyway. How about we do a speed tour now? Then in a few days you two can come back for a real viewing."

"Just go downstairs, Eleanor," said Granny. "We want to look at the place alone. We're annoying like that."

"I'm sorry. I'm not comfortable with that." Eleanor opened the bedroom door and entered. "Come take a look at the great light the apartment gets in the bedroom. Just try not to look at the blood stain on the carpet."

I leaned over and whispered to Granny. "Distract her. I'll see if I can locate any clues out here while you keep her occupied in the bedroom."

Granny winked at me. "Good plan, kid."

Granny charged into the bedroom and exclaimed, "This bedroom still smells like blood, Eleanor. We're going to need a rent decrease. And it has to be sizable. I mean, come on, for goodness sakes. You better be ready to wiggle more than you've ever wiggled in your life."

I let out a little laugh as Eleanor began arguing with Granny in her delicate and polite manner. Then my eyes darted around the living room. The place was just as Granny and I had left it. It didn't appear the cops had collected a single piece of evidence. I want to say I was surprised but my experiences in Pine Grove had taught me not to expect much from small-town police departments. They didn't have funding, they didn't have expertise, and if they were the best at what they did, they probably wouldn't have ended up in a small town in the first place. Maybe that wasn't fair to small town cops. But it had seemed true in Pine Grove.

I crossed over to a bookshelf at the far side of the room. Several books had been pulled away and tossed on the floor. The remaining hardbacks had titles like "Heavy Metal Guitar and Why it Matters," "Rock Gods Throughout History," and "How to Become a More Confident Man."

I ran my finger along the spine of the book about confidence. I muttered to myself. "What if Gerard wasn't everything he pretended to be?" I wondered how much of Gerard's rock 'n roll persona had been fabricated. What else could he have been hiding? Could he have been involved in something dangerous that no one in town would have expected?

I backed away from the bookshelf and my feet crunched on a takeout container from the *Big Baby Diner*. There were still a few French fries in the container. Wasting French fries is a cardinal sin in my book, so that was just one more thing to be suspicious of...

I heard Granny explode with a big, sarcastic laugh from the other room. "Save your breath, Eleanor. This place is a murder den. I don't care how good your cookies are, no one is going to rent it for the price you're asking."

"I'm so sorry you feel that way, Petunia. And I know you spent a lot of time in New York, where they talk to people rude, but I don't appreciate your tone."

Things were getting ugly but I hadn't found any clues. So I crossed over and poked my head into the bedroom. "Eleanor is right, Granny." I gave Granny a stern look to signal that she needed to keep Eleanor on her good side. "Back in New York, everyone talks that way. But in Southern California you need to be nice."

Granny slumped over with an exaggerated motion. "Fine. I'm sorry, Eleanor. I thought we were having fun and engaging in negotiation for sport. But I see now that I may have taken things too far. I never meant to insult you or your cookies. Will you forgive me?"

"Oh you don't need to apologize, Petunia." Eleanor smiled as if she had won a prize. "But yes, I accept. Now I'm sorry to rush you ladies out of here but I must get back to work."

Eleanor exited the bedroom, crossed to the front door held open for us to leave. "Do you have any other questions before you go?"

I smiled. I had an idea. "Actually, I do have a question... Smells like the trash hasn't been taken out of this apartment since before Gerard passed. Can I take it out for you?"

19

TRASH TALKING

*W*e stepped out onto the sidewalk and I held up my forearm to block my eyes from the sun. The transition from Gerard's stinky, dark apartment back into the real world was stark and jarring. "Now that we're back in California, I need to remember to grab my sunglasses before we leave the house."

"Who has time to worry about sunglasses when you're dragging twenty pounds of a dead man's disgusting trash?" said Petunia, gesturing at the trash bag I held in my other hand. "I know you're a nice person and that's hard for me to understand. But you don't need to go around taking the trash out for everyone you meet, kid. Especially the recently deceased. People are going to start thinking it's weird."

I put my non-trash hand over my heart. "Aw, you called me a nice person."

"So what? You know I think you're nice."

"Yeah, but it's not like you're running around giving compliments all the time. When they pop up, I like to take a moment to appreciate them. And so you know, I think you're nice too. You just don't want people to know it."

Granny put on her own pair of sunglasses with an eye roll. "Explain the trash."

I gave Granny a big, proud smile. "As far as I'm concerned, this isn't a bag of trash... It's a bag of clues. And it just might hold the key to this entire investigation."

I crossed the street toward the *Big Baby Diner*. Granny followed me. "Hold on a second. You can't dig through trash inside the *Big Baby*. We'll be banned for life. I can't live without my spaghetti tacos."

I called back over my shoulder. "I'm not going inside. We're going out back to the dumpsters."

A car honked as Granny scurried across the street and followed me toward the *Big Baby*.

"Listen," she said. "Stealing the trash was clever. If there's a clue to be found, that's a decent option. I mean, the guy didn't seem to throw away much actual garbage so maybe he threw away other stuff. The bag's full. But we can't dig through a bag of garbage in a public place like this. Someone might find us. And I for one don't want to explain why I'm digging through a dead man's sack of trash with my granddaughter to some unsuspecting member of the public."

"You stand guard," I said. "I'll slip into the fenced-in dumpster enclosure and root through the bag, careful and quiet. If someone comes, you make something up. All your years of playing poker have made you scary good at bluffing. We're going to need that skill in our investigations, perhaps starting now."

Before Granny had a chance to respond, I slipped behind the little wood fence that hid the dumpsters from the rest of the parking lot. Then I took a deep breath, peeled open the edges of the bag, and reached inside. The first thing I pulled out of the bag was half of a disgusting

Tupperware container filled with gnarly, fuzzy broccoli. I gagged. Granny poked her head into the enclosure. "What? Did you find something?"

I shook my head. "Rotten broccoli. What's going on out there?"

"All quiet so far."

I grabbed a broken piece of fence from nearby and used it to sift through the rest of the trash. The bag contained mostly food products. Half-eaten cheeseburgers. Cartons filled with curdled milk. Then I spotted something interesting… A yellow envelope, unopened, that had been stamped as "Past Due." I grabbed the envelope and took a closer look. It was from Toluca Lake Water and Power.

Interesting. If that past-due bill was any indication, Gerard had struggled with his finances and ignored warnings of impending financial collapse. I shoved the notice in my back pocket and resumed sifting through the trash. I'll spare you the details of the rest of what I discovered. Suffice it to say, the garbage had not been taken out of Gerard's apartment for a few weeks prior to his death. The guy was living like a wild teenage boy who had never been taught the art of housekeeping.

"Cluck, cluck, cluck," said Granny, in a strange imitation of a chicken. "Cluck, cluck, cluck. Alert, alert."

"What's going on?" I said.

"There's a kid coming toward me. He's wearing a *Big Baby* uniform and he's carrying trash."

I swallowed. Getting caught digging through the trash would be bad. I hadn't gotten to the bottom of the bag. So I tossed the broken piece of fence aside and started going through the remainder of the trash with my bare hands. At the very bottom of the bag I found a series of handwritten notes bound together with a paperclip. A quick scan of the notes revealed that they were written in the neat hand-writing of a woman. Had I hit the jackpot? Or was I too late?

"Um why in tarnation are you digging through the trash?"

I closed my eyes tight, put a big smile on my face and turned. There stood the employee Granny had warned me about. It was a teenage boy with acne and shiny, green braces.

And he looked mad.

20

DINE ON YOU CRAZY DINER

"That zit-faced kid was scary like Godzilla but you were incredible. I can't believe he bought your story." Granny laughed as she slid into a booth at the *Big Baby Diner*.

I sat across from Granny. "Why not? It was a plausible story. Grown women accidentally send their paper airplanes flying into dumpster enclosures all the time... Especially right before they eat breakfast." Granny gave me a skeptical look. I chuckled. "Fine. I'm lucky he bought my story. Happy?"

"Happier than I've been in years." Granny looked around the bustling diner. "I can't believe this is the first time we've been back to the *Big Baby* since we returned to California."

"We were busy setting up *Creature Comforts*," I said. "But you're right. This place is magical."

I looked around the diner. I looked around the restaurant. It was a classic Southern California diner with high ceilings, oversized red booths, big windows, and a long red counter near the front. The walls were decorated with photos of old muscle cars and pictures of Los Angeles from the 1950's. According to Granny, the place used to be the most happening spot in town and it had operated as a car hop back in the day. But it had remained successful over the years and it was packed with customers that morning. An old Elvis song played over the restaurant speakers and waiters and waitresses bustled by wearing white paper hats.

Granny grinned. "I had my first kiss at the car hop here. Have I ever told you about that?"

"A few times, yes," I said.

"I didn't think so. The year was... I don't remember the year. But I remember I was in Johnny Jacob's blue Chevrolet. It was a convertible. We ate with the top down. I got a double burger and fries and a strawberry shake."

"Yep," I said. "And Johnny got the same thing, right?"

"Let me tell it," said Granny. "Yes, Johnny got the same thing. Or, I guess I got the same thing as Johnny. I wanted to be feminine and girly so after he ordered I said that I would have what he was having. You know, to show that I thought he had good taste. But clearly he had good taste because he was there with me. Anyway, that's beside the point. I scarfed the burger in less than five minutes. So we spent the next thirty minutes necking. That's what they called the kissing back then. There was a lot of neck kissing, that's why. The kid was a terrible kisser. It was slimy. But I'll never forget it."

"Cute story." A voice rang out from above us. I looked up. It was our waitress. She was tall and skinny with long, blonde hair. And something about her looked familiar. I checked the name tag. Yup, it was Jess, one of my old friends from high school.

"Oh my goodness," I said, standing to give Jess a hug. "Jess. It's me, Amy."

I hugged Jess and she took a startled step backwards.

She turned her head to the side and studied me. "Amy! Wow. That is you. I should have known, you look exactly the same."

I laughed. "You look exactly the same. I haven't seen you in years. How are you?"

Jess shrugged. "Still working at the *Big Baby* so I could be better."

"Well you look cute in the uniform," I said. Then I turned and gestured to Granny. "Jess, this is my Granny, Petunia. Granny, this is Jess. We were close in high school."

Granny gave Jess a little nod. "So you were eavesdropping on that entire story, were you?"

Jess smirked. "It's a perk of the job. Trust me, there aren't many." Jess turned to me. "Please, sit down. Let me get your orders in before my boss freaks out."

I did as I was told and sat back in my seat. "Your boss, is it the same guy who used to own this place? The guy who ran it back in high school?"

"Yes. Apollo. Ex-marine, present-day pain in my rear. He is my worst enemy." Jess looked over both shoulders. "Whenever I talk about him I feel like he's going to pop up and fire me. Looks like I'm in the clear right now though. Anyway, our pancakes are still good. You used to love those."

"You remember well," I said. "Pancakes for me, please. With chocolate chips and some of that real maple syrup."

"I'll take the spaghetti tacos. Can I order those yet or is it too early?"

Jess smiled. "For Amy's Granny, I'll get the cooks to make an exception."

Jess turned and headed back toward the kitchen. For a brief moment, I could have sworn I was back in high school. Jess worked most weekend nights, so whenever I'd come in with other friends, Jess had been our waitress. Jess had hated the job even back then, so I understood why she seemed bitter to still be working there.

"Nice girl," said Granny. "But she should be careful how loudly she badmouths her boss. She can't be the only one eavesdropping in this joint."

I straightened my silverware and sighed. "You're right about that." Then I remembered the letters I had shoved into my pockets out by the dumpsters and I sat straight up. "I almost forgot!" I pulled the "Past Due" notice and the stack of handwritten letters out and slammed them down on the table. "I think I gathered useful information in the trash."

Granny let out an incredulous laugh. "You are something else, kid. I didn't think you were going to get anything from that pile of trash other than a venereal disease, but you've proven me wrong." Granny picked up the "Past Due" notice off the table. "Looks like the guy hadn't been paying his Water and Power bills. But I'm more interested in whatever these letters are." She grabbed the stack of handwritten notes that were bound together by a paper clip. "Have you read them?"

"I forgot I had them. Haven't read a word. But they look handwritten. And the handwriting appears to be feminine..."

Granny unfolded one of the notes and read it aloud:

"Hey G,

Can't wait until later...

Yours, Miss Lovey"

Granny looked up at me with widened eyes. "Miss Lovey?"

"Let me see that." I reached out and took the note. Sure enough, it was signed from someone who called herself

Miss Lovey. And the pink, cursive handwriting was absolutely feminine. I looked back up at Granny. "Read another."

Granny sifted through the stack of letters. "They're all similar. 'I can't wait until tomorrow.' 'Thinking about you.' 'Obsessing over your smell. Will you play me one of your songs tonight?' And every single one is signed from Miss Lovey." Granny tossed the notes down on the table and they landed with a soft thud.

I picked the notes up and wondered... Were we one step closer to the killer? And could that mean danger for Granny and me?

21

WOMANIZER, WOMANIZER

"*K*itty Kat told us the truth about Gerard's womanizing" Granny said. "The cheating probably started with *Liquid Staples'* first tour and continued from there on out. Musicians can't be trusted."

I stacked a few sugar packets on the table in front of me, thinking. "That's a strong, negative statement about musicians."

Granny shrugged. "I'm not going to apologize for offending musicians, Amy. They're all obsessed with feeling and emotion and passion. You think people like that make good spouses? Guess again. Read the autobiography of one famous rock star and you'll understand what I mean."

"Have you read a lot of rock 'n roll autobiographies?"

Granny nodded. "I've read enough. The upsetting thing is, Gerard Crimper wasn't a rock star. But he apparently still insisted on living the adulterous life of a celebrity. What a scumbag."

"I don't think someone's level of fame should dictate whether or not it's OK for them to cheat on their wife," I said.

"Of course not," said Granny. "I'm just saying the guy has some nerve! And I can't believe he found more than one woman to hit the hay with him."

"Hold on one second." I grabbed the stack of letters and sifted through them. "It's possible these notes are from Sandra. Maybe Lovey was a cute little nickname he had for her."

"You're being too optimistic, Amy. We're dealing with a murder investigation here. Sometimes you need to look away from the bright side and seek darkness. That sounds extreme but I speak the truth. People, lots of them, are evil. That's why I don't feel bad taking people's money at the poker table. If I don't win their cash, they'll probably use it to hurt someone, someway, somehow."

"That's an interesting justification for your gambling," I said. "And pretty misanthropic."

"Do you want to fight me?" Granny asked.

I laughed. "No. I'm sorry. It's possible that you're right. My tendency to see the bright side of everything may not be helpful right now. It's more than likely Miss Lovey is one of Gerard's mistresses. I mean, I've never been married for forty years, but do people who have been married that long often write each other such steamy letters?"

Granny let out a gravelly laugh. "Not in my experience. The last few years of your grandfather's life, the two of us only spoke about NASCAR and what was for dinner. I'm not saying all couples are like that but plenty of them are. Romance has a tendency to flatten out unless both people try to keep it around."

"So you're right about Sandra then," I said. "She lied to us. And she's our number one suspect."

Granny nodded. "I think so, yes. The woman is a hair dresser. She has an eye for detail. There's no way he pulled one over on her like that. She knew the guy was cheating and I'll bet you anything she hated him for it."

"But did she kill him? That's the main question here. Even if Sandra was fully aware of this Miss Lovey, that doesn't mean the affair angered her enough to kill. I mean, it sounds to me like Gerard had been a cheater for years, if not decades. If Sandra was going to kill him for it, wouldn't she have taken the opportunity sooner?"

"That's a decent point," said Granny. "So let's decide who our suspects are."

Jess approached, carrying our food. She set the food down on the table and looked over at me. "Are you two discussing suspects for something?"

"We're playing an online game," I said, smiling too broad. "It's an interactive adventure where you need to solve a crime."

"Sounds kind of fun," said Jess. "Can I play? I'm looking for any opportunity to mentally escape the prison of my job."

"You're a perky one," said Granny.

Jess returned Granny's sarcasm with a perfect deadpan. "Thank you. I was a cheerleader in high school. Captain of the squad."

"I detect your sarcasm and I appreciate it," said Granny.

I could tell Jess had to fight back a smile. "Thank you. I appreciate your gruff energy and laugh that sounds as though you're currently smoking a cigarette inside your throat."

I took a bite of pancake. The pancakes tasted just as they had way back in high school... Fluffy, moist, chocolatey and buttery. "I appreciate these pancakes."

"Anything else I can get you ladies?"

"We're good for now. The next time you come over here

maybe you can deliver one of those high school cheers for us," said Granny. "Go, team, go!"

"I'll do my best," said Jess, walking away.

As soon as Jess had left earshot, Granny leaned over toward me. "That was close. We're going to have to be a little more careful if we're going to discuss our investigations in public. People in small towns gossip and are always eavesdropping. It's not just the waitresses, either."

"You're right," I said, shoving more pancake in my mouth. "I would care more but these pancakes are the best things that have happened to me in quite some time."

Granny grabbed a spaghetti taco of her plate and took a huge bite. "These tacos are good too. Just as I remember them."

I waited for Granny to swallow and chase the big bite with a sip of water. Then I got back down to our proverbial business. "So to summarize... I think we should decide who our suspects are."

Granny wiped her mouth and took another sip of water. "OK. First of all, Sandra. She's the estranged wife of the dead man who was cheating on her."

"Next suspect is Miss Lovey, whoever she is" I said. "Gerard had been courting her. He had probably been waiting for her that night with the champagne. But something went wrong. Maybe she wasn't the only mistress. Maybe she's the one who got jealous."

"The third suspect is you," said Granny.

I lowered my fork and narrowed my eyes. "Excuse me?"

Granny shrugged. "I don't think you did it. I'm just saying."

"You know I didn't do it. We were together when we discovered the body. And I'm your granddaughter."

Granny held up her hands in apology. "I know. I'm

simply observing that as far as the cops are concerned, you're a suspect. You found the body and Gerard scorched your brand-new business with his mean review."

"Fair point." I grabbed my phone and opened it to a popular review site. "I wonder if Gerard ruined any other local businesses with his silver tongue."

I entered Gerard's name into the search bar on the review site. Sure enough, the top search result was Gerard's most recent work... His zero star review of *Creature Comforts*. But Gerard had left twelve reviews besides his review for my shop. Every single one of those twelve reviews was for the *Big Baby Diner*. And every single one complained about the owner, Apollo, by name.

As if on cue, a waiter dropped a plate across the restaurant and a large, imposing man rushed over and loudly scolded the waiter. The man was enormous, almost seven feet tall, and he was terrifying.

The man was Apollo.

*G*ranny and I agreed Apollo seemed like a decent suspect in Gerard's murder. Gerard's reviews were harsh, and it seemed the two men despised each other. So we went up to the cash register in the front of the restaurant to pay, and we set a little trap for Apollo.

Once the older woman at the register handed me my receipt, I furrowed my brow and acted confused.

"I'm sorry," I said, "I saw an advertisement online that said there was a manager's special this week. It said that every meal was 50% off for the next seven days, no questions asked. But it looks like you charged me for the full price of our meals."

The older woman took a painstaking amount of time to retrieve her glasses from her purse. Then, with great effort, she perched her glasses on the edge of her nose and took a close look at the receipt. "Yes. I've charged you for chocolate chip pancakes and spaghetti tacos."

The woman handed the receipt back to me as if she had proven a point. But, unbeknownst to her, we were only at the beginning of my plan. I handed the receipt back with a smile. "I'm so sorry. Would I be able to speak to the owner about this?"

The woman turned and screamed back toward the kitchen at the top of her lungs. "Apollo."

Both Granny and I jumped back a few feet. I don't think either of us expected the woman to scream with such ferocity. She had been so quiet and slow up to that point. Although I suppose we all have a bloodcurdling scream buried somewhere inside us...

The large, intimidating man I'd spotted earlier hurried out of the kitchen and towards the cash register. I recognized the man as Apollo, the owner of the *Big Baby*. Like I said, Apollo had been running the place since my high school days. He looked the same as he always had. Big, muscular, a luscious head of wavy black hair. But he was slightly less muscular and slightly more bald than he had been ten years prior. That's the way things often seem to go.

I caught Jess's eye as she walked past us and Apollo hurried toward the counter. In that passing glimpse, I was transported back to my high school days. I remembered the way Jess would imitate Apollo's hurried walk and gruff demeanor and I would laugh. It took a lot to keep from laughing that day. But again, I had a ruse I needed to uphold.

"Hello, ladies," said Apollo in his slight Greek accent. "Is there a problem?"

"My granddaughter read an advertisement on the Internet that said this meal should be half off," said Granny. "Are you some kind of liar? You're charging us full price. I wouldn't have come here if it wasn't for the sale."

Apollo knitted his brow. "I'm confused. As owner and general manager of the *Big Baby Diner*, I create and advertise all of our sales events myself. I didn't create the special discount you're requesting. Are you sure it was for this restaurant?"

"Yeah, we're sure," said Granny. She nudged the elderly cashier. "Can you believe this guy? He thinks old people can't tell the difference between one restaurant and another. I'm insulted."

Apollo stammered. He looked surprised and confused.

"What's the matter, mister?" Granny demanded. "Did you think I was too old to be insulted? You're never too old to be insulted and you're never too old to be jealous and you're never too old to get mad. Don't you forget it."

I put my hand on Granny's arm. Sometimes she was like a runaway train. I would need to remember that and keep her on track in our investigations. Hopefully she wouldn't derail us. Or this investigation would end up a train wreck. Alright, enough train stuff.

"It's OK, Granny," I said. "I'm sure this gentleman is confused, that's all. I'm sure if he thinks about it, he'll remember the sale."

Apollo's face reddened. "There was no sale."

"The ladies say there was a sale," said the cashier.

"There wasn't." Apollo slammed his hand down on the counter and a tiny figurine of a big baby clattered onto the floor. Apollo bent and scooped the big baby up, returning it to its place. "I'm sorry, ladies. You seem quite nice. And I thank you for your business today. If you like, as a courtesy, you can dine this morning for free. But it's important to me that you know the sale you're referencing never existed. I can't have you spreading false information about my restaurant all around Toluca Lake. Can you promise me that?"

"We're not going to promise you anything, you crook," said Granny. "And stop insulting my intelligence as an elderly woman!" Granny turned back to the cashier. "This guy is unbelievable."

"He lets me read on the job during slow times. It's nice."

"Oh yeah, right. He lets you read on the job because he knows full well he's not paying you a fair wage. This is elder abuse. Who knows what will unravel if we pull out the thread of this disgusting, ugly sweater."

"I said you could eat for free," Apollo said. "What do you want?"

"Admit you ran the ad," Granny said.

Apollo gritted his teeth. "I didn't run the advertisement."

"You know what, I can prove it." I pulled out my phone and pretended to type out a search. "*Big Baby Diner*. 50% off sale." Secretly, my phone was already preloaded with Gerard's bad reviews. But I pretended they'd popped up out of nowhere. "Oh. Look at this. I search *Big Baby Diner* and tons of horrible reviews come up. And it looks to me like every single review mentions you by name." I pointed out Apollo's name on my phone. "Apollo, right?"

"Well will you look at that," said Granny.

Apollo muttered a few words but I couldn't make them out. I leaned forward to hear better. "What was that?"

"I've never seen any bad reviews."

"Look for yourself then." I held the phone out to Apollo and he took it. I studied his face as he scrolled through the reviews. Although I had expected Apollo's eyes to widen with rage upon reading the reviews, his shoulders drooped and his face sagged. "I've — I've never read these. I didn't know they were there."

Apollo handed the phone back to me. "I'm sorry. I need to go. I have a restaurant to run." Apollo shoved my phone back into my hands, turned, and hurried toward the rear of the restaurant with his head buried in his hands. I watched him go, confused. "Is he crying?" I asked.

"Kind of looks like it," said Granny.

Seconds later, Apollo disappeared into a back room and slammed the door closed behind him. I stood there, dumbfounded. I wondered if Apollo had truly been surprised by the bad reviews or if he had played up his emotions to hide the fact that he had murdered the reviewer...

"What should I do with this bill?" the cashier asked.

Granny handed the woman a wad of cash. "We'll pay the whole thing."

23

FLUFFY'S TAIL, PART THREE

*T*hursday morning I had plenty of time to think. Too much time to think, for a cat like me, can be a bad thing. It can be the kind of thing that gets you into trouble. But Amy and Granny had an early morning, out doing who knows what, and they had dropped me off at *Creature Comforts* to be looked after by a peculiar woman named Betsy.

Now, Betsy had shown interest in me at first. But it wasn't the kind of interest I liked. She picked me up by my chubbiest spots, she held me close to her heaving bosom and she spoke in a voice best suited for newborn, human infants. "Goofy, goofy, goofy," she had said. "Kooky, goofy."

She had continued by calling me Bubble Boy, Mr. Bubbles, and the cutest, sweetest little kitty on planet Earth.

Don't get me wrong. I had grown used to attention from peculiar women over the course of my life. Being a fluffy cat, that's par for the course. But few ladies had treated me with such intense and ferocious energy since I'd been shorn by Amy. The old lady and Amy had been kind to me and they had petted me and loved me. But neither had freaked out over my cuteness and, to be honest, that's how I preferred it.

Lucky for me, Betsy had quite a few animals to groom that morning so, although she might have liked to, she didn't have time to squeeze me by my chubby parts for long. After just a few minutes, she set me on the floor with a little pat on the bottom and told me to relax. "You're the shop cat, now," Betsy had said. "Just be cute and be nice to customers and before you know it, you'll be an Internet celebrity with thirty million followers."

Don't get me started on the Internet.

Older cats have told me about a time before the Internet existed. When I was growing up, I was told stories by my great, great grandmother cat about humans who were almost never holding phones. She told me that humans used to always have their hands free for petting, feeding and loving. Great, great grandmother cat didn't know then that I'm not the lovingest cat around. Still, the time she described sounded sweet and charming, even to a cat like me. So I yearned for those days, even though I had never seen them. Maybe, in one of my previous nine lives, I'd known the glory of BWWW. (that's Before World Wide Web) and I just didn't remember.

Gerard Crimper had always been on his phone, Googling his own name and the name of his horrendous band, *Liquid Staple*. What's the point of a staple that's liquid anyway? You can't staple anything with liquid. And you can't staple liquid to other liquid. Don't get me started on *Liquid Staple*.

Anyway, back to Betsy. Betsy was an attentive groomer but she lacked the skill and grace of Amy. So I spent most of the morning watching as Betsy struggled with one animal after another. It was funny, watching her get soap suds everywhere, over and over again. Once, it seemed the spray hose had control of Betsy, rather than the other way around. It dragged her from one side of the room to the other, drenching everything in sight.

When I got bored of watching Betsy wrestle with animals and soap and everything in between, I padded across the shop and jumped up to the ledge by the window. *Creature Comforts* had a quaint spot all the way at the end of Main Street. And my spot in the window was even more quaint. I found a sunny spot and laid down. I watched an attractive young couple stroll by, hand in hand. The woman pointed at me and I could hear her say, "Let's adopt that one."

I hissed. She moved on. I settled back into the sunny spot on my window ledge. "This is Fluffy's ledge now," I thought. "And I will defend it against all forces, good or evil. I will have this ledge until the day I die and no one else will ever rest here."

The gentle hand of the sun pressed down on my back until I was lying completely flat in that sunny spot. My eyes began to close of their own volition and a wave of sleepiness overtook every inch of my closely-shorn body. Then, just as I closed my eyes for what could have been the last time, I spotted a flash of movement on the sidewalk outside. Jumping to my feet, I pressed both front paws against the window. "What was that?" I meowed.

"What's going on over there, Mr. Fluffers?" Betsy called out. "What are you all upset about"

Stupid woman. I wasn't upset. I was intrigued...curious... driven. Betsy crossed to me and rubbed the back of my neck. I'll admit it. It felt good. I felt my interest in whatever had moved outside the window begin to wane. Then it happened again. As quick as a flash, something scurried across the sidewalk. My ears stood on end. Where did it go? And what was it?

Betsy laughed. It was the chortle of a woman who has spent far too much time eating chips straight out of the bag. "Oh. Now I see what you see, Mr. Fluffy. A little mouse."

My eyes widened and I looked up at Betsy. Could she be right? Could this silly woman have spotted a mouse before me? Betsy pointed out the window. "There's the little mouse again. And now he's just sitting there."

I whipped my head around and looked out to the sidewalk. Betsy was right. The mouse was sitting there, looking up at us. Seconds later, a gaggle of obnoxious pedestrians came along and the mouse darted into a little hole in the side of the building across the street. And it was at that moment, I had what I believed to be the biggest breakthrough in the case of the missing tuna...

I realized there was a mouse in my house. And it had been stealing my food.

24

SOAPY DRAMA

*W*e went from the *Big Baby* straight back to the pet salon to get to work. When we entered, Betsy was chasing a beagle around the shop, yelling in frustration. "Get back here, Harry Potter. Quit running away on me or I shall summon He Who Must Not Be Named."

I looked around. The beagle had knocked shampoos and other products all over the floor. Betsy was red-faced and sweaty. Fluffy was clawing at the front window in desperation.

Betsy didn't notice when Granny and I entered so I cleared my throat. "Hey Betsy. Everything going OK in here?"

Betsy lunged after the beagle and missed. "Things are going great, boss. Just playing a little game with Harry Potter, here. He's a rambunctious fellow but we're buddies."

Betsy was a friend, sure. But she was also my employee. I wanted her to feel my confidence so I played along with her white lie. "That sounds good to me. Harry's owners will be so happy that we sent him home all tired out for a good night's sleep."

"Exactly." At that point, Betsy was on her hands and knees, under a table.

"Looks to me like you lost control of a finicky dog who doesn't like getting groomed," said Granny. "I don't think we should tell any of the customers about that. They'll sue us for malpractice or something." Granny turned to me. "Do you have malpractice insurance?"

"Pretty sure that's just for lawyers and stuff but I'll look into it."

Granny let out a short, sharp whistle. The beagle darted out from somewhere behind Betsy and jumped into Granny's arms. Granny raised her eyebrows. "That's why they pay me the big bucks."

Betsy stood and acted nonchalant. "Oh, cool. You're done playing for now, Harry Potter? That works for me. I was getting bored anyway."

Harry Potter looked at Betsy with his big, adorable brown eyes. She retreated back behind the counter and started cleaning up the mess the two of them had created.

Granny took over grooming Harry Potter and I helped Betsy clean. As we worked, Granny and I told Betsy all about the updates in the investigation. Betsy hung on every word with the attention a rabid fan would give an important boxing match. Her jaw dropped when I got to the part about Apollo rushing into his back office in tears. "I always knew I hated that guy," said Betsy. "We're thinking the tears were fake, right? Crocodile drops! He murdered Gerard because of the bad reviews. That stinking, ratty weasel man. I bet he murdered Gerard with a chef's knife or a frying pan. Typical restaurant owner. Couldn't even invest in a Glock like a respectable killer."

"We already know the guy was killed by a speaker," said

Granny. "Follow along, Betsy. You're dragging the whole operation down."

Betsy scoffed. "I'm not dragging you down. If anything, I'm dragging the operation up with my insightful questions and unique perspective on life. How many detectives do you know who've been consistently eating bologna for lunch every day for thirty years? Plain bologna. Bologna on a plate with no cheese or anything."

I cocked my head and looked at Betsy. "I never noticed that. I guess you do eat a lot of bologna."

Betsy crossed her arms. "Every. Day. No questions asked."

Granny sized up Harry Potter and washed behind his ears. In her care, the dog was docile and calm. "Eating bologna every day for lunch doesn't qualify you to solve mysteries, Betsy. It just makes you a freaky lady who's obsessed with the poor man's lunch meat."

"It's the most luxurious lunch meat," said Betsy. "And the only one for me. If you disagree, let me hear why. I'll fight you over this. I've done it before."

"Who have you fought about bologna?" I asked. "Actually, nevermind. Let's get back to Apollo for a second if we can." I gathered a few boxes of organic dog treats from where they had fallen on the floor and stacked them back on the shelf. "Maybe he was being genuine. It's possible he's just not a tech savvy guy, and his business seems to be doing fine. So maybe the reviews really were news to him."

Granny toweled Harry Potter off with a nice, clean, white towel. "I'm skeptical of any man who cries, real or fake. Call me old-fashioned, but I like a man who keeps it in, you know? Lets his emotions bottle up for years until he barely recognizes himself in the mirror."

"...you like that?" I asked.

Granny shrugged. "Oh yeah. Your grandfather never expressed a single feeling to me in our entire relationship. Anyway, whether or not Apollo was putting us on, we've got no evidence against him. We need to keep thinking about suspects."

Betsy gave one affirmative nod. "Sounds right to me, Petunia. Who do we investigate next?"

Suddenly, the door chimed and Officer Mike Fine entered the shop, leading a German Shepherd on a leash. The German Shepherd was wearing a little police ascot . The intention probably was to make the dog look intimidating but it was the cutest thing I had seen all day, including the moment Harry Potter had licked Granny's face and she giggled like a little girl.

"Good morning, ladies," said Mike. "Did I hear someone say the word investigation?"

I swallowed and gave Mike a tight smile. We were going to have to be much more careful if we wanted to stay under the radar investigating murder in such a small town.

25

A DOG'S PURPOSE

*M*ike returned my tight smile with a curious look. "I did hear someone say investigation, right?"

I stammered and Betsy stepped forward, chest out and chin held high. "I'm the one doing the investigating! Yup. I'm investigating a bologna shortage in Southern California. My supermarket ran out of my favorite brand and I need to find out why."

Granny put her head in her palm. "This bologna thing needs to stop, Betsy. People are gonna start calling you the bologna freak."

Mike laughed. "No, no, it's fine. Lunch meats are too slimy for me, but I think that's an admirable investigation." Mike turned to me. "It's funny, every time I see you we end up talking about deli meats."

I cringed. "Yeah. I guess we do. Although that's more gross than funny if you ask me."

Betsy held out her hand and Mike shook it. "Name's Betsy. Good to meet you."

"I think we've met before, actually," said Mike. "We went to high school together."

"I don't recall," said Betsy. "Sorry. I was a little boy crazy in high school. You must not have caught my eye."

Mike gave Betsy a smile. "Good to know. Your friend Amy caught my eye back in high school, actually. We had chemistry together."

"Romantic chemistry or the boring kind?" said Betsy.

"The boring kind," I blurted. "I had no idea I had caught anyone's eye back in the day."

"Well you did," said Mike. "And now you've moved back to town, and you're trying to catch it again."

My face reddened. I wasn't accustomed to that kind of attention from gainfully employed bachelors and I wasn't sure how to handle it. So I did what I always do when I feel uncomfortable...I turned my attention to the dog, knelt down beside him and gave him a pet. "Hello, mister! Don't you look like a distinguished gentleman? What's your name?"

"Right. How rude. I forgot to introduce you to Officer Carmichael."

I gave the dog a big pat on the back. "Officer Carmichael. Good to meet you."

Mike shifted his weight from one foot to the other. "Yeah. The problem is, not a lot of people feel that way about Officer Carmichael. Not since he's developed his...stench."

I rolled my eyes. "People are so ridiculous. They get all upset when a dog starts to smell like a dog. But have no fear, that's why *Creature Comforts* is here. Would you like to try our Powerful Pampered Pet service? That includes hair care, nail care, and a doggie massage."

"I think I'd like one of those for myself," said Mike.

I laughed, maybe a little too hard. But Mike had a funny way of saying things. Also, his square jaw and flirtatious attitude was making me a little more giggly than usual. And the broad shoulders. And the perfect smile. Something tells me I might have been lost in Mike's smile for a few seconds too long because Granny elbowed me hard in the side. "Amy. Let's run the officer's credit card and process the order already." Granny looked over at Mike. "Sorry. She gets distracted around good looking...dogs."

"I get it," said Mike. "Occupational hazard at a pet salon. But this guy is about to get even better looking, thanks to the three of you."

"That's right," said Betsy with a smile. "Once we're done with him he's going to be like hot like Gerald Ford."

"Was Gerald Ford an attractive president?" said Mike.

Betsy grinned. "Oh yeah. I had posters of him all over my wall in high school. I know, he wasn't exactly our vintage, but I liked his big, bald head."

"She really did," I said, remembering Betsy's oddly presidential bedroom. "It was strange."

I rang Mike up as Betsy led Officer Carmichael over to the grooming table. Then, just after the purchase was complete, Mike leaned toward me. He had a serious look on his face. "Hey, would you mind if me, you and Granny spoke in private for a few minutes?" Mike glanced over at Betsy and then back at me. "It's about Crimper."

I nodded and gave Mike a carefree smile, but my stomach knotted up like a pretzel. My first instinct about Mike's arrival in the shop had been correct. He was there because he had questions about Gerard's murder. Or he suspected me and Granny were the killers. I should have known. Officer Carmichael didn't smell bad at all. I wanted to run out back, jump into a red convertible with Granny and speed into the distance like Thelma and Louise. But I knew my desire to escape was irrational. We were innocent, so we had nothing to fear. At least in theory. If only the wrong man or woman had never been arrested for murder before. If only.

Thirty seconds later, Granny and I followed Mike out of the shop and onto the sidewalk. I'd tell you about the weather, but you probably can guess by now. It was sunny. So sunny, in fact, that Mike put on his sunglasses. "Look, my boss wants me to ask you some more questions about that day you found Gerard. This isn't coming from me. You know I love you both."

"I know you love my granddaughter and you're coming on a little strong." Granny crossed her arms. I blushed.

"Nobody said love," said Mike.

"You just said love," said Granny. "You can't take it back now. You love both of us. So why are you acting like we're suspects in this murder?"

Mike held up both his hands. "No one is suspecting you. I don't suspect you of anything. I just want to confirm a few details."

"That's fine." I gave Granny a pointed look. "We know you're just doing your job and we'd be happy to help."

My eyes met Mike's for a few seconds. His gaze seemed to thank me for my understanding but also seemed slightly...seductive? Or maybe it was romantic? It's hard to say for sure. The last two guys in my life had been neither seductive nor romantic. And neither of them had been as complimentary of me as Mike had been in our first two meetings since my return to Toluca Lake. But I needed to stay focused, so I looked away from Mike, back out at the passing traffic. "Go ahead and ask your questions."

It turned out Mike just wanted to review everything that happened that morning in excruciating detail. He asked us why we went to Crimper's apartment and why we went inside, and he tried to get us to say exactly what time everything had happened. Granny was curt and blunt, as always. But I tried to be helpful because, at least at that point, I thought the cops had just as much of a chance at finding the killer as we did. And I did not want to impede justice.

After about ten minutes, Mike folded up his little notebook and slid it back into his pocket. "OK. That's all I've got."

"That's all?" said Granny, emphasizing the word all. "You kept us out here for an eternity. I think I got sunburn on my precious scalp. Do you know how much of an issue that can be? I'm an old woman. I don't have time to sit around itching my head."

Mike laughed, apparently thinking Granny was making a joke. Granny did not return the laughter. Mike swallowed loud. "I'm not trying to get your head burned. I'm sorry, ma'am. But I do have one more order of business here. And remember, this is coming from Rotund, not from me. He's the bad cop. I'm the handsome, friendly cop with the adorable dog and kind demeanor."

"Spit it out, Officer Handsome," said Granny.

Mike winced. "Yeah. I deserve that. Pretty weird to call yourself handsome."

"What is your last order of business?" I said, the pretzel returning to my stomach.

"Ah, well, the chief and Detective Rotund wanted me to, um, warn you. We can't have any amateur detectives in this town. If you run some kind of investigation while we're also investigating, things will get messy. And, according to

Rotund, when things get messy... Sometimes the wrong people get arrested for the crime. His words, not mine."

Granny took a step toward Mike. "Is that a threat?"

Mike met Granny's eyes. "Not at all. But, unfortunately, it's the truth."

26

BOLOGNA CHRONICLES

As soon as Mike's squad car disappeared down Main Street, Granny and I went back into *Creature Comforts* and she turned to me with a determined look in her eye. "We're not dropping that case, kid."

"I wasn't thinking we would, either," I said. "Now, after that conversation with Mike, we have no choice but to continue. We're seriously suspects in this thing!"

"I can't believe Officer Handsome threatened you like that. He threatened us."

"He was following orders. And let's call him Mike, OK? Or maybe Officer Fine. No, Mike. Mike's good."

Granny shook her head. "I don't like people who follow orders like that. The thing about orders is that they're up to interpretation. He could have told us Rotund's message without actually threatening us."

"Maybe he has genuine concern for our well-being," I said, seeking the brightside. "Think about it... If Rotund is as impulsive and suspicious as Mike claims, maybe Mike believes it's in our best interest to lay off the case. Maybe he doesn't want the two of us to end up in jail."

"Whatever," said Granny. "At the end of the day, we're on the same page."

"Wow," I said. "You just said two clichés in a row. At the end of the day. On the same page."

"So what?" said Granny. "I'm not a writer. This isn't a book report. This is real life. I want to solve the murder so I can get back to playing poker, smoking cigars, and belching like a real lady."

Betsy piped up from behind the cash register. "You speak the truth, sister. Women should be allowed to belch. It's our inalienable right."

Granny sighed. "As soon as you agree with me, Betsy, I realize I've gone too far."

"I'll take that as a compliment." Betsy smiled.

Granny turned back to me. "Look, we got distracted by the crybaby restaurant owner at the *Big Baby*. But we had a great clue before that."

I pointed at Granny. "You're right." I pulled the stack of handwritten letters from my pocket. "The letters from Miss Lovey. They were buried at the bottom of the trashcan. Whoever wrote these might be involved in the murder."

"Too bad Lovey is such a common pet name," said Betsy. "Oh, that's funny. It's not a common name for pets. But it's what people who love each other call one another. I've heard. I wouldn't know because I've never been in love. Waiting for my Prince Charming, no matter how long it takes. But I've seen it on TV and movies."

"You'll find someone, Betsy," I said. "That Adam guy is obsessed with you."

"Oh, I know," said Betsy. "The men of Toluca Lake can only resist my pheromones for so long."

Granny marched up to the counter and looked right at Betsy. "You need to stop talking for a few minutes. Every time you open your mouth we get sidetracked with some kind of crazy Betsy moment."

"Sometimes a sidetrack is the only track that's available," said Betsy. "Amy knows. She knows everything about tracking."

"You make a good point, actually," I said. "We can't only think about the obvious with this investigation. We need to investigate alternative solutions, alternative paths…"

Granny opened a bag of treats and fed a few to Officer Carmichael. He gobbled them up like the German Shepherd he was. "OK. Unconventional thinking. I can get behind that. In fact, I almost got a masters degree in unconventional thinking back in the 60's. But I didn't, because that would've been too conventional."

"So what now?" Betsy said.

"Now we think, unconventionally," said Granny. "Which means no talking."

For a few seconds, we all thought in silence. Granny fed Officer Carmichael more treats. Betsy dried up the grooming area and tossed the towels in the laundry pile. I looked over at Fluffy, who seemed to be caught up in his own deep, contemplative thought. Then Granny's eyes widened. "Oh my goodness. I can't believe I didn't remember this. The answer is here in front of us."

"What is it?" I asked.

"Back when I was a lunch lady at Toluca High, Gerard Crimper was dating a girl named Elizabeth Love. I don't know how I forgot! Those two were hot and heavy. I remember because I would always have to break the two of them up when they were French-smooching in the middle of the cafeteria. It was too graphic. Eleventh graders could see that stuff. But those ninth graders were barely thirteen. You know?"

Betsy draped her cleaning towel around her shoulders. "So you think this 'Miss Lovey' is actually Gerard's ex-girl-friend, Elizabeth Love."

Granny nodded. "Makes sense to me. A lot of men get hung up on the girls they liked in high school." Granny turned to me. "Like you and Officer Handsome."

"We barely even knew each other in high school," I said.

"I didn't know him at all," said Betsy.

"We covered that during the Bologna Chronicles," said Granny. She turned back to me. "So what do you think?"

"I think... Why would Elizabeth Love sign her name as Lovey on the notes? That's weird."

"The handwriting is all feminine and swirly," said Granny. "I think the notes say 'Love,' not Lovey. And I think Liz is our girl."

"I think I'm hungry," said Betsy. "Anybody want a sand-wich? I'm gonna put an order in with the mayor."

"One second." Granny leaned toward me. "Am I on to something or what?"

I bit my bottom lip. "You're onto something."

"Good." Granny grinned. "This is the part where I tell you that I know exactly where to find her."

27

BAR NONE

*A*pparently, Elizabeth Love opened a bar in Hollywood shortly after she graduated from high school. Granny was convinced Elizabeth still owned and operated the bar and she wanted me and Betsy to head out that night to investigate. I wanted Granny to come with us, and I insisted all day, but she refused my invitations. Then, just before I headed out to the bar, I gave it one more shot.

"Are you sure you don't want to come, Granny? It'll be so much more fun if you're there!"

Granny kicked her feet up on her kitchen table and grinned. "Not a chance, kid. I'm going to be at the *Commerce Casino* from 9 PM until three in the morning, taking money from all the tourists with a smile on my face. Now spin around and show me your backside in those jeans. You need to look hot and spicy if you're going undercover for a mission at a bar."

"I'm not going undercover. And if all goes well, we'll only be there for a few minutes. The plan is to walk in, find this Miss Lovey, have a quick conversation, and leave. I could wear my pajamas if I wanted."

"This is a Hollywood joint, kid. If you're not looking hot the bouncer won't let you in the door. Now do the spin."

I looked down at what I was wearing. Tight blue jeans that Granny had picked out with a little tank top and a jean jacket. I hadn't worn the tank top or the jacket since high school and I felt ridiculous. "Don't make me spin."

Just then, Betsy burst into our house with her arms spread wide. She was wearing a strange, sleeveless sweater and a flannel skirt. "I'll spin for you all night long, Granny."

Granny shielded her eyes. "Please don't. Your whole look is a crime against fashion and possibly humanity."

I laughed. "I think you look great, Betsy. I forgot how 'Betsy your sense of style is when you're not at work."

"My tiny house should have reminded you. That place is turned all the way up to Betsy." Betsy gave me the up and down. "You look like you're on your way to a *Backstreet Boys* concert. I like it."

I turned to Granny. "Betsy likes it. Isn't that good enough?"

Granny poured herself a cup of coffee and took a sip. "Just get out of here already. And if the bouncer won't let you in..." Granny handed me a $20 bill. "Bribe him."

Listen, I'm sure Elizabeth Love's bar was a hotspot in the 80's, but I could only assume the place had gone downhill in the ensuing years. The bar's brick exterior was dirty and crumbling. A neon sign that said "LOVE'S BAR AND GRILL" blinked sporadically. And the bouncer Granny promised was nowhere to be found.

Betsy and I stopped a few feet short of the entrance and put our hands on our hips. Betsy scrunched up her nose.

"Can this be the right place? Granny had me thinking we were headed to *Studio 54*. I broke out my best flannel skirt for this occasion."

I looked up at the blinking sign. "Love's Bar and Grill. This is it."

Betsy clapped me on the back and took a deep breath. "I'm sorry to say I don't think this is going to be much better than the time we saw the *Backstreet Boys*. But few things are." Betsy pulled the door open for me. I entered and she followed close behind.

The inside of the bar was far more charming than the outside and I quickly realized the crumbly exterior was part of the charm. Granny had clearly been misinformed about the type of bar *Love's* was, however. It was less *Studio 54* and more *Cheers*. In fact, the place looks a lot like the bar from the TV show, complete with a shoehorn bar and a big, burly bartender. Sports played on the TV behind the bar, everything seemed to be made of walnut or oak, and every table came complete with a little bowl of peanuts. The place felt like it was stuck in the past but in a good way. "This spot is actually really cool," I said.

Betsy nodded. "Totally. And I can't believe how crowded it is! I'm getting sweaty just looking at these people."

I surveyed the scene. Betsy was right. Happy people packed the bar from one wall to the other. A young couple cheered at something that happened in some sporting event. A group of middle-aged ladies were huddled together, whispering and giggling at the far end of the bar. A few cops played pool in the back of the room.

I leaned forward to get a better look at the cops. "Hold on a second. Is that Mike back there?"

Betsy stood on her tippy toes and peered into the crowd like a ship captain. "Oh yeah. There's Officer Handsome. About to sink the eight ball, if you know what I mean."

"Do you mean he's literally playing pool and shooting at the eight ball?"

Betsy winked at me. "He's up."

Ugh. I thought the rules of small town living didn't apply once you left your small town. But there Mike was, in all his glory, sinking the eight ball without breaking a sweat. "Let's just try to make our way to the bartender and ask where we can find Elizabeth Love. OK? I don't want to talk to – –"

Betsy waved in Mike's direction. "Mike. Officer Handsome! Over here."

I hung my head. "Betsy, no."

"Relax," said Betsy. "It's rude not to say hi."

I blushed as Mike came toward us through the crowd. He smiled a little bigger than normal and walked a little looser than normal. I put two and two together when I spotted the beer in his hand. Mike spread his arms wide when he saw us. "Betsy and Amy. I should have known the two of you would be at the coolest place in town. It's so good to see you here."

I stared at the space created by Mike's big, open arms. Was the guy inviting a hug or was I crazy? I shoved my hands in my pockets to play it safe. "Hey, Mike. Yeah. Good to see you, too."

Betsy gave Mike the hug I resisted. "You smell great, Officer. Like leather and the law."

"Thanks, I guess," said Mike. "Hey so what are you two doing here?"

"Long day at work," I said, maybe a little too fast. "We had a beagle named Harry Potter that went rogue."

"Oh no. Did he jump off the grooming table, hunting for the Golden Snitch?"

My eyes widened. "Harry Potter fan?"

"Isn't our entire generation?" Mike asked. "And kind of the entire world?"

"What's your favorite book?"

"Book 1."

"Easy answer," I said.

"What's yours?" said Mike.

I looked down and mumbled. "Book 1, book 1."

Mike pointed at me. "I knew it. The origin story is an unbeatable classic. Nothing is more satisfying than seeing Harry get out from under the stairs and begin to reach his true potential."

"I totally agree," I said, reconsidering Mike's mimbo status. "It's a classic story and it gets me every time."

Betsy shoved her fingers in her ears. "Spoiler alert, spoiler alert."

I looked over at Betsy. "You were talking all about He-Who-Must-Not-Be-Named before, with the dog..."

"But I haven't finished the series! I started reading 'em late in life. For a long time I was against wizards." Betsy looked over at Mike. "I dated one for a while. He put a spell on me and had me whistling through my teeth for a week straight. Totally ruined my job interviews. Anyway, that's why I never got around to reading Harry Potter until I was older."

"That's amazing," Mike and I said at the exact same time. Then we laughed at the exact same time. Then we caught each other's eyes at the exact same time.

Thankfully, Mike broke the awkward jinxes. "Let me get you two ladies a drink."

"We're feminists," I said. "How about we get you a drink?"

Mike held up his beer. "I would accept but this is full."

A moment later, the three of us were lined up with our elbows on the bar, first Mike, then me, then Betsy on the end.

Betsy nudged me with her elbow and whispered. "Officer Handsome is looking extra hot tonight. You guys have that witch and wizard chemistry going on."

I spoke out of the side of my mouth to Betsy. "Keep it down."

Mike leaned on the bar and looked down toward us. "What're you ladies talking about?"

"Drinks," I said. "I'll have a double shot of whiskey on the rocks." I swallowed. Why had I said that? That's too much whiskey for a tiny lady like me!

"Wow. Really was a tough day with Harry Potter, wasn't it?"

"Yeah," I let out a nervous laugh. "Better make that just one shot of whiskey. With a splash of water. Got ahead of myself there."

Betsy licked her lips. "I hate whiskey. Burns like a fire ant going down. But I drink it to look cool. Same for me, please."

Mike chuckled and turned to flag down the burly bartender. As he ordered, I scanned the room, looking for someone who might be the notorious Miss Lovey. I couldn't spot anyone who might have been Miss Lovey, and a ball of warm anxiety filled my stomach.

"Excuse me for a second," I said. "I'm going to head to the ladies room." I gave Betsy a meaningful look, meant to signal that I was continuing the mission. Then she gave me one of her famous winks and I slipped away.

There was a long hallway toward the back of the restaurant. The men's room was on the left, the women's room was on the right and a third door at the end of the hall was labeled "Back Office." I looked at that door to the back office and narrowed my eyes. "There you are, Miss Lovey. Got you."

I crossed to the door, grabbed the handle, and wiggled. The back office was locked.

"Can I help you?" a baritone male voice asked.

I turned around. It was the burly bartender, towering two feet above me and scowling down. I gave him a nervous smile. I had been caught trying to enter the back office and I would need to play it off.

"What did you say?" The music in that back hall was loud, so I had to yell to be heard over the speakers.

"I said can I help you," the man repeated.

"Oh. Yes, thank you. I'm looking for the owner of the bar."

28

AFTER MIDNIGHT

I stepped into the living room around midnight, tossed my keys on the little table by the door and peeled off my tight jeans. Once the jeans were beside me in a crumpled pile on the floor I let out a big sigh of relief. "That's so much better."

"Not for me."

I shrieked and turned around. Granny was sitting in her chair, reading a poker book and petting Fluffy. "Would you mind putting on some pajama pants or something? Fluffy is an impressionable cat."

I hurried into the bedroom to find pants and called out to Granny through the open door. "I thought you were going to be out playing poker until the sun came up."

"The casino was dead. Came back home to study probabilities and brush up on my Omaha high/low theory. I won't bore you with the details but that game is going to make me rich. Tourists just don't know the ins and outs the way I do."

I found a pair of pajama pants covered in cute little polar bears and pulled them on. Then I grabbed an old *Toluca Lake High Schoo*l T-shirt, threw it on and shuffled back out to the living room. "Those poor tourists. I bet they never suspect a card shark to be hiding in a Granny like you."

Granny turned the page and didn't look up. "Yup. That's my secret weapon. One of my many secret weapons." I flopped down on the couch beside Granny's chair and put my feet up on her armrest.

Granny nudged my feet away. "Get those stinky things away from me."

I wiggled my toes. "Granny. My toes are beautiful, not stinky."

Granny shoved my feet away once more, that time with a laugh. "Remove your feet, or I will remove them for you."

I giggled and sat up. "So do you want to know what happened at the bar or not?"

"I was waiting for you to spill."

"You could have asked, you know," I said. "Besides, before I had a chance to say anything, you made me put on pants."

"Pants are a requirement in this home. While you're living under my roof, you're keeping your underwear under there." Granny gestured to my pants area. "Once you're gone, who knows what the rules will be. Probably I'll be No-pants Petunia."

Over the next few minutes, I told Granny all about what Betsy and I had experienced at the bar. Granny was shocked to hear the place didn't have a bouncer and she seemed disappointed that her knowledge of nightlife had fallen over the years. She asked if the bar had been crowded. I confirmed that there had been lots of people there but I didn't mention Officer Handsome, I mean, Mike. Granny and I needed to figure out the next step in our investigation and I wasn't in the mood to discuss my nonexistent love life any further. Then I got to the part of the story where the bartender caught me trying to enter the back office. Granny scooted to the edge of her seat and widened her eyes.

"So did you talk your way out of it? Did you find Elizabeth Love? What'd you learn?"

I took a deep breath and let it out. "Sadly, I failed. I couldn't make it into the office with the guy standing right there. And I wasn't able to locate Elizabeth Love."

Granny hung her head like I had just missed the buzzer beater in a basketball game. "So you didn't make any progress in the investigation. Next time just say that before you tell me the whole story!"

"I'm sorry." It hurt to disappoint Granny, but there was nothing I could have done. "What do you think we should do next?"

Granny stood up from her chair. "I need to get my beauty rest. Let's sleep on it and reconvene in the morning." Before I had a chance to respond, Granny turned, shuffled into the bathroom and closed the door behind her. She could be abrupt like that but I didn't mind it.

"You're such an efficient communicator, Granny," I called out.

"Don't talk to me while I'm in the bathroom."

I let out another laugh, then crossed over to Puppy's pen and knelt down beside it. Puppy was asleep with his adorable little head resting on a stuffed dog toy. Those were the first moments since we had gotten him that I had seen him lay still. It was a marvel that such a peaceful puppy led such a chaotic life during its waking moments. "Good night, Puppy," I said. "Tomorrow morning, we'll get back to solving this mystery."

The next morning, I managed to slip out of the house without waking Granny. I wanted to get a head start at *Crea-*

ture Comforts and I wanted to respect Granny's request for beauty rest.

I spent the hour or so before opening stocking our little shopping area with pet treats, leashes, and take-home grooming products. As I worked, I thought about Gerard and the mysterious Miss Lovey. I wondered what might be the best strategy to find Miss Lovey and speak with her. Should we ask around and find out where she lived? That might raise suspicion among the townspeople. So maybe it would be a better idea to go back to the bar and sit there until an older woman showed up. But Granny and I had a business to run. There didn't seem to be a clear answer but I refused frustration when it knocked on my door. There was no point wasting time with worry or concern. That was something I'd learned over and over in my life. The most important thing was to make careful decisions, have confidence in yourself, and take action when necessary.

A few minutes before the shop was scheduled to open, the front door buzzer sounded with a harsh annnnkkk. I knitted my brow and crossed toward the door. Who was there? I hoped someone wasn't having a problem with a pet.

As I reached to unlock the door, I saw that my early visitor was my sister, Megan. She was wearing a full pantsuit, drinking a supersized cup of Starbucks, and looking at me with an impatient smile. Mr. Buttons waited by her side on his leash. "Open up, Amy. I've got a huge merger negotiation in less than an hour and I still need to get my nails done before the meeting."

I opened the door and Megan pushed her way inside like a tornado, holding up her nails as she walked past me. "See these? They're a disgusting mess. I can't possibly see anyone other than you with my nails looking like this. I had to walk here with my hands in my pockets which is difficult to do while holding a leash."

I looked from Mr. Buttons to Megan. It seemed like Megan had a problem but it wasn't clear what the issue was. I knew from past experience that I had likely done something wrong in Megan's eyes. But I ignored the little pretzel in my stomach and gave her a smile. "What's going on, Megan? Are you just popping in on me to say hi and complain about your nails?"

"Of course I'm not popping in on you. I don't pop in on people. I think it's rude. What if you were in your underwear or just sitting down to dinner?"

"That would be strange considering this is my business. Besides, the whole point is I want people to pop in on me. That's why I got the old *Priscilla's* location."

"Stop bragging about your location, Amy. I have a serious problem."

I blinked a few times in confusion. "OK."

Megan pointed at Mr. Buttons. "I hate this haircut. At first, it was fine. But over the past few days I've realized you did a bad job. I need you to fix it."

Granny pushed past Megan entered the shop. She was holding two cups of coffee and handed me one. "No returns on haircuts, Megan. Leave your sister alone. Hair grows back most of the time. Mr. Buttons will be all better before you know it."

"Good morning, Granny. Look at my nails."

"They look great."

"No they don't, they look terrible."

"So are you returning your nail polish, too?" Granny chuckled. "You're a piece of work, Meg."

"Stop playing favorites," said Megan. "I know you like Amy more than me, but can't you be a little less obvious?"

"I'm not playing favorites. If I was playing favorites, I would only be talking to the dog." Granny gave Mr. Buttons a nice, firm pat. "Women are crazy, aren't they?"

"You're a woman, Granny," I said. She waved me off.

Megan's phone rang. She checked the screen. "This is work. I need to go." Megan gestured in Mr. Button's vague direction. "Fix this. Thank you."

Seconds later, Megan was gone. Mr. Buttons looked up at me and Granny with a helpless look in his eyes. Granny took him off the leash and led him back to the grooming area. "You hang out here for a second," she said. "I need to have a conversation with your Aunt Amy."

I walked over and placed my hands on my head. "What's up?"

Granny turned back at me and grinned. "I know where we're going to find Miss Lovey."

29

LIQUID STAPLES

*P*erhaps this isn't a surprise, but there were very few people at Gerard Crimper's memorial service. A notice of the service, which was held at *Park's Funeral Parlor* just off Main Street, had been posted the day prior in the *Toluca Tribune*, as was the custom with all local burial services. Although typical Toluca Lake funerals attracted everyone in town, and often for no other reason than offering free food and gossip, it seemed Gerard just wasn't well-liked in the community.

Granny expressed confidence that we'd find Elizabeth Love at the service. So our plan was to lay low and wait for the perfect moment to approach her. But that was difficult because so few people were in attendance. As soon as we entered the lobby at the funeral parlor, for instance, I made accidental eye contact with Gerard's widow, Sandra the hairdresser. But I looked away quick enough that she didn't approach.

"This is the worst funeral attendance I've ever seen," said Granny in a hushed tone.

Betsy craned her neck and looked around. "Do you think there's going to be food after?"

A tall, balding elderly man approached. He was prim and proper, wearing a three-piece suit. The man had a head that was a bit too small for his body. And he wore thick bifocals, which were perched on the end of his nose. "Petunia. Is that you?"

"Dirk!" Granny smiled. "It's been forever. I was hoping I might see you here."

Granny hugged the man and he smiled. But then he wiped the smile off his face and replaced it with a grim frown. "It's certainly terrific to see you but sad under these circumstances. Were you a friend of Mr. Climpet? I mean, Crimper. It's Crimper, right?"

"Crimper, yeah. No, I didn't like the guy," Granny said. "But I've been out of town for a few years and I'm trying to make the rounds. Back in the day, funerals were a social event in Toluca Lake."

"They still are most of the time." Dirk leaned forward. "This fellow was not the belle of the ball, so to speak. But I'm being rude, I haven't yet greeted your granddaughter." Dirk turned to me and gave me a half bow. "Dirk Stein, editor of the *Toluca Tribune*. I knew you when you were young. So good to have you back in town."

I smiled at Dirk. "Great to meet you as an adult. I like your suit, it's very sharp."

"Thank you. I have thirty identical suits hanging in my closet. If you ever see me and I'm not wearing a suit just like this, send me away to the mental hospital and never let me out.

"I'm Betsy," Betsy said, apparently feeling left out of the conversation. "Remember me? You interviewed me when I won the discus throwing championship back in high school."

"Betsy, of course. I never forget a face or a name or a hairstyle like yours. Are you still throwing discus?"

"No. I'm working over at *Creature Comforts* now. If you have a pet that needs grooming, bring it by. We pamper pets like no other!"

Dirk gave Betsy a polite laugh. "I spend far too much time grooming myself to have to worry about an animal. If you ever see me in the streets and I'm with the dog or a cat, once again, please assume I've lost my mind and need to be sent away, preferably somewhere warm and with extra padding on the walls."

There were a few moments of silence as Dirk stepped back and we all looked out over the funeral parlor lobby. Sandra spoke to an elderly woman. A few older folks milled about. There wasn't much going on.

"Hey, Dirk," said Granny. "You know everyone around this town. Do you remember the Love family?"

Dirk stroked his chin. "Let me think. As a matter of fact—"

Before Dirk had a chance to finish his sentence, a bearded funeral director stepped out into the lobby. He had a monotonous, morose voice which was fitting for the occasion. "Everyone please join us in the viewing room. Thank you."

The small crowd shifted into the viewing room. In the shuffle, we were separated from Dirk. That disappointed me because the quirky man was interesting. Want to know what disappointed me more? Granny, Betsy, and I were ushered to the seats right beside Sandra Crimper. Granny took the spot immediately to Sandra's right. As soon as Granny settled in,

Sandra turned to her. "What are you three doing here? You didn't care about Gerard."

"We're here to pay our respects," said Granny. "Besides, funerals used to be social events in this town."

"Gerard was a very private person." Sandra jutted out her chin. Her eyes watered. She dabbed at them. The whole moment seemed performed and inauthentic.

Granny played along with Sandra. "I know everyone's probably said this already, but I'm sorry for your loss. We all are. This must be so hard for you, especially considering that you were cutting hair the night Gerard was killed."

My heart skipped a beat as I awaited Sandra's response.

"Why are you bringing that up?" Sandra asked. "You sound like the police."

I leaned forward to look over at Sandra. "Oh my goodness. Have the police been questioning you? That's terrible."

Sandra narrowed her eyes and looked from Betsy, to me, to Granny. "There's something off about the three of you. I'm going to figure out what."

A bell chimed and the funeral director stood up in front of the small crowd. He said a few words and then stepped aside. Then a middle-aged man took the funeral director's place at the front of the room. He was wearing an ill- fitting black suit and he had a long, droopy face. The man's hair was perfectly parted to the side and he had a nervous energy.

His hands shook as he pulled notecards out of his pocket and arranged them in his hand. Then the man delivered the most dramatic eulogy I had ever heard and our case broke wide open...

30

SAYING A FEW WORDS

*T*he man's chin quivered as he delivered his eulogy. The following is a word for word recounting of what he said, best I can remember.

"When I was a kid, funerals were only something that happened on television. I would be watching an action movie, alone in my room, and someone would die, and there would be a funeral. It was never the hero who died but maybe a friend or mentor. The ensuing funeral was always somber but meaningful. It always felt like the hero needed to attend the funeral in order to summon the strength to finish their mission and to save the day. They say that we all think of ourselves as the hero of our own lives. I'm Bruce Willis. You're Bruce Willis. So is your brother and so is that other guy. We all think other people die, and we get to live. We all think funerals are only there to teach us, to help us grow, to help us reach our full potential. So these past few days I've been thinking a lot about what Gerard Crimper's death may teach me. But I can't come up with a single lesson here."

At that point, the man choked up. His voice broke and tears streamed down his cheek. After a few seconds, he gathered himself and continued.

"I think that's fitting, though, because Gerard Crimper was a man who wasn't interested in teaching others during his life. He didn't want the people around him to reach their full potential and he didn't care who died, as long as it wasn't him. They say even the villains in action movies think of themselves as heroes. I'm not sure if Gerard was a hero or a villain in his own mind. I'm not sure he ever had a single moment of introspection. He had no depth as a person, but he didn't have much depth as a villain, either."

I looked over at Sandra. She glared at the guy delivering the eulogy. If she could have killed him with that look, I think she would have.

"Look no further for evidence of Gerard's narcissism and lack of depth than the lyrics to his songs. Or, if you don't have time for his music, just browse the titles. 'I Am a God.' 'The Mirror and Me.' 'Never Going to Die.'"

The man looked over in the direction of Gerard's casket.

"Gerard, you were a deadbeat dad. Now you're just...dead. Good riddance."

As the man uttered his final words he threw his notecards down and stormed out of the room. Granny, Betsy, and I jumped to our feet and followed.

31

MOTORCYCLE DIE-ARIES

I believe anyone can accomplish anything they put their minds to. How did the pyramids get built? Human determination. And the same goes with landing on the moon. Anything can be achieved with the right mindset, strong thinking, and perseverance.

That being said, it's hard to keep up with a motorcycle if you're driving a big, clunky grooming van. Nonetheless, Granny, Betsy, and I pursued the man who'd delivered the eulogy as he zoomed out of the parking lot on an old Harley. I had set my mind to catching him. And I didn't intend to fail.

The Harley maneuvered between a city bus and the sidewalk like a mouse slipping under a door. Granny slapped my arm. "Get a move on, Amy. I should have known better than to let you drive on this chase. You operate a motor vehicle like a grandmother."

"You are a grandmother! And I'm doing my best. I can't fit through the gaps like him."

Betsy stuck her head up between us from the backseat.

"You can if you put two wheels up on the sidewalk." She pointed up ahead. "Petunia's right. He's getting away."

I stuck my head out my window to get a better look at the motorcycle. The eulogizer was three blocks ahead of me, stopped at a red light. "OK, ladies. I hope you're ready to see my stunt driving." I stepped on the gas and veered into the wrong lane, barreling straight toward oncoming traffic. Once I got around the city bus, I pulled back into my own lane with a screech. The bus honked at me but I ignored it, keeping my foot down on the gas.

Granny thrust her fist in the air. "That's how you do it, Amy! Take no prisoners. Drive like your life depends on it because if you don't solve this murder we could all go to jail for life."

"Me too?" said Betsy.

I made eye contact with Betsy in the rearview mirror. "At this point you're an accomplice. Sorry."

Betsy tightened her topknot. "No need to apologize. We're a team now, ladies."

I spotted another opening in traffic. I shot between two cars. Suddenly, I was in the right lane and the motorcycle was in the left lane, next to me. I winced. "Shoot! Now I'm too close. Don't look at him, don't look at him."

"Too late. I made eye contact with him for a few seconds. His eyes got all wide and freaked out." Betsy shrugged. "Sorry."

The motorcycle took a hard left turn into a residential neighborhood. Suddenly, we were out of traffic and things were quiet. A teenage girl walked a Doberman Pinscher. A gaggle of high school boys rode their bikes, yelling back and forth to one another. An ice cream truck was parked on the corner up ahead.

"Ice cream. Can we stop?" Betsy licked her lips.

"Not a chance," said Granny. "This is a high speed chase, remember?"

I let off the gas. "Our speeds are not so high anymore. I can't go too fast in this neighborhood, it's disrespectful. The guy who gave the eulogy has even slowed down and he just publicly denounced his own father at his own father's funeral."

Granny squinted and leaned forward to get a better look at the motorcycle driver. "You're right. But I don't understand. How is the guy ever going to get away if he drives so slow."

"Looks to me like this is going to be a war of attrition," said Betsy.

Granny looked back at Betsy. "What's that?"

"I have no idea but it sounded right," said Betsy.

I grabbed the wheel at ten and two and ran my fingers over the ridges in the leather. "With determination and perseverance anything is possible. If we stick with this guy for long enough, he'll give up. He'll pull over and talk to us."

"Remember at this point he doesn't have any idea who we are," said Granny. "We're lucky if he doesn't call the cops on us."

"Gerard Crimper's ghost should call the cops on him," said Betsy. "That eulogy was brutal. I mean, I'm sure Gerard was a bad dad but goodness me. That was the worst eulogy I've ever heard, and I've heard hundreds."

"Hundreds?" I said to Betsy. "How many funerals have you been to?"

Betsy shrugged. "Enough."

I narrowed my eyes and followed slowly as the motorcycle took a right turn, and then another, and then a left. Over the next few minutes, I created more distance between my van and the motorcycle. My hope was that he would think he had lost us and let his guard down. Maybe he could convince himself that he had been imagining things and the van had never been following him in the first place. After about a dozen turns, I slowed to a halt and hung my head. "Have either of you spotted the motorcycle in the past minute or two?"

"I told you we were going too slow," said Granny. "You created too much space, now we're never going to see him again. We're going to have to go back to town and ask around and find out his address and his name and that's going to raise suspicions and—"

Betsy pointed out the window. "Isn't that his bike right there?"

32

NO BIKES ABOUT IT

"You're right. That's the bike our fugitive was riding. This is so weird. I didn't expect him to be running away to a cute little house." I glanced at the house in front of which the bike had been parked. The home was gray with cute, yellow shutters and there were lots of flowers in the yard.

"I don't care about the house," said Granny. "What's much more interesting to me is the mailbox."

My eyes widened as I looked at the mailbox. There, written in beautiful calligraphy, was the name of the family I presumed lived inside the house... The Love Family.

"This is huge," I said. "That kid... That man who was riding the motorcycle said Gerard was his father. But, based on that mailbox, it seems the man's mother is Miss Lovey! We should have stayed at the funeral! This means she was definitely there!"

"I doubt it," said Betsy. "If that guy's mom was at the funeral she would have stopped him from talking about his dead dad that way, at least that's what I think. In other news, have you ladies been wondering about Gerard's grave? I wonder if he got something south-facing. They say a south-facing grave is nice because it keeps you cool in the summer but you get plenty of sunlight in the winter. Oh, here I am rambling about graves again. I'll stop. Sorry."

Granny turned back and looked at Betsy. "Stop and never start again. "

Betsy shrugged. "Not going to make any promises, Petunia. I'm my own woman."

"Excuse me, ladies?" I pointed toward the front of the house. The man from the funeral was standing on the steps with his arms crossed. "I think maybe we should go talk to him."

The man stood motionless as the three of us climbed out of the van and started toward him. His eyes were sharp and angry, just like his posture. But I didn't let that intimidate me. We were there on the behalf of the truth and truth doesn't back down from anyone. I gave the guy a big wave and my happiest smile. "Hello, sir. My name is Amy and these are my uh, employees, Petunia and Betsy. I just opened a pet salon in the area and I'm going door to door to promote my services. Do you have any fur babies?"

"I have a snake." The man uncrossed his arms and placed his hands on his hips. "But he doesn't require much grooming."

Granny held a finger up. "Technically I'm a co-owner of the salon, for the record. I'm not an employee."

I fought back the urge to roll my eyes. Granny didn't need to correct me when she knew my story was fiction. But I supposed her nit-picky attitude was realistic and could help sell my story. I was wrong.

The man stepped off the porch. Betsy, Granny, and I stopped a few feet away from him, about halfway up the path toward the door.

"You're all wearing black. Were you just at my dad's funeral?"

"No. Black is the dress code at the pet salon." Betsy smoothed out her black blouse. "I like it because it's slimming."

"Black uniforms. Sounds like a happy place." The man took another step toward us. "I know you followed me here."

I winced. By that point, I had committed to my story, so I decided to double down. "First of all, I'm so sorry to hear your dad passed. You said you were at his funeral earlier today?"

"Did you follow me here from the funeral?" the man's voice grew insistent.

"The truth is," I said, "business at *Creature Comforts*, that's my shop, hasn't been going well. That's why I've been going door to door today, trying to find new customers. But we've knocked on a dozen doors so far and no one has been home. So I decided I was going to follow someone to their house to approach them about the business. It was wrong, I know. I probably shouldn't be soliciting in the first place. But I'm desperate. And studies show motorcycle riders are more likely than most to own dogs."

"That doesn't make sense," said Betsy. "If you own a dog, you need a nice big car to take them around in."

"Maybe the studies are wrong," I said. "Anyway, I'm so sorry for disturbing you, sir. And I'm sorry about your dad. May I ask his name? I'd like to uh, make a donation in his honor to a charity of your choice."

"We love charities," said Granny. "Giving is essential, that's what I say. Giving is living."

The man scoffed. "Don't bother donating any money in my dad's name. He was the least generous man on the face of the earth. The guy had a big nest egg, I know it. But he wouldn't even help me pay for my new teeth."

"What's the matter with your old teeth?" Betsy asked.

"Too small. I hate them."

Betsy nodded. "I get that. They do look tiny."

"Betsy," I said.

"No, she's right," said the man. "Thank you for being honest. I've been plagued by these minuscule teeth my whole life. I always have to smile with my mouth closed in pictures. It's embarrassing. And my dad owed me the money for those teeth. I mean, what about child support?"

"Not sure that applies once you're a grown man," said Granny.

"Maybe not legally, but it's the right thing to do," said the man. "It's ridiculous. The guy was barely around. Jackie needs new teeth! And he needs someone to pay for them."

I turned my head to the side. "Hold on one second. Are you referring to yourself in the third person?"

"Yeah," the man said. "That's cool again."

Not sure it was ever cool, but I held my tongue. "So you're Jackie Love. You own *Love's Bar and Grill*."

The guy turned up a hand. "That's right. But the place is in disrepair. It's not raking in the new teeth money. That's what parents are for."

I noticed the flowers in the window box near Jackie. "Does your mom live in this house with you?"

"No. And she won't pay for my teeth because she says I'm perfect just how God made me. Crazy, right? No one is perfect."

"If she doesn't live here, where does she live?" said Granny.

"She comes up in the summer but not for long. Spends most of her time in Boca."

My mind raced with all the possibilities and implica-
tions behind what Jackie was saying. Was he telling the
truth? Was he lying? It was hard to say for sure.

But I had one last question for Jackie. "Has your mom
been back to Toluca Lake recently? Like...maybe in the last
week?"

33

MURDER MATH

"*I*f the kid says his mom hasn't been in town for weeks, Miss Lovey can't be the killer," said Betsy. "It's simple murder math."

I parked the van in the lot behind *Creature Comforts* and climbed out. The others followed.

"You have a point, but I'm not so sure." I put on my sunglasses. "Do you two want to grab a bite before we head into the shop?"

"I'll grab several dozen bites if you're buying, boss." Granny grinned.

I groaned. "You're still upset I said you were my employee. It was spur of the moment and I was telling a lie."

"It was offensive, Amy," said Granny. "We opened this place together. In your mind, are you my boss? That's how it seems to me now. It seems like that's how you think of things."

"I think of you like a grumpy queen who answers to no one," said Betsy.

Granny gave Betsy a thumbs up. "That's more like it."

"I think of you as my equal, Granny, in every way." I

looked over to Betsy. "The same is true for you, too. Sure, you don't own this place, but you're valuable in a priceless way."

Betsy beamed. "That's the nicest thing anyone's said to me all week. I'm like a prized pig, aren't I?"

"Sure," I said. "If that's what you want."

"For the record, I think of you as an employee, not as an equal and not as a pig," said Granny.

Betsy gave Granny a deferent nod. "Yes, my Queen."

Granny shoved her hands in her pockets and began walking down Main Street, away from the salon and toward the central hub of town.

"Where are you going?" I called after her.

"Donuts," Granny called back.

Betsy and I caught up to Granny just as Granny entered *Eleanor's Bakeshop*. Two teenage girls sat at the front window, sipping coffees and gossiping. But other than them, and Eleanor behind the counter, the place was empty. Eleanor didn't look up from her work or offer a friendly greeting as we entered. And when we got closer I noticed that her face was long and sullen.

"Hey there, Eleanor," I said.

Eleanor looked up from the cake she was decorating and squinted, almost like she didn't recognize us. "Oh. Amy. Petunia. Betsy. I'm sorry, I didn't see you come in. Have you been standing there long?"

Granny and I exchanged a confused look, then I glanced back to Eleanor. "We entered just a few seconds ago," I said.

Eleanor let out a distracted laugh. "Oh. I've got my head in the clouds again, I suppose."

"You look depressed." Betsy put her elbow on the counter. "What's going on in that brain of yours, Miss Eleanor?"

Eleanor wiped her hands on her apron. She sighed. "You're an astute observer of the human condition, Betsy. The proof is in the pudding, as they say. And my pudding has been drab ever since my upstairs neighbor passed. It's lonely without someone up there."

"You're a much sweeter person than I am," said Granny. "I think I would relish the peace and quiet."

"Don't get me wrong, the quiet is nice, certainly. But Gerard came in every morning and asked for my biggest chocolate chip cookie. That's what he had for breakfast, a cookie." Eleanor laughed to herself. "I don't think I appreciated the guy when he was around. Anyway, here I am going on and on when you three look hungry. What can I get you?"

We each ordered a strawberry donut and a coffee. As Eleanor retrieved the donuts from the glass case, she continued our conversation. "Amy, have you given any consideration to the apartment upstairs? I've got the apartment all cleaned up and painted, if you'd like to take a second look. I even pulled up the carpets to showcase the hardwood floors underneath."

I stammered. It was hard for me to fathom what Eleanor was saying. I thought Gerard's apartment was an active crime scene. I feared my interest in the apartment had spurred Eleanor to take unnecessary or even illegal action. Moving forward, I thought, I needed to consider the consequences of my actions during these investigations. I tried to let that sink in.

Granny, as was often the case, said what I was thinking. And she didn't mince any words. "Eleanor! You can't clean up an active crime scene."

Eleanor offered Granny a reassuring smile. "The police said I could do whatever I wanted in that apartment, so don't worry." Eleanor pointed at crumbling tiles on the ceiling above the cash register. "Workers are going to come later this week to fix my ceiling, too. I figured I might as well try to kill as many birds with as few stones as possible now that I'm in the renovation state of mind."

"The cops are not investigating this crime anymore?" I asked. "They're the ones who told you to gut the apartment and to throw away all the evidence?"

Eleanor set the donuts down on the counter with a careful motion. Her eyes widened. "I hope I haven't done something wrong."

I took a deep breath and steadied my voice. "You didn't do anything wrong, Eleanor. I'm sorry. I suppose I'm a little too invested in the investigation. Toluca Lake, the place in my memory...felt safe. And I want it to feel that way again. I want this case closed."

Eleanor gave me a little nod. "I understand. But I heard that your town in New York had murders all the time. Seems you might have gotten used to it by now."

Betsy looked off into the distance. "You never get used to seeing the darkest parts of man, Miss Eleanor. Each time the horror feels new and the pain is deep and true. Nothing can prepare the human psyche for murder." Then Betsy turned back, grabbed her donut from the counter and took a bite. "Yum, sprinkles!"

34

DONUT GO IN THERE!

We sat on a bench outside the bakeshop, ate our donuts, and talked.

"This is why we need to be active in the investigation," said Granny. "The police have dropped everything. Seems to me they're not even considering this a murder anymore. No offense, but Officer Handsome might be missing a few million brain cells."

"We both know Mike doesn't make the decisions in the department. Rotund makes the decisions. And, occasionally, I suppose Samuel has something to say. Mike is just a rookie cop."

"So you're not mad at him?" Betsy asked, taking a big bite of donut. "The guy just threatened you and told you to stop investigating. Now, it turns out, he's not even treating this as a crime."

"I'm frustrated with the police, sure. It's clear to the three of us that this was a murder, so it should be clear to them. But I don't have time to be mad at a man I'm not in a relationship with."

"That's fair." Betsy eyed the donut in my hand. "You gonna eat that or frame it for posterity?"

I laughed and took my first bite. The donut was light, flaky and delicious. "My goodness, this is so good! How is this so incredible? The jelly is like...divine."

"New York has pizza," said Granny, "Southern California has donuts and tacos."

"I will never speak ill of *Patty's Pizza*," I said. "But you're right. It's not like New York pizza. And New York donuts are nothing like Southern California donuts."

"They don't even have independent donut stores in New York," said Granny. "All they've got is that corporate junk." She took another bite of her donut. "Eleanor does it right. But there are a dozen places within an hour drive of Toluca Lake that do donuts even better. I'll take you one day. Maybe after we solve this case." Granny washed down her bite of donut with a big sip of coffee. "What are we thinking about this Jackie kid, by the way. Trash talked his dead dad. Clearly harbors resentment. Seems like a killer to me."

"That's a big jump," I said.

Betsy mumbled what sounded like a long, run-on sentence with her mouth full of donut. Then she looked at us like she had made an incredible point.

"Swallow and try again, Betsy. Neither of us speak donut," said Granny.

"I said I'm not sure if I trust much of what that guy said," said Betsy. "There was something off about him. I felt it in the bottoms of my feet, which is where I feel all my hunches."

"I'm not sure if we can trust him either," I said. "But the fact I find most interesting is Jackie's claim that his mom isn't around anymore. That little house where Jackie was living is so cute and so well-maintained. But Jackie himself is neither of those things. So if his mom isn't home, who is keeping the property so pretty?"

"That is an interesting point," said Granny. "All of his tooth chatter distracted me from the house. But it looked like whoever lives there takes a lot of pride in the place. Maybe he lied. Maybe he knows his mom killed his dad but he's trying to keep the attention off of her to keep her out of jail. Or maybe they teamed up for the killing!"

"OK, so that's one theory," I said. "But now let's consider...what if Jackie was telling the truth? If Miss Lovey is not in California what do we make of those love letters?"

Betsy finished her coffee in one, big gulp. "Maybe Gerard and Miss Lovey were pen pals. That's so romantic. They were writing one another love notes from thousands of miles away, holding each other in their hearts despite the distance."

"That's possible," I said. "And that theory actually makes a lot of sense. If Miss Lovey was in town all the time she wouldn't need to write Gerard letters. But if she's in Florida or something, maybe letters were their cute way of communicating and keeping the flame alive."

"But these were notes, not letters, right?" said Betsy. "Didn't they all say stuff like 'I'll see you later' and 'Can't wait for tonight?'"

"That's true," I said. "Good catch. But Miss Lovey still could have written the notes if she'd been in town recently."

"So the question is: did these two stay hot and heavy all these years?" said Betsy.

"I thought the two of them dated in high school and then broke up. I remember when I was a lunch lady in the cafeteria, they would always be Frenching in line for Taco Tuesday. And their breakup was a big deal when it happened. She cried. He cried. It was embarrassing." said

Granny. "But they must have gotten together at some point after graduation to conceive Jackie, right? So maybe they kept the flame alive all these years."

I took a deep breath and sat back. A mother strolled past us, pushing redheaded twins in a nice stroller. The twins were subdued, half-asleep and relaxed. I would have felt the same way after eating that donut if the murder investigation wasn't keeping me on edge.

Then I had a thought and jumped to my feet. "Maybe Sandra found the letters, and it made her angry enough to kill. Think about it! Sandra and Gerard have been married for decades, right?"

Granny nodded. "That's right."

"But what if Gerard was hung up on his first love, Miss Lovey? Maybe Sandra always knew that Gerard's flame still burned for Miss Lovey. Then Sandra found the letters and everything got out of control from there."

"But who were the flowers and champagne for if Gerard and Sandra were on the rocks and Miss Lovey was in Boca?" Betsy asked.

"A third woman," said Granny. "Smart money says this guy was playing lots of girls at the same time. What a bucket of trash."

"But we should stay focused on the two women we know about now," I said. "We need to confirm Sandra's alibi. She said she was working that night. If she wasn't she might need to be in jail...for life."

35

STUCK IN QUICK SANDRA

*G*ranny called *Sandra's Salon* and put the phone on speaker.

A woman's voice answered the phone at the salon after two rings. "*Sandra's Salon*. How can I help you?"

"Yes, hello," said Granny in her sweetest 'little old lady' voice. "My name is Marla Mavis Maplewood. I get my haircut there by Sandra."

"This is Sandra." I pictured Sandra with the phone between her shoulder and her ear, typing into the computer as she spoke. "I'm sorry, what did you say your name was?"

"Not important." Granny winced, probably regretting giving such a strange, specific name. "Well, I'm sorry to say, I'm calling today because I have a problem with you and your salon. It's an issue that I'm hoping you can resolve."

"Just tell me the problem, ma'am," said Sandra. By that point, my mental image of Sandra had her looking annoyed, no longer typing on the computer or twirling anything.

Betsy leaned toward Granny. "Accuse her of the murder straight out and see how she responds. We'll gauge her reaction that way."

Granny held her finger to her lips to silence Betsy, then she turned back to the phone. "I'm just going to come out with the truth, Sandra. The haircut you gave me is bad. When I first got it, it was fine. But it's been a few days now and I no longer feel the same. It's not holding up."

I chuckled. Granny was using the same complaint with Sandra my sister Megan had used with me about Mr. Buttons. It pleased me that there was some good use for Megan's ridiculous complaints.

"And you said your name was Marla Mavis? Mavis like the discount tire company?"

"I don't know any tire companies. Quit changing the subject! I want my money back."

"Calm down, ma'am. Look, I can't guarantee every haircut I give. At the end of the day, it comes down to personal preference. You were sitting in the chair watching me the whole time. If you didn't like what I was doing you should have said something during the cut. I can't make your hair grow back how you'll like it."

"You're right, you can't make my hair grow back. But you can give me free haircuts for life."

"Why do you want free haircuts from someone who ruined your hair?"

"I'll...give them away as gifts to people I don't like."

I laughed out loud. Granny glared at me and I went straight-faced again.

"I need to be compensated for my heartache and grief," Granny went on. "I had to go to my sister's birthday party with this haircut. No one said anything mean but I could tell they were thinking it. A woman's hair is her identity in the world. So much is said by your hairstyle. Are you clean or dirty? Are you old or young? Do you care about how you present yourself in public or do you not care? Well, Sandy, I care. And I need you to make it right."

"Hold on a second, I have a customer here." Sandra had a muffled conversation with someone at the salon. We couldn't hear much other than the music playing over the speakers. I think it was a song by Carrie Underwood. I liked her songs and bobbed my head along. Granny looked at me and I gave her a half-hearted thumbs up.

After a minute or two, Sandra came back on the line. "Alright, ma'am. When were you here for your haircut?"

Granny smiled a mischievous little grin. "Monday night."

"Then I didn't cut your hair."

Granny's eyes widened. "How do you mean?"

"I was off Monday night, lady. If you got your haircut here that night you're looking for Kitty Kat or one of my other girls."

"Is this not *Sandra's Salon* in Lexington, Kentucky?" Granny asked, in her most confused old lady voice, suddenly adding a southern accent to the mix.

"No, it's not," said Sandra, sounding annoyed.

Granny let out a little polite laugh. "OK. Nevermind. Bye now!" She hung up the phone and looked over at me. "You know what this means, right?"

"So Sandra was lying about her alibi," I said, that familiar lump forming in my throat. "We need a plan."

36

LATHER, RINSE, REPEAT

*N*othing helped me think like working with animals. And I got to do a lot of thinking that afternoon, because I had grooming appointments with several adorable pets. First came Floppy, an older King Charles Spaniel with a long tongue, big ears, and a perpetually wagging tail. Floppy had that classic spaniel smell to her and those big, adorable eyes that almost looked like a cartoon. And, like many of my spaniel clients, she was relaxed and happy throughout her grooming appointment.

Floppy chilled out during her bath. She napped while I cut her hair and she rolled on her tummy during her ear cleaning. Once I was through with her, she looked ten years younger, ten pounds lighter, and as happy as could be. "You're a good girl, Floppy. Your owner is lucky. Maybe one day I'll get a King Charles Spaniel, just like you."

That day I also had the pleasure of working with the most adorable toy poodle you have ever seen. Her little bark sounded like squeezing a toy. And I gave a Border Collie such a great haircut that his owner, a middle-aged mother, teared up. Apparently it had been quite some time since she had seen the collie's big, brown eyes.

All the while, I mulled over our predicament in the case of the murdered rock and roll guitarist. Granny had confirmed Sandra was lying about her alibi. But it was unclear whether or not that meant Sandra was the killer. People lie all the time, for so many different reasons. So I made a mental list of all the possible next steps we could take in the investigation.

At the top of the list? Gather more information about Sandra Crimper.

We needed to deduce whether or not she fit the mold of the killer in this case. What was her reputation around town? Was she known to have a temper? Did she have enemies? Had anyone seen her and Gerard arguing in public in recent weeks?

I wondered how we could get close to Sandra's loved ones without alerting her. Then I had an idea. Once the Collie left with his teary-eyed owner, I walked over to the front counter, where Betsy and Granny were working, and I launched my plan.

"Hey Granny. When I was growing up the older ladies around Toluca Lake and North Toluca played bingo every Saturday night. Isn't that right?"

"You're correct there, kid. I loved those games, cuz if the ladies at bingo didn't get enough adrenaline pumping from playing their squares, I was able to recruit them for poker. Bingo girls are easy money and they love the thrill of the hunt."

"Is that game still running?"

Granny nodded. "Oh yeah. Dirk calls the numbers. He's probably they're getting set up right now. Game starts in five minutes. Don't tell me you want to play..."

"I'm down for bingo," said Betsy. "B-I-N-G-O, B-I-N—"

I shook my head. "Not tonight. But can you call Dirk? I want to know if Sandra is there with her mother or sister. If she is, that means her house is empty. And if her house is empty—"

Betsy's eyes widened. "If her house is empty we can break and enter."

"We don't have to break but yes, we can enter," I said.

I turned back to Granny. She already had her phone to her ear. "Dirk. No, I'm not coming. Listen, is Sandra Crimper playing tonight?" Granny stopped and listened. "I'm just wondering, don't worry about it. She is there? Great. And who is she with?" Granny listened again. "Interesting. I'll tell you later. Be a dear and don't mention this phone call to anyone. OK, bye."

Granny hung up the phone. "Sandra's playing bingo with her mom. Says her sister's home sick with the sniffles."

Betsy snapped her fingers in disappointment. "If the sister's home that means we can't break or enter."

"I think that's OK." I looked over at Granny with a little smirk. "How long does bingo usually last?"

Granny shrugged. "Two hours. Two and a half, if anybody tries to cheat and there's a brawl."

I gathered my things to go. "That should be plenty of time."

37

BINGO WAS HER GAME-O

*W*e exited the pet salon at a brisk pace, eager to grab a moment to speak with Sandra's sister in private. But when we got out to the sidewalk, I stopped dead in my tracks.

The street was lined with vendors selling food and drinks and crafts. And hundreds of people wandered the sidewalks and strolled down Main Street, which had been closed to traffic. I turned to Granny. "Is today a holiday I forgot about? It's not July already, is it?"

Granny chuckled. "They call this First Saturdays. The first Saturday of every single month, they shut down the street and have a party like this."

Betsy's eyes lit up. "It's incredible, Amy. Small town living at its pinnacle. Everyone in town congregates, if they're not playing bingo, of course. It's a great way to try new restaurants and see your neighbors. I think *Liquid Staple* provided the music once or twice, in fact. They were so...metallic."

I scrunched up my mouth, feeling a little disappointed. "I wish I had known. We could have set up a table down the street to help get the word out about *Creature Comforts*. I don't want to have to go door to door to promote the business for real."

"You're not going to have to do that," said Granny. "Business is trickling in, despite Crimper's scathing review. That guy was such a catastrophe of a human. May he rest in peace or whatever."

"One time, when *Liquid Staple* played this event," Betsy said, "he got so drunk he tried to play the guitar upside down. Poor Mayor Tommy had to escort Crimper off the stage personally. Crimper demanded an egg and cheese sandwich as Tommy pulled him away. It was embarrassing for everyone."

I sighed. "On the one hand, I'm proud of Tommy for becoming the youngest mayor in all of California. On the other hand, it's disappointing he's become nothing more than a glorified sandwich boy."

"Well said, Amy," said Granny. "Our mayor the sandwich boy."

I spotted Mike over by the entrance to the *Big Baby*. My nostrils flared. "Look at Mike Fine, just leaning there. Do you think he's on-duty right now?"

"He's wearing the uniform," said Granny.

"I can't believe he's standing around at a street fair instead of investigating the murder. It's absurd."

Betsy nudged me. "Hey Amy? If you keep talking like a jilted lover, it's going to be hard for you to keep pretending you're not into the guy. Besides, I thought you said it wasn't his fault."

"He's his own man! If the police department isn't doing a good job, he should say something."

"The heart of a woman can never be tamed," said Betsy,

once again looking off into the distance like some kind of poet. "And shame on any man who tries to tame her."

Betsy's words were all the motivation I needed. Seconds later, I was elbowing my way through the crowd, carving a direct route toward Mike. When he first saw me, he smiled and waved. But then he must've gotten a good look at my face because he slowly lowered his hand almost like I was holding a gun. A few seconds later, we were face-to-face.

"Hey there. You're looking sparky today," he said.

"Don't give me that. What's the deal? First you threaten me about investigating the murder, and then the cops drop the investigation altogether. Either you're not doing your job or you're not taking a stand when you should."

"Oh I can't take a stand on anything. First of all, I'm not that kind of guy. Surprising, maybe, because I'm a police officer. But I like this job because I like to take orders, not give them. A big promotion is not in my future."

"You said you wanted to be detective."

"OK, true. I'm just saying, I'm not trying to boss people around as a police officer. I do what I'm told. And in this case I was told to drop the investigation. Apparently we don't have the resources for this case."

"More like you don't have the brainpower," I said.

Mike laughed. "You do not shy away from confrontation. I don't remember you being that way in high school."

"My only memory of you from high school is when you put straws up your nose and acted like a walrus." I crossed my arms. Part of me wondered if I was letting my anger run too far. But it was too late. And what was that Betsy had said about taming a woman?

Mike slapped his knee with delight. "Straw walrus. That was my claim to fame in high school. Can't believe you remembered that. You must have been really into me back then."

"I was not 'into you.' You said you thought I was pretty. I was just doing my schoolwork and keeping my head down."

Mike held up his hand and gave me a kind smile. "Look, I'm just playing with you. But I know that there are times to play and there are times when you need to be serious. So seriously, I'm sorry. I'm just trying to avoid a future as a deli man. I don't want to end up like the mayor."

The door to the *Big Baby* swung open and Detective Rotund emerged, shoving a chili cheese hotdog in his mouth. He stopped walking and widened his eyes when he saw me. Then he swallowed his bite of hotdog, wiped his mouth and stood tall, seemingly embarrassed that I just witnessed him eating like a slob. His French accent was extra ridiculous when paired with the hotdog. "Amy. Happy First Saturday. If you're looking for fine cuisine, I would recommend the chili cheese hotdog from the *Big Baby*. Surprisingly elegant and refined, no?"

I scoffed. "Yeah, whatever. I'm sure that's the exact type of cuisine they serve in Paris. Except the hotdogs come on croissants." I emphasized the word cuisine to make it clear I was mocking him.

Rotund looked from me, over to Mike, and then back again. He stroked his chin. "There's tension here. Mike, you are tapping your left foot. You do that when you're feeling tense or in dangerous situations. Madame, your jaw is set tight and your arms are crossed. That body language can be translated across the globe and understood by all."

"Amy was just—" Mike began. But Rotund held up his hands to stop Mike.

"No need, Officer Fine. The lady was pressing you about the death of the road-worn guitarist." Rotund handed Mike the hotdog without taking his gaze off of me. "It was an accidental death. We know beyond the shadow of a doubt. But if you'd like to keep snooping with your tiny little nostrils, I'm sure we can take a closer look at you and your grandmother and your little friend. Has one of you brought death upon this town? Is that why the weird one has been shopping for graves?"

I opened my mouth to speak but no words came out. Instead there was only a light, choking sound. Rotund was more perceptive than I thought. It was clear the three of us had made an enemy of him. I tried to tell myself none of that mattered but deep down I knew I was wrong. And Rotund would never stop being a problem for us.

38

FLUFFY'S TAIL, PART FOUR

*A*my dropped me at Petunia's apartment before she and the others headed out into the world on their investigation, and she went on and on about Crimper's murder the whole way home. The woman was hot on the trail of the killer. At least that's what she thought. Point being, she was distracted, and she had no suspicion that my food was being eaten by a little mouse. Mice are tricky. They're deceitful. They don't care who they hurt or how.

Puppy barked his infernal bark when Amy entered the home. She quickly unzipped my carrier and let me out. She hurried over to Puppy to shower him in undeserved attention, as usual. I hurried to my food bowl. You guessed it. Someone or something had nibbled my leftovers while I was out. Mouse!

I turned away from the half-eaten food in disgust. Amy approached, rolling her eyes. "Let me guess? You want a fresh bowl of food. You are such a little prince. But I wouldn't have it any other way."

She opened up a can of grade-A tuna, my favorite. She turned the can upside down into my bowl and it plopped out nice and clean. Amy squeezed the scruff of the back of my neck and leaned over to better pet me. "OK, Fluffy. Have fun while we're gone. Make sure Puppy doesn't go too crazy."

I bit my sandpaper tongue to keep from laughing in her face. Did Amy really think I had any control over that crazed canine addict?

Seconds later, Amy was out walking Puppy to give him some exercise. Then she deposited Puppy back in his area and left for the night. Was I lonely? Not a chance. Very few cats need companionship of any sort. Loneliness is weakness and I am anything but weak. It was quiet in the house as Puppy slept, sure. But I liked the quiet. I liked it, I tell you.

I left half of my food untouched and pure, straight from the can. Then I hopped up on the couch, from where I had a perfect view of my food dish, and I watched. And I watched. And I watched.

Nothing happened for the longest time. The hands of the clock ticked in a way that seemed slower and slower with each passing second. A siren blared outside the apartment but I barely noticed. Someone walked with heavy footsteps overhead.

One hour into my stakeout and I hadn't made any progress in my investigation. I jumped off the couch and smelled my food. I don't need to tell you it smelled delicious. It took all my willpower not to devour all the remaining tuna in one, big bite. I stepped back and thought. Why wouldn't the mouse eat the food I had left out? Was the rodent smarter than I had suspected? Did she know the food was a trap?

Of course. The mouse saw me sitting on the couch, keeping a careful watch over the tuna. No thief would rob a home with the owner sitting in the living room, holding a gun. I needed to lull the mouse into a false sense of security, let her think I had left for the night. So I got to work disguising myself.

One after another, I dragged and clawed at the blankets in the living room and piled them onto Granny's armchair. Two afghans, a fuzzy blanket, and a couple hand towels, for good measure. Then I crawled into the pile of blankets and hid myself beneath them. I waited 30 seconds, then I stuck just my nose and my eyes out from under the blanket. It was the perfect hiding spot and from there, I knew I would catch the perpetrator in action. If I didn't, that would be fine too. I was comfortable under those blankets. And this cat right here? He loves getting comfortable.

Spoiler alert... I fell asleep. So let's pick up this tale when I woke with a start an hour later. I leapt out from under the blankets, setting them flying in every direction. In two large lunges, I was at the edge of my food bowl. My tuna had been nibbled. And those nibbles were significant. And it looked like they had been perpetrated by a mouse.

I heard stirring in the walls. The hair on my back stood. I spun in a fast circle. There the sound was again. The unmistakable sound of little feet running through the walls. I jumped on the kitchen counter. Was the sound behind the stove? No. Higher. I jumped onto the hood of the stove but slid down the stainless steel, landing back on the counter.

The sound continued. Lightning quick footsteps, so fast they sounded like 1000 fingernails tapping at once. They were above me, then behind me, then above me again. I leapt across the counter and listened as the footsteps started from the right side of the room, then travelled all the way to the left. Then I concluded...the footsteps were for sure coming from somewhere above me.

My senses were heightened, thankfully. I zeroed in on

those footsteps with exact precision. I followed the sound with my eyes up to the top left corner of the kitchen. There, imperceptible to most eyes, human or feline, I saw it...

A tiny mouse hole.

I grimaced. "So that's where you're launching your attacks from," I said. "Not for long, little mouse. Not for long."

39

A GRAVE CONCERN

*B*etsy needed to go sign papers for her future grave site, so just Granny and I continued on to Sandra's place. The goal was to speak with Sandra's sister, to gain information that might more clearly implicate Sandra in the murder of Gerard Crimper.

It was a short drive to North Toluca but the trip took almost twenty minutes. Most of the main streets were closed for First Saturdays so we had to wind our way over to North Toluca on the backstreets. If we weren't chasing down a killer, I would have enjoyed the drive. The backstreets of Toluca Lake are flower-lined, peaceful, and quiet. But I was too anxious to enjoy the beauty. Plus, Granny kept tapping me on the arm and urging me to go faster.

After what felt like two dozen eternities, Sandra's mom's house came into view. Granny clutched my wrist so hard I thought she might break it. "There it is. Slow down."

I took my foot off the gas and cruised to a stop in an empty parking spot about two blocks from the house. "Ready?" I said.

"Not really," said Granny. "I mean, do we have an exact plan?"

"We have the element of surprise," I said. "Sandra's sister doesn't know we're investigating this murder. We'll use that to our advantage and we'll find out where Sandra really was Monday night when she was pretending to be at the hair salon."

"OK," said Granny, unbuckling her seatbelt, "let's make it rain, partner."

"Make it rain? What does that even mean?"

"Stop picking apart my powerful lines," said Granny. "It means... Let's do something great. I don't know."

Granny popped out of the van and walked toward the house. I let out a little chuckle, then followed behind.

I knocked on the front door, using the *Shave and a Haircut* rhythm to signify I was a friendly visitor. No one came to the door. Granny nudged me out of the way. "Let me have a shot at this."

She knocked so hard the frame of the house rattled. Granny was a small lady but she packed a mighty punch. Once she had finished knocking, Granny stepped back and looked at me as if to say, 'See how much stronger I am than you?'

I gave her a little nod. "Great job, Granny. You should enter a strongman contest."

We both stood there waiting for another thirty seconds. No answer. Then a voice called out from behind us. "Are you ladies looking for someone?"

I spun around to find a large, smiling man looking over at us from the front steps of the adjacent house. He was wearing a black T-shirt emblazoned with Shakespeare's face, a pair of saggy sweatpants, and sandals.

"Hi." I smiled. "I'm Amy and this is my granny, Petunia.

We're looking for Sandra Crimper. I heard she was staying here with her mom and sister?"

"Those girls aren't at home tonight," said the man. "Are you in the business?"

Granny squinted at the guy. "What business?"

The man chuckled. "The entertainment business. I'm a writer, actor, producer. Grammar is my passion. I'm playing one of the pigs in the *Three Little Pigs* at the North Toluca theater next month. You should come. Tickets are only $37.50 if you buy through me."

Granny scoffed. "Forty bucks to see some guy play a pig? That's insane."

"It's important to support the arts in Los Angeles," said the man with a surly tone. "People like me keep the entire economy of North Toluca and the surrounding towns afloat. And I play that pig with nuance and subtlety. If you don't cry, I'll give you half your money back."

"No thank you. And I know I'll cry, from the pain," said Granny.

I gave Granny an annoyed look. She refused to return my glance but I could tell she knew her behavior bothered me. When you're trying to lay low and investigate a murder, I would imagine that it would be best to refrain from insulting the neighbors. I wasn't sure why Granny didn't feel the same way.

"My Granny is just playing with you, sir. She's a huge supporter of the arts and the truth is, we were already planning to get tickets for that performance. We're on a special theater mailing list so we get access to early tickets for all the good shows in the area."

The man gave me a pleased smile. "I figured you two were messing with me."

"That's right." I turned and looked right at Granny. "Isn't that right?"

"Yeah, sure, whatever. Can't wait to see you play a subtle pig."

"As luck would have it, I have two tickets in my pocket right here. You can pay in cash or you can pay online. Would you like Friday, Saturday, or Sunday matinee?"

"We'll take the Friday," I said. "And I have cash."

I did my best to avoid wincing as I handed the man $80 in cash and accepted the tickets. But I decided I would go to the play and use the opportunity to drum up business for *Creature Comforts*. Once the man had my money in his hands he scurried back into his house with a polite thank you and closed the door behind him. Granny grumbled. "We just got mugged, Amy. I've gone my entire life without being the victim of a mugging and you ruined my streak."

"I had to do something. That guy was going to call the cops on us if you kept insulting the arts. We're trying to stay under the radar here."

"What difference does it make?" Granny asked. "No one is home. Either that, or Sandra's sister is dead in that house, just like Sandra's ex-husband was dead in his."

"Please don't be so dark," I said. "No one is dead in that house. They're all out living their lives, having a good time. And this is an opportunity for us."

"Opportunity how?"

I gave Granny a mischievous smile. "We're breaking in."

40

BREAKING THE FOURTH WALL

We crept around the side yard, staying low so that the writer/producer/actor next door wouldn't be able to see us. Within seconds, we were around the back of the house. My heart pounded in my neck like a tribal drum. The yard was small and exposed on every side. If the actor went out into his backyard, he would be able to see us. The same was true for the neighbor on the other side of the house.

"So close to your neighbors in North Toluca," said Granny.

I held my finger up to shush her as I crept toward the back door like a cat burglar. Burglar would be a funny name for a cat, I thought. I quickly filed that away for another time. Because the stakes were high and that drum in my neck was thumping harder and harder.

I reached out to try the knob on the back door. My hand got closer and closer until—

There was a sound from the actor's yard, like his back door opened and closed.

I dropped to the ground and Granny fell to her knees beside me. We held still for a moment. Then what sounded like a portable radio resounded from the actor's backyard. Next came the sound of a beer cracking open. I crawled over to the fence that separated the yards. I rose to a crouch while remaining quiet, and peered over the fence, allowing only my eyes to rise above the dividing line. Sure enough, the subtle little pig was shirtless on a lawn chair, reading what appeared to be a script and drinking a cocktail in a can. He was so close I could read that his can contained a piña colada. That sounded good to me but not at the moment. I ducked back down and turned to Granny. "He's out there. We need to stay quiet." But Granny wasn't there. I looked back toward the house. She was standing at the back door, holding it open, smiling. She beckoned for me to follow her inside, and I did.

Granny closed the door with a gentle touch and we stepped into what appeared to be a family room. There were two antique couches, an old record player, and a TV along the wall. The place smelled like mothballs and macaroni water. "How did you get in here?" I asked.

"They had one of those plastic rocks where you hide keys," said Granny. "Those things are so stupid. Everyone knows what they look like. I used the key and walked in. Was there anyone over at the neighbor's place?"

I nodded. "The pig man was drinking a piña colada from a can."

"There's a sentence I hope I never hear again," said Granny.

"Looked pretty good to me."

"The piggy or the cocktail?"

"The cocktail, Granny." I gestured around the living

room. "Now let's stop gabbing and try to find something that might help in this investigation. This is a small house so it shouldn't take long to search the place."

Granny crossed the room and looked at some photos on the wall. "Sandra's mom sure is obsessed with herself. All these pictures show her performing in local plays. I wonder if she's in the pig theater you signed us up for."

"When did you get so against supporting the arts?" I said. "Live theater is important."

"I agree," said Granny. "I just don't think watching that man play a nuanced swine supports real theater."

"OK fine. Let's focus. Look for notes or date books, stuff like that. We need to figure out where Sandra might have been at the time of the murder. Or maybe we can find something that will reveal more about her relationship with Gerard. With so much conflicting information about the relationship, we need clarity and we need it now."

"This couch is comfortable."

I turned around. Granny was reclined on the couch with her feet up on the arm rest. "If I had a cocktail in a can I would be one happy camper."

"Granny. Stop fooling around."

"OK, OK," said Granny. "I'll look more in here and I'll check out the kitchen. You go to the bedrooms."

I nodded, and headed down a corridor that I assumed led to the bedrooms. There were three doors along the hall. I entered through the door at the end of the hall first. It led me into what appeared to be the master suite. The room was pink from floor to ceiling. There was a beautiful, midcentury modern dresser along the wall with a matching mirror, which I loved. And there were photos of Sandra's mom on every surface.

First there was Sandra's mom on stage, dressed as a

pickle. Then there was Sandra's mom on stage dressed as a wicked witch. Then there was a photo of a hand wearing an engagement ring. I assumed the hand belonged to Sandra's mom since the photo was from an ad for diamonds. The place was like a museum. I gave it a quick search but didn't find anything that pertained to Sandra or Gerard, so I moved on.

The next room was bare except for a few sparse pieces of furniture, including a bed and a desk. There was a large, leather suitcase propped up on the desk. A few scattered pieces of clothing spilled out of the suitcase. All the clothes had floral designs and I thought I recognized a couple pieces from what we had seen Sandra wearing earlier.

Sure enough, the tag on the suitcase had Sandra's name on it. I gingerly opened the suitcase further and sifted through the clothes without disturbing their order. "Come on, Sandra. Give me something. You have to be hiding something."

I kept digging through the clothes for a few moments. "Talk to me, Sandra. Tell me what happened. Tell me what you did."

A soft voice whispered from someplace that felt like it was somewhere above me. "I killed my husband. I hated him. It felt so good to get rid of him."

I shrieked, stumbled back and fell onto the bed. Granny entered the room, cackling. "Amy. You're too easy to scare."

I pressed my palm to my chest. "This is a high stakes investigation, Granny. I was already nervous. You can't do that to me."

Granny helped me up from the bed. "Alright, I'm sorry. But look, I think this place is a bust. I didn't find anything in the kitchen but a pot of old macaroni."

"I knew I smelled macaroni water," I said.

"I take it you haven't found anything either, based on your conversation with a woman who wasn't here."

"There's one more room left to search." I pointed at the closed door across the hall. "I bet Sandra's sister is staying in there."

Granny and I entered that third room with big, confident steps. After she'd scared me, my jitters calmed quickly. Funny how life works that way sometimes. So I had a renewed sense of drive and determination.

The last room, unlike Sandra's, was packed with furniture and personality. That made sense, considering that Sandra's sister was a full-time resident of the house and Sandra was just a visitor. I looked over at Granny. She was already sifting through the dresser. "How old is this sister?" Granny inquired.

"Not sure," I said.

"She has some adventurous lingerie. And a lot of perfume. I'm assuming she's somewhere around Sandra's age."

"Older women often have active romantic lives," I said.

Granny shrugged. "Not me, thank goodness."

"Detective Rotund seems interested in you. In his arrogant French way."

"We both know that guy is barking up the wrong tree, Amy." Granny held up a pair of underwear and dangled them toward me. "There's less fabric here than a handkerchief."

"Just keep searching. And try not to judge."

"I can try but we both know that's not possible with me," said Granny. "Where is this woman, anyway? Dirk said the sister was home sick."

"That was according to Sandra," I said. "We already know Sandra lies."

I opened the sliding closet door to reveal a row of clothes hung according to their colors. There were some noticeable gaps in the closet, with bare hangers in between the clothes. "Is this closet color-coded?"

"You bet it is. This woman had too much time on her hands. I barely have time to code my clothes between dirty and clean."

I chuckled. "I know what you mean. Also, when are a pair of jeans actually dirty? You can wear them a few times in a row without anything bad happening. Unless there's a stain, I don't wash them."

"And now you've told me too much," said Granny.

I sifted through the clothes in the closet, gradually moving from the reds to the oranges to the yellows. Finally, I got to black. I wasn't sure what I was looking for but then I found something that caught my eye...an old letterman jacket with a logo for the *Toluca Lake Ladies Bowling Association* on the back. I pulled the jacket out and held it up for Granny to see. "Look how cool this jacket is. I wish I could buy it from her."

Granny shook her head. "So strange to me how your generation wants to dress like old women. I can't believe that's trendy now. I saw a girl the other day wearing a housecoat with a belt and high heels. And she had glasses but I swear they weren't prescription."

I stepped back and looked at the jacket. "I think it's fun and retro." I was about to put the jacket away when a detail on the front left chest caught my eye. "I also think this jacket might be the clue we've been looking for."

Granny walked over to me to get a better look at the jacket. "What do you mean?"

I pointed at the name embroidered on the jacket and Granny read it aloud. "Lovey." Granny looked up at me.

"Wait... The name on the jacket matches the letters we found in Crimper's garbage? Why?"

I let out a sigh. "I'm not sure. But we need to find out."

41

HEAVENS TO BETSY'S

*B*etsy swung open the door to her tiny home before I even had a chance to knock. "Took you forever to get here. What's going on? What happened?"

"A lot. Can I come in?"

Betsy gestured for me to enter. "I thought you'd never ask. Where is Granny?"

"She went home awhile ago to feed Puppy and work on his training regimen. By now, I think she's probably back at the casino or maybe hosting a game at *Toluca Gardens*? Hard to keep track." I entered Betsy's house, kicked off my shoes and flopped down on the couch. "Do I smell...beef?"

Betsy smiled. "Good nose. Me and mom had roast beef for dinner. I've got enough leftovers to feed myself all week. I can't wait to eat roast beef for every meal."

"Sounds...delicious? Are you off bologna already?"

"Bologna is just for lunch," said Betsy. "Say the word and I'll beef you up."

"No beef for me, thanks."

"Then get talking." Betsy crossed the room, sat on the

couch beside me, and rested her chin in her palm. "I want to know what happened at Sandra's mom's house."

Over the next few minutes, I told Betsy everything that had happened at Sandra's mom's house. Betsy had a few strange questions about the actor next door and seemed oddly intrigued by the pig play. Then, when I told her about the jacket emblazoned with the name 'Lovey' she stood up and grabbed her hair. "So that tells us everything we need to know. Sandra's sister was having a secret affair with Sandra's husband. Something went wrong, maybe Gerard threatened to tell Sandra about the affair, so the sister killed him. Now she's on the run but tragically left her trendy bowling jacket behind."

"Hang on, what do you mean she's on the run?"

"Well isn't it obvious? She wasn't at bingo, she wasn't at home either...she's in the wind. A killer on the lam."

"OK, slow down." I bit my bottom lip. "Yes, Lovey could be our killer. That's one theory. That's what Granny also thought, at first. But then she and I talked more about it and realized this whole affair with the sister theory gives Sandra even more motive than she had before. We already knew Sandra and Gerard were on the rocks. What if they had started repairing their relationship and then Sandra found out Gerard had been romancing Sandra's sister?"

Betsy nodded. "You're right. I'm ashamed I didn't see it sooner. Sandra is the killer. She found out her husband was getting with her sister and she snapped. Classic. I've changed my mind already."

"Don't get ahead of yourself though, Betsy." I crossed to the window and peeked out the blinds. I wasn't sure why, but I had a sudden feeling we were being watched. Thankfully, no one was out there. I turned back to Betsy. "Jackie Love remains a suspect as well."

"Right," said Betsy. "Jackie hated his dad because his dad wouldn't pay for Jackie's new teeth. And what did we decide about Jackie's mom? The lady who is down in Florida? Did you confirm that she has been down there all this time?"

"I'm not sure we need to confirm her whereabouts," I said. "Yes, it seems Jackie's mother and Gerard were involved at some point. That's where Jackie came from, obviously. But now that we know Sandra's sister went by the name Lovey? Seems to me she's the more likely killer than a woman with the last name Love. We haven't identified any motive for Jackie's mom to have killed Gerard, other than hating him."

"Everybody hated that guy. Unless they were involved in a romance with him," said Betsy. "Or I guess sometimes because they were involved in a romance with him. Part of this whole mystery is figuring out why so many women were attracted to Gerard Crimper."

"The heart wants what the heart wants," I said.

Betsy flopped back down on the couch. "I guess. But the stomach wants what the stomach wants, too. And my stomach never wants rotten, expired food. Gerard Crimper was rotten."

I sighed. "And now he's expired."

Betsy suddenly sat straight up. "Wait one second. Before you go off hunting for Sandra's sister... Have you confirmed that Apollo was telling the truth? What if he knew about Crimper's reviews but was playing dumb?"

"We've talked about this. Apollo's reaction was extreme, yes, but it didn't seem obviously fake. Besides, a few bad reviews is hardly enough to kill over. So many other people have bigger, scarier motives in this investigation."

Betsy crossed to the kitchen, took out some aluminum foil and began wrapping her leftover beef. "Sounds to me like you know what you need to do next."

"Help you store the leftovers?"

Betsy put the tinfoil down and placed her hands on her hips. "No, Amy. You need to find Sandra's sister, Lovey. And you need to find her fast."

42

TEND THE GARDEN

*T*he next morning, I woke up to the sound of workers mowing the grass at the *Toluca Gardens* Apartments. It was 6 AM on a Sunday. I groaned, covered my head with a pillow and yelled into it. "I need my own place!"

I shuffled out into the kitchen with quiet footsteps and started the coffee without turning on any lights. Fluffy was sitting on the counter, looking up toward the ceiling. It looked like he was plotting something. "What are you looking at?" I said.

Fluffy narrowed his eyes and swished his tail. I shrugged. None of us will ever truly know the secret lives of cats. That was unfortunate, especially because Fluffy probably knew what had happened to Gerard Crimper.

As the coffee brewed, I walked over to check on Puppy. He was bouncing off the tiny gate in his area, filled with energy. His little tail wagged so fast it looked more like a vibration than a wag. I crouched down and unlocked the gate. Puppy jumped into my arms and licked my face. I fell back onto my rear laughing. "Oh my goodness, Puppy. OK,

OK. Calm down. What's going on? Do you need to go to the bathroom?"

A few minutes later, I had the answer to that question. As soon as I strapped on Puppy's leash, he darted out of the apartment complex and headed over to his favorite tree on the sidewalk outside. The tree wasn't much more than a sapling but it was pretty and I could see why Puppy had chosen it as a bathroom. After I cleaned up after the cute little dog, he and I started off on our morning walk around the block. The only sound for miles was the lawnmower at *Toluca Gardens*. The morning was misty and gray and peaceful. A couple cars drove past us but they were going slow, almost, it seemed, out of respect for something. As we rounded the corner back toward *Toluca Gardens*, I nearly walked straight into Granny. She was wearing a teal sweatsuit and pumping her arms as she walked. I laughed. "Watch where you're going, lady."

Granny removed tiny headphones from her ears. "Amy. You're awake. Don't be offended by this, but I'm shocked."

"The lawn care guys were right outside my window this morning. I'm surprised you're awake too. I was tiptoeing around the house, trying not to disturb you."

"I've been power marching through the neighborhood for almost an hour. And I've been up since before 5 AM. Us old folks don't need sleep. It's our superpower."

"One of your many superpowers," I said.

"Don't butter me up, kid." Granny looked down at Puppy. "Did our little business man here do his business?"

"He did."

"And how about you?" Granny asked.

"Oh," I said. "Um, I haven't gone to the bathroom yet this morning but I'm hoping for something later."

Granny shook her head. "I'm not talking about the bathroom, Amy. What's going on with the investigation? Any idea what you want to do next?"

I rubbed my temples, embarrassed. "Wow. OK. I shouldn't have assumed you were talking about my bowel movements, I guess. Actually, yes, I think I have a plan. Talked it over with Betsy last night."

"I don't trust any young person who goes grave shopping for fun. But what's the plan?"

I gave Granny a little smirk. "We're going back to the hair salon."

Granny and I got home a little while later, then we got ready to leave and we headed out for *Sandra's Salon*. OK, first we stopped to grab a cup of coffee to go from the *Big Baby*. But the place was empty so we were in and out in less than five minutes.

At that point, it was still only 8 AM. The salon didn't open until nine. So Granny and I walked around Toluca Lake to take in the morning air. Granny told me all about a big poker hand she won. She got deep into the statistics and probability. And she told me all about how she knew one of her adversaries had been bluffing. Apparently the kid was shaking his leg under the table and kept checking his watch. Granny has an eye for stuff like that. I liked to think it was hereditary.

We got to the mall a few minutes after 9 AM. It too, was empty. But there was a line of women standing outside of *Sandra's Salon*, anxiously awaiting their hair appointments.

Granny scoffed. "Southern California women love hair, makeup, and beauty, don't they?"

"I think you mean, 'don't we?'" I said with a smile.

"Listen, I might have lived here for many years, but I'm not one of those preening creatures like the women by the salon. The Los Angeles I grew up in was rough and gritty. I don't think there was a single plastic surgeon here back in the day. If you wanted a new nose, you got it in a street fight."

"Somehow I think plastic surgery might be more precise," I said.

"More precise, more boring." Granny crossed her arms. "What do we do now?"

"My 'Plan A' was for us to talk to Sandra but she's too busy for that. 'Plan B' involved a quick convo with Kitty Kat, but I don't see her in there. So I'm not sure what to do next."

"We're here to find out if Sandra knew Lovey had been involved with Sandra's husband, right?" Granny asked.

I nodded.

"I say we go in there and we talk to Sandra, straight up. Sometimes you need to hit people with the truth like a ton of bricks. See how they respond. See if they get fidgety. Like that bluffer I fleeced last night."

I bit my bottom lip. "We need to be more delicate than that. Sandra is already on to us. And she pretty much hates us. Besides, the salon is too busy. We can't talk to her in front of all those people and there's no way she's going to step outside for conversation when there's such a big line."

A strong, female voice rang out from behind us. "Amy's right. Sandra's too busy to talk right now. And she hates you two."

Granny and I turned around to find Kitty Kat standing behind us, eating a yogurt sample from one of those tiny white cups. She smiled. "You're better off talking to me. But make it quick, I'm already fifteen minutes late for work."

Kitty Kat led us to the food court and the three of us sat down at a small, silver table. All the restaurants at the food court were closed because it was so early. It was eerie to see them all locked up behind metal gates. Plus, all the lights in the food court were off. So the place had a tense and dangerous energy.

Kitty Kat sucked the last drops of yogurt from the bottom of the tiny white cup. "The strawberry flavor is so good. And you get as many samples as you want, so I never have any need to buy yogurt."

"That is the beauty of free samples, I guess," I said.

Kitty Kat pulled a napkin from her shirtsleeve and wiped her mouth without looking up at me. I got the impression she was waiting for me or Granny to initiate the conversation. Fortune favors the bold, and the beautiful, so I dove right in. "You know we're investigating Gerard's murder, don't you?"

"It wasn't hard to figure out."

"Does Sandra know?" Granny said.

Kitty Kat shook her head. "Don't think so. But she doesn't trust either of you. As far as I can tell, that's a problem for the two of you."

I leaned forward. "Why? Does Sandra know who did it?"

Granny cleared her throat. "Is Sandra the killer?"

Kitty Kat shrugged. "I don't know. The thought has crossed my mind. Like I said, the two of them had been having trouble. But I don't know why Sandra would have killed Gerard now. It was kind of out of the blue."

I looked over at Granny and then back at Kitty Kat. "We just found out that Sandra's sister, who went by Lovey, was involved with Gerard. We think it might have something to do with the murder."

Kitty Kat shook her head. "No. That can't be right. Sandra has known about Lovey and Gerard forever. That was why she left him the first time. They had been working through it, supposedly. Messy business. Can you believe it, one pitiful guitarist sleeping with two women in the same family?"

"That's what we're saying," I said. "What if the two of them, Sandra and Gerard, had been working through things and then Gerard went back to Lovey without telling Sandra?"

Kitty Kat shrugged. "I don't know. I just don't think Sandra would kill over the whole sister thing after all this time. The guy has been running back to Lovey every couple years throughout his marriage to Sandra. Lovey is a drug to him. Sandra had grown numb to the affair. She didn't have any fresh rage about it. No, if she killed Gerard, it had to have been for another reason."

"But you think it's possible," I said. "You think Sandra is capable of murder."

"I think most hairdressers are capable of murder," said Kitty Kat. "We're a feisty bunch. We talk too much, we learn secrets we shouldn't learn, we own sharp scissors..."

I scooted my chair in. The squeak echoed throughout the cavernous, empty food court. "You seem so casual about all of this. Does it not freak you out that your boss might be a killer?"

"No. She doesn't have any reason to kill me. Though she might if I don't get to work soon."

"Do you know Sandra's sister, Lovey?" I said. "Do you think she's capable of murder?"

"I already said, I think everyone is capable of murder."

"You said you think all hairdressers are capable of murder," said Granny. "IS Lovey a hairdresser?"

"Well I want to change what I said," said Kitty Kat. "I think we've all got evil in us. For some of us, that evil is deep down. For others, it's right at the surface. I'm somewhere in between. Sandra is somewhere in between, too. I don't know Lovey well, so I can't say about her."

I sighed. "Thanks."

Kitty Kat stood to leave. "Sure. Look, I really need to get to work."

I reached out to stop Kitty Kat from going. "Wait. We've been looking for Lovey but we haven't been able to find her. First, we heard she was sick, but she wasn't home like she was supposed to be. Now we're under the impression she might be away on a trip somewhere. Do you have any clue where she might've gone?"

Kitty Kat smirked. "You've been looking for Lovey in all the wrong places."

"Sure," I said.

Kitty Kat tossed her little yogurt cup in a nearby trash-can. "The Kirsch family has a little bungalow in Malibu. They've had it a hundred years or something crazy. That's the only place I can think of. You want the address?"

43

MALIBU AMY

*D*epending on traffic, it could take anywhere from one to three hours to drive from Toluca Lake to Malibu, California. But the drive was always worth it. Malibu, although part of Los Angeles, felt like another country or another world. The sun shone more gently there. People smiled more broadly. And all the children were blonde-haired, blue-eyed, and kissed by the sun.

The address Kitty Kat had given us led to a small beach-side community called the Malibu Flats. Traffic hadn't been bad that day so the drive had only taken us about one and a half hours. Still, the GPS voice notifying us that we were nearing our destination thrilled me.

"Make a left. She wants you to make a left," said Granny, referencing the lady who lived inside my GPS. "You, Amy."

I did as I was told and a little security booth came into view beside a sign for Malibu Flats. I sighed. "Security."

Granny snapped her fingers in annoyance. "Dang. We should have known. These Malibu people don't like to commingle with the rest of us. What are we going to do now?"

"Not a problem, Granny," I said, rolling my window down as I approached the booth. "I've got this."

I waved at the middle-aged lady who was staffing the booth. Her khaki pants were hiked well above her belly button, her long blonde hair flowed halfway down her back, and her nose was oddly young looking and perfect, maybe thirty years younger than the rest of her face. I thought back to Granny's comment about plastic surgery and fistfights and swallowed my laughter. "Good morning, Miss. I'm Amy from *Creature Comforts*. Here for a pet grooming appointment at the Kirsch house."

The woman typed into a little computer. "Pet grooming, pet grooming... I don't see you here."

"Figures. My Granny here booked the appointment and she's always getting things wrong." I did my best to sound annoyed as I turned to Granny. "See? This is why we need to send you to a home. You keep costing us business. You're a liability. This lady doesn't have any record of the appointment. I'm sorry, Granny. I can't afford someplace nice on a groomer's salary. You're going to be eating Jell-O every meal for the next few years but I'll visit when I can."

Granny's chin wobbled. "No, Amy. Don't send me to a place like that. Jell-O makes me crazy. I swear I called the Kirsch people!"

The long-haired woman looked over at Granny, then to me. "Everybody calm down. No one here needs to be sent to a home. I make little mistakes like this all the time. And it's possible there's a glitch in the system. You go right ahead. Have a good day, OK? You too, Granny. And uh, watch your back."

Granny smiled brightly like a Christmas tree. "Thanks. Bye-bye."

The woman opened the gate and I cruised into the little

community. Granny slapped her knee and laughed. "Nice job, kid. I loved the part about the Jell-O, brilliant. How was my performance?"

"Disturbingly convincing. You did great, Granny. No wonder you're such a shark at the poker table." I pointed out the window, where I could see slivers of the ocean poking out between adorable little cottages. "Look at this neighborhood, by the way. Gorgeous."

"Makes sense this place has been in the Kirsch family for generations," said Granny. "Because there's no way a failed actor could afford a getaway in Malibu like this."

The GPS pinged. "You have arrived at your destination." I looked out the window. We had stopped in front of the most rundown house in the neighborhood. It was a yellow cottage with peeling paint. The lawn was brown and patchy. And the windows had been boarded up. I scrunched up my nose. "Is this the right place?"

"Just because you inherit a nice house doesn't mean you have the money for upkeep. There's a car in the driveway."

I looked. Sitting in the driveway was a rusty old Volkswagen Beetle in worse shape than the home. "I don't think that vehicle functions, Granny," I said. "No way did Lovey Kirsch drive that thing here from North Toluca."

"You're not a mechanic, Amy. You're an animal person and, as of a few days ago, you're an amateur sleuth. But I've seen junkier cars run for thousands of miles."

I hopped out of the van and circled the little Beetle. There was a current inspection sticker on the front window. "You're right, Granny. Maybe this thing functions. This sticker doesn't expire for another ten months." I cupped my hands against the driver side window and looked inside. "Plus, there's an empty Coke can in the cup holder and it's got the new design from this year."

Granny put her hands on her hips and looked up at the house. "So Lovey Kirsch is inside this crumbling beach house." Granny looked back at the *Creature Comforts* van, then returned her gaze to the house. "What are we going to do, tell her we're here to groom her yard?"

I chuckled. "We've dodged our way through enough little conversational obstacles by now, Granny. You need to have faith. I believe in you. Do you believe in me?"

"Not really," said Granny.

With my hands on my hips, I looked over at her.

"Fine, Amy," said Granny. "I believe in you and I wouldn't want to be in this dangerous situation with anyone else. Does that make you happy? I think you're a strong, independent woman who is capable of anything. I'm proud of how well I raised you and how well your dad half-raised you out in the desert. But don't forget I had to undo a lot of damage he did on your character. So everything you are, for the most part, is thanks to me."

"I didn't expect that speech," I said. "Are you done or is there more?"

Granny nudged me out of the way, charged up the front walkway and knocked on the front door. Once again, she used her house-shaking knock. That time I was afraid she might bring the roof down but we were lucky because the structure remained intact. We waited a few minutes but no one came to the door. Granny knocked again. Again, nothing. The windows on either side of the front door were covered by boards so we couldn't get a look inside. Granny tried to pry one of the boards away from the other windows on the front of the house but they were nailed in tight.

"What are we going to do now?" Granny said.

I gestured around the side of the house with my head.

"Let's walk around back. Maybe the guest of honor is suntanning or swimming in the ocean."

My jaw dropped as we rounded the house. There we were, face to face with the Pacific Ocean. Back in New York, I had grown to appreciate the Hudson River. I loved how it stretched between cute little towns all up and down New York, how it flowed into the city and divided New York from New Jersey...I might have even claimed that I liked the river more than I enjoyed the Pacific Ocean back in California. But at that moment in the Kirsch's backyard, feet away from the water's edge, the Hudson River was the farthest thing from my mind. The Pacific Ocean is endless and powerful. It's more mysterious than the Atlantic, maybe because on its waves you can sense the far east and Hawaii and all those islands in the South Pacific. Maybe because the shoreline is dotted by striking, barren cliffs. I wasn't sure what gave the Pacific its allure. I'm not an oceanographer or a nature reporter. All I can tell you is standing there, looking at the water, I was breathless. A small smile flickered across my lips. "Look at that."

Once again, Granny pushed past me. "Yeah, yeah. It's the ocean. So what? We're here on a job."

I chuckled and followed Granny a few steps out onto the beach, then we both turned around and looked at the back of the house. I pointed toward the back window. Half of a large pane of glass was covered with boards. But on the other half of the window, the boards had been pried off and they laid splintered on the ground. "Maybe Lovey forgot her key and had to break into her own house."

Granny wrung her hands. "Or maybe someone else broke in looking for her."

There was a sliding back door so of course I tried that first. But it was locked. So I climbed into the broken window.

Sometimes being tiny is very convenient like that. Then I opened the door for Granny and she came inside.

The bungalow was dark and shadowy. We were in some kind of weather-protected back porch or all-seasons room. Blankets were covering a few pieces of wicker furniture. But there was another Coke can sitting on the floor. And it had the new design, just like the can from the Beetle.

I opened another door and we stepped into the proper interior of the home. Everything in there had also been covered in blankets. I swallowed. "Hello? Lovey? Miss Kirsch? I'm a friend of your sister. Visiting from North Dakota." I said the words North Dakota in an accent and tried to keep up the accent as I continued speaking. "Yeah. California is so nice. Sandy said I should look you up. I've got my Granny here, too."

"I'm not from North Dakota so I talk normal," said Granny, rolling her eyes at me.

We entered a small, closed-off kitchen. There was a passport out on the table. I flipped it open. The passport belonged to Anna Lovey Kirsch. She was pretty, with blonde hair like her mother and sister. But she looked to be at least fifteen or twenty years Sandra's junior. Beneath the passport was a printout of a plane ticket. I picked up the ticket and read the details aloud. "This is an American Airlines flight from Los Angeles International Airport to Brazil. It left yesterday."

Granny approached and stood by my side. Her little brown eyes darted over the paper. She spoke in a hoarse, concerned voice. "I don't know if we're safe here, kid. Maybe we should—"

I shook my head. "We need to keep looking. We need to find out if something went wrong. We'll stick together."

I took Granny's hand and led her down a small, dark

corridor. There were two doors. I opened the first door, which led to a simple bathroom. Old, dusty beauty products dotted the bathroom counter, the liquids separated into creepy oils and colors. There was a toothbrush that looked out of place among the beauty artifacts. It was brightly colored, with a tongue scraper on the end. The toothbrush looked newer than the rest of the items.

I stepped out of the bathroom, keeping Granny's hand in mine, and walked down the hall, toward the only other door. The door was open half an inch. I nudged it further open with my toe. We stepped into a large, master bedroom. Dust was suspended in the air, trapped in beams of light which entered the room through the cracks in the boarded up windows. The place felt frozen in time. The tribal drums had found their way back into my throat from my heart.

Granny tightened her hand in mine. The bed was unmade. The dresser had been knocked over. The television was on the floor, screen broken. The whole scene was disturbingly similar to Gerard Crimpers' apartment the day we found his body.

I crossed to a closet at the front of the room, flung open the doors and couldn't believe what I saw. The woman from the passport, Anna Lovey Kirsch, was dead.

She had been shot between the eyes.

44

LOVE IS DEAD

I stammered and stumbled backwards. "Lovey Kirsch... That's... That's..."

Granny gripped my arm tight just above the elbow. She pulled me close. "Another dead body. Another victim. Poor girl."

I took a deep breath to steady myself. "Let's take another look around the house and see if we can find anything that feels like a clue. I mean, we already found the plane ticket and the passport, but besides that."

"Works for me," said Granny. "But do you think we're safe? What if the killer is—"

I shook my head. "The blood is already dry. Besides, we would have heard someone stuff the body into the closet when we got here. And there was a layer of condensation on the window I climbed through, so the window hadn't been disturbed for at least a few hours before our arrival."

"That's my little tracker. I guess your dad deserves credit for some stuff. OK. Let's keep looking." Granny squeezed my arm even tighter. "But I'm not letting go of your arm."

The boarded-up home took on a creepier and creepier

energy as we searched. And the longer we stayed in the house, the more uneasy I felt. Gerard Crimper was a hated man and it was easy for me to imagine plenty of good reasons someone might have wanted him dead. But I had never heard anything bad about Sandra's sister, except for maybe the fact that she had been cavorting with her sister's husband... which, to be fair, wasn't good.

Granny and I searched the beach cottage with careful precision but we didn't turn anything up. As I sifted through junk mail on the kitchen counter for the third time, I realized we needed to make a change. "Let's get out of here. Search outside."

And for two or three minutes, Granny and I stood out behind the house, allowing the breeze to sweep over us as we listened to seagulls overhead. The cool ocean breeze calmed me. And as we stood there, I imagined generations of the Kirsch family in the exact same spot, appreciating nature just like Granny and me. The thought swept over me like a powerful wave. Tragedy had befallen the family and it could all be traced back to Gerard Crimper.

There was a small picnic table on the back patio. I sat on the table and put my feet on the bench, looking toward Granny. "First theory: Sandra snapped. Killed Lovey in a desperate, jealous rage."

"I thought it," said Granny. "And we've discussed the possibility before."

"But I'm not sure if that's a good theory," I said. "Kitty Kat says Sandra had known about the affair for years. So why would she have snapped and killed Gerard now? Besides, does Sandra strike you as the type of woman to kill her own sister?"

Granny shrugged. "That's not a type of woman I've ever imagined before. Can't say."

"Also," I said, "Sandra has been around town lately. She would've had to be gone for quite a while to drive out here, kill her sister and get back to Toluca Lake without anyone realizing she had left. And Lovey was shot with such precision, right between the eyes. If Sandra lost her mind after years of jealousy and acted on her emotions, the murder scene would indicate that. She wouldn't have shot her sister between the eyes. She would have bashed the girl over the head with a vase or something more impulsive."

Granny sat at the table beside me. A seagull landed on the patio where Granny had been standing. It looked right at us. "What're you staring at, Mr. Seagull?" I said. "Do you have an idea? Is there something we're missing?"

The seagull flew away with an unhelpful caw. Granny picked at a worn spot on the table. "I have a couple theories we haven't discussed."

"Shoot."

"Poor choice of words, kid." Granny kept picking at the table but didn't look up. "We need to think about who might have wanted both Gerard and Lovey dead. Other than Sandra. Lovey had that plane ticket to Brazil, right? Maybe she figured out who killed Gerard and thought she might get murdered just for knowing. So she was planning to escape. But the killer couldn't stand to let Lovey leave the country with the knowledge of what the killer had done. So they murdered Lovey, too."

I nodded. "That might be what happened. Or maybe Lovey killed Gerard, then someone who loved Gerard — someone like Sandra or Jackie — found out, so they killed Lovey to avenge Gerard's death."

"You said it yourself... Lovey didn't have any motive to kill that creepy weirdo. And I doubt his cheated-on wife or estranged son would make the effort to carry out a revenge killing on Gerard's behalf."

I shrugged. "Well, Lovey had no motive we're aware of. But Gerard was terrible to women everywhere so I'm sure she resented him for something."

Granny climbed down off of the table, crossed to the house and closed the sliding door. Then she turned back to me. "So what do we do now?"

"There were roses and champagne at Gerard's place," I said.

"So what?"

I turned back to Granny. "So let's go to the flower shop and find out who they were for."

45

FLUFFY'S TAIL, PART FIVE

*H*umans get to go on trips. They get to go on vacation. They get to spend the afternoon in Malibu, pretending to investigate a murder while they sip on umbrella drinks on the beach.

Cats don't often get to go anywhere. Sometimes we stay with family friends, where the house is confusing and different, and the food bowl smells like Cheerios. Other times we're sent to so-called pet hotels while our parents go away on vacation. Those pet hotels are particularly ridiculous. You humans do the craziest things. Do you feel guilty for pampering yourselves while leaving your pets at home? Sure, send them to some place called a 'hotel,' and that will make things right.

You have to be kidding me. News flash: you're going to a hotel. I'm going to a boarding house with fake grass and fake sunshine and fake people whose only friends are cats. Not my type. Note to the wise among you: pet hotels are a no-no. Personally, I'd rather be set free in the forest while you're off in Boca or Miami or San Diego. At least in the wild I can return to my feline roots and reclaim my throne as the king of the jungle.

Anyway. Petunia and Amy went off to Malibu, as I said. They left me alone in the home with my tormentor, Puppy, and my other tormentor, the mouse. Puppy amused himself by barking at a lamp for a full hour after Amy and Petunia left the apartment. I stared him down and gave him my most evil of evil eyes but that did little to calm the tweaked-out, drug-obsessed lunatic. I'll admit, I was too focused on the puppy for that hour. My annoyance with the dog was my weakness...and the mouse took advantage.

Puppy eventually decided the lamp was not a threat and fell asleep. Then, once he had been still for a few moments, I crossed back to my prized bowl of tuna. It had been nibbled. I wanted to yell at the dog but I knew it was my own fault. I'd let my guard down. I'd missed my opportunity to catch the mouse when she was out of her hole, and I'd paid the price in tuna.

I looked around, eyes darting from one corner of the room to the other, then up to the mouse hole near the ceiling. But not a creature was stirring in the house, you know how the expression goes.

The night prior, the mouse had spent the evening in the cupboard, nibbling Amy's secret stash of cookies. The cupboard was too high and isolated, so I couldn't jump to it to catch the mouse in the act. But I heard the nibbling. And the nibbling enraged me.

The mouse attacked when darkness fell over the streets of Toluca Lake. A less noble cat than myself might wish illness, death, or a cruel trap upon such a devious creature. You should know, I never wanted to harm another living thing. Except tuna. But 'do no harm' is part of my code. Part of my ethics. It's who I am.

So what was the goal with the nefarious mouse?

I wanted her out of the home. Perhaps Petunia could set the rodent free in a garden or in the house of one of her enemies. I just wanted my tuna...every morsel...and I wouldn't rest until the future of my fish was secured for me.

But by that point, I felt the mouse was playing games with me. Darting out when I wasn't looking, nibbling, and then disappearing. It was my own fault. Puppy was distracting. And sometimes he did this little thing with his eyes that made my heart feel soft. Nevermind. I take that back. I don't have a heart. I don't have emotions. And there was no way I was going to make friends with that puppy or cuddle up against it for warmth or do anything like that.

Everyone thinks that cats and dogs should be friends and fall asleep together because of the Internet. It's not natural. Strike from the record anything I said about the puppy being cute. He was a drug- addicted deviant. OK? Do you understand me?

Good. Back to the mouse. As I stood at the lip of my bowl, looking down at the tiny divots which had been caused by the tiny little teeth of the mouse, I hatched a plan. I would no longer be distracted by the dog or by the wind or by my very feline nature and tendency toward distraction.

No. My plan was to stay awake all night, listening for the sound of the mouse in Amy's secret stash of cookies. Then I would climb to the top of refrigerator and brave a death-defying jump across the kitchen, onto the top of the cupboard. From there, I would open the door and slip into the secret cookie area like Tom Cruise in *Mission: Impossible*. I would trap the mouse in the cookie box.

And then everyone would see the face of evil incarnate.

46

A FLOWER FOR YOUR THOUGHTS

"So what did the flower guy say?" Betsy scratched behind the ears of an old beagle. The beagle sat there and took the scrubbing without so much as a flinch. I hope I'm that agreeable when I get older, I thought. What was that beagle's name again? Killer? Quick? Shotgun?

I shook out my arms. Clearly, the murder investigation was preoccupying my mind. "I'm sorry. I zoned out for a second there. What did you say?"

"I asked what you learned from the flower guy," said Betsy. "But I'm also wondering how his shop was looking. Did it seem like he needed business? Do you think he'd give me a discount if I ordered my own funeral bouquet for an undisclosed date in the future?"

I looked at Betsy like she was nuts. "Betsy. You need to stop worrying about your own funeral."

Betsy switched to the beagle's other ear. "I know. You're right. The thing is, Mom and I have been planning to go grave shopping for months now. So that little girls trip wasn't out of the ordinary at all. But—"

"Yes it was, Betsy."

"I'm talking here!"

"Sorry," I said. "Continue."

"So the grave shopping wasn't strange. But then Crimper got murdered and I found myself consumed by the need to prepare for my own demise, including, as I mentioned, funeral bouquets. Forget I said anything."

"That's going to be tough to erase from my memory, Betsy. It's one of the strangest things I've ever heard someone say. But you're healthy, right? There's nothing wrong with you or your mom?"

"Mom's as strong as an ox. I'm as strong as a bull. Between the two of us, we could probably plow sixty acres a day. Not that either of us would want to do that, we're both pretty sedentary by nature."

"OK. Good."

"So did the flower guy help with the investigation or what?" said Betsy.

"I haven't gone to the flower shop yet. Granny's coming at lunch and we're heading over then."

Betsy grinned. "Can I come?"

Granny arrived at *Creature Comforts* at 12:30 PM, just in time for our lunch hour adventure. She'd been at home, working on getting Puppy to sit. Puppy, however, still seemed to prefer standing. Or jumping. Or barking at lamps.

The door chimed when Granny entered and she winced. "Can we get rid of these bells on the door? Every time I walk through here I feel like a Christmas elf. I'm short enough without the reminder."

I laughed. "I'll take those off the door later. Are you ready for the flower shop?"

Betsy emerged from the back room and gave us two thumbs up. "I'm ready."

Granny groaned. "She's coming?"

"I know you love me, Granny." Betsy crossed to Granny. "Give me one of your famous hugs."

"My hugs are only famous because they happen so infrequently. And today is not your lucky day."

Betsy shrugged. "Fine. I'll settle for a firm and businesslike handshake."

Granny shook Betsy's hand.

Betsy beamed. "You love me so much."

Granny let go of Betsy's hand and turned to me. "Are we going or not? Because if we're not doing the investigation today I'm going to go to the casino."

"You know you technically work at this pet salon, right?" I said.

"I'm technically a co-owner of the pet salon, Amy. And owners come and go as they please."

Granny turned, pushed open the door, and exited. Betsy followed. I said a quick goodbye to the pets in the kennels and then hurried after them.

We entered the flower shop to find a gruff older gentleman arranging a bouquet of roses at the back counter. The guy was wearing olive green pants and a heavy sweater. He had a large nose and pouty lips, kind of like Robert De Niro. And he had the attitude to match. "Hi. I'm a little busy. Come back later."

I stepped forward. "We won't take too much of your time. I just have a quick question. But I don't need to make an order or anything."

"So you're not here to spend money. You're here to interview me? I thought Dirk was the only writer at the *Toluca Tribune*."

"This isn't a newspaper mission, mister," said Betsy. "It's way more interesting than that. Have you ever thought of yourself and wondered if one day you might become an international man of mystery?"

"No. I hate mystery. I like sports. And cigars. Barbecue is also good. Not a lot of good barbecue in Southern California, though."

"That's not true," said Granny. "You just need to know where to look. You never had *Roscoe's Chicken and Waffles*?"

"That's southern food but it is not barbecue."

"They've got plenty of barbecue there. You don't know what you're talking about. And you have a thick New York accent. What do you know about barbecue anyway?"

The man set his bouquet of roses aside and looked over at Granny. "I'll tell you what... Hold on a second... Petunia?"

Granny narrowed her eyes. "Do I know you?"

"It's me, Nathaniel. We were neighbors for years. You won $600 from me in a poker game one night."

Granny pointed at the guy. "Nathaniel, of course. You check/raised me on the river with bottom pair. I pushed all-in and you called. I'll never understand that move."

"And I'll never understand anything you just said. That's probably why I lost."

"I didn't realize you owned the flower shop here in town. That used to be my gig in New York actually. Owned a flower shop in a little town called Pine Grove."

"You're kidding. I opened this place up a few years ago in my retirement. You may not know it from looking at me, but I love flowers. I love the way they smell, I love the way they feel. They're so delicate." Nathaniel put on a pair of glasses and I suddenly noticed he had kind, blue eyes. "How can I help you?"

"My uncle used to buy flowers here all the time for my

aunt. But now my uncle is dead and my aunt is sad. We're trying to cheer her up, but...she won't tell us what kind of flowers he used to buy. So we were hoping you could tell us," I said.

"That's strange," said Nathaniel. "Why wouldn't your aunt tell you?"

I began to speak again but Granny held up her hand to stop me. "It's OK, Amy. This guy paid me all $600 he owed me, no questions asked. He can be trusted."

Nathaniel narrowed his eyes. "Alright, now I'm getting concerned. First this lady tells me I'm a man of mystery or something. Now you're talking about whether or not I can be trusted. What's going on here?"

Granny looked at me, almost as if she were requesting permission. I trusted her judgment of character more than anyone I had ever known. So I gave her a little nod. Then Granny turned back to Nathaniel and told him all about Gerard Crimper and the flowers. She didn't officially confirm we were investigating the murder or that we didn't trust the cops to solve it, but she might as well have. Nathaniel didn't bat an eye at Granny's story. But when she was finished talking, he simply shook his head.

"Why are you shaking your head like that?" said Granny. "I told you we need to know who he bought flowers for. There must have been a note."

Nathaniel nodded. "Of course there was a note. There was always a note with Gerard. But I need to be discrete. It's part of the flower man's code of honor. You can't violate that."

"Absurd," said Betsy. "You're not a doctor or a therapist. You sell flowers. All due respect, kind sir, I'm sure you do beautiful work and I look forward to using you for my funeral one day—"

"Betsy," I said in a stern tone.

"No, Amy, he needs to hear this." Betsy crossed the shop and got right in Nathaniel's face. "Dead bodies are piling up in Toluca Lake, Mr. Nathaniel. This town, once quaint and charming, is becoming a veritable death sentence for all those who walk the streets. Do you have a wife? Children? Grandchildren?"

Nathaniel nodded. "All three."

"Then you're going to share this information and you're not going to think twice about it."

Nathaniel stammered. He appeared to have been shaken by Betsy's stern tone and crazy eyes. "I—I couldn't help you even if I wanted to. Crimper wrote all the notes by hand. And he was in here buying flowers three times a week. The guy had more girlfriends than I could count. And they all thought they were exclusive."

Betsy took Nathaniel's hand in hers. "You've done the right thing here today, Nate. I'll call you about the funeral arrangement later."

"Are you sick?" said Nathaniel.

Betsy shook her head. "Not at all."

47

BILLY GOAT GRUFF

Granny wanted to go to the *Big Baby* for food. But Betsy and I were in the mood for baked goods and coffee. So we outvoted her two to one and we all three went to *Eleanor's* for lunch. There were a few guys fixing Eleanor's ceiling behind the counter. She was supervising the work, so we ordered with the other girl who worked there and we sat down.

"These construction guys smell terrible and they're making so much noise," said Granny. "I knew we should've gone to the *Big Baby*. They haven't done any work on that place in thirty years. That's exactly how I like my restaurants."

"Old and unimproved?" I said.

"Authentic and charming. And don't pretend like you don't love the *Big Baby Diner* more than anyone in this town, Amy. We all know you do."

I laughed. "It's true. I do. But I already told you I was in the mood for a pastry. And Betsy was with me. This is a democracy."

Granny grumbled something about how she should

have become a communist when she had the chance. I made a mental note to continue that conversation later. But for the time being, we needed to discuss the flower shop man, Nathaniel, and the new information we had received about Gerard.

I sipped my coffee. "So that was an interesting conversation with Nathaniel. Sounds like we were right. Gerard Crimper was running around with all sorts of women, not just Sandra and Lovey."

Betsy licked her teeth. "But how can we figure out who else the creep was dating? Should we go back into his apartment and look for more love notes from different women?"

"No point," I said. "The cops already gave Eleanor the OK to clean it out. The place doesn't have a trace of Gerard Crimper or the murder any longer."

Eleanor approached with a smile. "Hello, girls. So good to have you back." Eleanor gestured at the unopened box of pastries on our table. "Are you three planning on admiring the box or were you going to open it and eat the treats inside?"

"We're going to eat the treats." I opened the box and pulled out the croissant I had ordered. Betsy pulled out the blueberry muffin she had ordered. And Granny pulled out her oversized oatmeal raisin cookie.

"I'm going to be honest with you, Eleanor, I didn't want to come here for lunch," said Granny. "But these two outvoted me and I missed my chance to join the Soviets back in the 60's."

Eleanor let out a little titter. "You crack me up, Petunia. So nice having you back in town. I love seeing you girls and your smiling faces. You let me know if you need anything else."

"As a matter of fact, I do need something." Granny

gestured at the construction workers over by the counter. "Can you get these guys to leave? They smell like tobacco, body odor, and last night's beer. And they're making such a racket it's ruining the ambience."

I buried my face in my hands, embarrassed by Granny's brash request. She had no shame in asking for what she wanted.

"They should be out of here soon enough. But I don't want to scare them off before the job is done. That little spot in the ceiling has been leaking for so many years. I never wanted to get it fixed while Gerard and Sandra were living up there. Didn't seem right, causing such a racket right under my neighbors' feet. But now that the place is empty, I can finally cause all the racket I need."

"What was the leak from?" I said. "Was there a hole in the roof or pipes or something?"

"Pipes," said Eleanor. "Leaky pipes. They're always trying to bring me down."

"If pipes are the problem, you're going to need a plumber in here to figure out where the water is leaking from," I said. "And if it's the roof that's the issue, you should call a roofer. I admire how proactive you're being, getting the tiles repaired, but if you don't address the source of the problem then the problem won't stop."

"I've already got a call in to Paul the plumber. But I couldn't stand looking at that crumbling ceiling tile a minute longer. Paul says it shouldn't be a problem." Eleanor gave us a polite little smile as she hurried back toward the workers.

Betsy took a big bite of her muffin and crumbs spilled all over the table. "You really gave that little old lady the third degree about her broken ceiling tiles, Amy."

I bit my lip. "I guess I kind of did. I must be in investigation mode or something. Did it seem like she was offended?"

"You talked about the woman's leaky ceiling like she was too stupid to understand simple repairs," Granny said. "But Eleanor is sweet and, if I'm being honest, a little dumb. So I doubt she was offended."

"Granny," I said with a scolding tone. "Don't talk about people that way."

"You're the one who got into it about the ceiling," said Granny. "Anyway, what's next with this investigation?"

I broke off a piece of my croissant. I did my best to avoid spilling crumbs everywhere as Betsy had, but I failed. Crumbs are par for the course when you own a bakery, I suppose. But I still felt a little bad. "Like you said, any one of Gerard's love interests might have snapped and killed him. By the—"

"Petunia," said Eleanor, from over behind the counter. "You're still planning to call me when you have another poker night, right?"

"Sure, sure," said Granny. "No problem."

Granny flashed Eleanor a thumbs up. Eleanor returned the gesture with a thumbs-up of her own. Then she disappeared to the back of the shop with a broom in hand. Granny turned back to me. "Gross. I think I might've made a friend. What were you saying, Amy?"

"I was saying any one of Gerard's girls might have snapped. But Sandra was his wife." An image of her face flashed through my mind. "Her eyes are shifty, aren't they? And she's lied to us at least once or twice so far."

Betsy tossed the wrapper of her muffin into the empty box. She leaned forward. "So you think we need to have one more conversation with Sandra Kirsch Crimper?"

"That's right," I said. "And I think it might be extremely dangerous."

48

OLD WIVES' TALE

*S*andra opened the door wiping tears from her eyes. "Why are the two of you at my house now? I heard you were at my place of business. You came to my husband's funeral. You chased my stepson down when he got upset and ran off. What do you want with my family?"

I shifted my weight from my left foot to my right. It wasn't clear to me how to proceed. For some reason, I didn't expect Sandra to be upset or confrontational. But Granny and I needed information so I pressed on. "We can explain all that. But first... Are your sister or your mother home?"

Sandra shook her head and dabbed at her eyes with a tissue.

"Good," I said.

"What's that supposed to mean?" Sandra's eyes hardened.

"OK, Mrs. Crimper. Or, Ms. Kirsch," I said. "You've noticed that Granny and I have exhibited odd behavior around you since your husband died. The truth is..." I took a deep breath. Was I really about to do this? "We have good reason to believe that the Toluca Lake Police Department is not treating your husband's death as a murder. We found the body. We know he was killed by someone, and that someone is still on the streets. Justice is important to me and my granny, so we're trying to solve the murder."

Sandra lowered the tissue from her eyes and crumpled it in her hand. "You want justice for Gerard."

"We want justice for everyone in Toluca Lake. What happened to Gerard wasn't right." Granny leaned to the side to get a look past Sandra, into the house. "Do you mind if we come inside and talk?"

Moments later, we were seated around the small table in the kitchen. Granny and I each made a few comments about the decorations in the house and how lovely the home was. I wanted to make it clear that I had never been there before but I might have been overcompensating, and maybe Granny was too. But Sandra was too upset to notice anything off about us.

"My sister was murdered too," she said. "They found her in our Malibu house. I guess the police got an anonymous tip."

I snuck a look over at Granny. That anonymous tip had come from me. It was nice to know the tip had led to action. I looked back at Sandra. "What horrible news. I'm so sorry you're going through all of this."

Sandra ripped a little piece of paper out of a magazine and folded it up real tiny. I studied her face as she folded. Granny and I were there to determine if Sandra could have killed Gerard or Lovey. The woman in front of us had red eyes, sagging with exhaustion and sorrow. But that didn't mean she couldn't have killed.

Sandra put the folded up piece of paper to the side and

looked at me. "A lot of people hated Gerard. There were so many I can think of who would have wanted him dead. Have you been thorough in your investigation? Have you learned anything useful?"

"We have leads. Also, for whatever it's worth, Amy and I believe that there is good in everyone. Sure, the guy wasn't the most popular fellow in Toluca Lake. I'm not the most popular lady, either."

Sandra let out a little laugh. "People around here didn't understand that he was a true artist. He was temperamental, sure. But there was so much beauty in that man. Even when he was playing his guitar at top volume, annoying me, I saw that beauty. Gerard had a big heart. And yes, we had issues. But I knew in my heart, we were going to get past them." Sandra looked down and grabbed her temples with her hand. "I have no idea how my sister got wrapped up in all this."

Granny looked over at me and then back at Sandra. "You don't?"

It seemed Granny, like me, was confused. We both thought Sandra had known all about Lovey's affair with Gerard. But if Sandra didn't know that Lovey had been involved with Gerard, Sandra had less motive than we had thought.

"The two of them weren't connected in any way," said Sandra, sniffling. "Other than through knowing me. In fact, they weren't even friendly. Lovey despised Gerard ever since the moment I met him. She refused to be a bridesmaid in my wedding as a form of conscientious objection. The two barely spoke. They barely knew one another."

Granny sat back in her chair and let out a deep breath. "I'm surprised to hear you say that, Sandra. Because, and I'm only saying this because we all want justice here, we've heard that Gerard and Lovey were...intertwined."

Sandra furrowed her brow. "I don't understand."

I spoke in my most gentle tone. "I don't know how to say this, Sandra. Your husband and your sister were in love."

49

KICKED TO THE CURB

*S*andra shoved me out the front door, then held a broom overhead and threatened to bash Granny if Granny didn't follow me out. Perhaps it's needless to say, but Granny followed me...fast. As Granny and I hurried out to the van, Sandra screamed at us. She said we were slanderous liars. She accused us of murdering Gerard. She cursed us for defiling the name of her dead sister.

Seconds later, Granny and I were flying down the road in the *Creature Comforts* van, buckling our seat belts as we drove away.

"Go, go, go," said Granny. "She's following us with that broom."

I glanced in the rearview mirror. Sure enough, Sandra was running after the van, looking like a villager with a pitchfork the way she was carrying that broom. "It's OK. She can't catch up to us. We made it out."

I made a sharp turn and sped up, just to be safe. Granny let out a stressed sounding laugh. "That was bad. I don't think we did a good job back there, Amy. We insulted a grieving woman!"

"Listen, I don't think we handled ourselves the best we could have, but we're trying to solve a murder here. And we only treated Sandra that way because she has lied so much over the course of this investigation. Plus…she deserved to know about her sister's affair with her husband. Don't you think?"

"So you still think she might be guilty?"

"I think the way she chased us with that broom demonstrated a lack of stability and an abundance of rage."

Granny rolled down her window. "The woman is grieving, Amy. Her husband and her sister were both murdered. Of course she's enraged."

"We still don't know where she was the night Gerard died. Without that information we can't dismiss her as a suspect, not yet."

Suddenly, bright lights shone through my back window and almost blinded me. I held up my arm to block the light and looked in my rearview mirror. A big, black Jeep was behind us and Sandra was at the wheel. She slammed on the gas and revved up her engine.

"Oh my goodness, Granny. She's chasing us!"

Granny turned around to look at the Jeep, then she looked over at me, eyes wide. "Drive like you've never driven before, little girl."

I slammed my foot on the gas and took off down the suburban street. Granny gripped her armrests and sat back. "Faster. She's coming around on my side! She's driving on the sidewalk."

I looked over. The Jeep was indeed up on the sidewalk. Sandra's window was down and she was shouting expletives at me and Granny. "Looks like we found our guilty party," I said.

"Yeah! Now make a getaway before she kills us too!"

I made one quick turn and then another. Sandra stuck with me. Finally, I saw my opening. We were headed toward train tracks and the gates were lowering because the train was approaching. I went faster. Granny gripped my arm. "Amy, don't do it."

I tightened my grip on the wheel. "Don't have a choice, Granny."

I crossed the train tracks one second before the train came barreling past. As soon as I was safely through, Granny and I burst out in relieved laughter. Sandra got stuck behind me, waiting for the train to pass. I let out an adrenaline-filled exhale. That was close.

I cheered and kept speeding. Where? I wasn't sure.

"You did it," said Granny. "You almost killed us, but you did it."

I let out another laugh and so did Granny. Then I heard the sirens behind me. I checked my rearview mirror and there was a police squad car with its cherry lights blazing. I hung my head. "We might have celebrated too soon."

I rolled down my window as a police officer approached. I heard the voice before I saw the face. "Pretty wild driving for a pet grooming van, miss."

I looked up at the cop.

Yeah, you guessed it. It was Mike Fine. He had a tiny smirk pulling at the edges of his mouth. "Are you two in the middle of an action movie I'm not aware of?"

I gave Mike a big smile. "It's a long story."

"I'm not a big reader."

Granny leaned forward. "So what? Stories come in all forms. Not just books. There's TV shows, movies, plays."

"I like action movies," said Mike.

"That's the second time you've mentioned action movies in this short conversation," I said.

Mike scratched his head. "I guess so. What can I say? I'm a typical man."

Granny leaned even further forward. "As a typical man, do you think maybe you can let us go with a warning because Amy is such a pretty girl?"

"Granny," I said.

Mike laughed. "Sure, I think I can do that." He squatted down so he was on my eye level. "But you need to stop snooping around this closed investigation."

The tribal drums went rat-a-tat-a-tat in my throat. "We're not doing any snooping."

"I heard you stopped by Gerard's apartment again," Mike said.

"Every girl needs a place to live."

"I also know for a fact you've been by the Kirsch house in Toluca North. What did you say to that lady? She seemed pretty mad, chasing you through the streets like that."

I squinted up at Mike. "You saw all that?"

"I saw bits and pieces. You were going so fast I lost you a few times. So I took the service road, cut you off on the other side of the tracks."

"Not a bad idea," I said.

"I see a lot of action movies."

Granny groaned, probably feeling impatient with the light flirting. "Give us a ticket or let us go. I need to go to the bathroom."

"I'll let you go this time because of the prettiness," said Mike. "But stop tracking this killer. We're onto you."

"It sounds to me like you're still tracking the killer yourself," I said. "But I have this distinct memory of you telling me the cops were dropping the case. Did I hallucinate that?"

Mike stood and patted the hood of my car twice. "Get out of here. Keep your noses out of other people's business."

I drove away, going the speed limit. Suddenly, I realized I had no idea where I was headed next. All I knew was that my knuckles were white and danger could be lurking around any corner.

50

EX-COMMUNICATED

I don't know how it happened, but that night I ended up with Puppy in one arm, and my laptop open to Facebook as I looked through old pictures of me and Furball, my ex. Sometimes I just ended up there when I was feeling lost, confused, or lonely. There were so many pictures. Me and him at the Grand Canyon. The two of us at Disney World. So many photos of us giggling together in the wilderness. We were happy in the photos. Smiling. But looking at the pictures that night did not put a smile to my face. Still, I scrolled and scrolled and scrolled. A few times, Puppy wiggled around, probably trying to stop me from this futile pursuit, but his cute little motions did nothing to sway me.

I only snapped out of the doom scroll because my phone rang. It was Betsy. "Hey Betsy."

"Get on your dancing clogs because I'm having a dance party at my place. Twenty minutes. Be there."

The photo on my laptop showed me and my ex eating at a fancy restaurant somewhere in New York City, I think. I felt my stomach knot up with sadness when I looked at it. "I'm not sure I'm in the mood for dancing tonight."

"Please can we save time in this conversation by just cutting to the part where you say you're going to come over to my dance party?"

"Let's see—"

"Bring Granny, too."

I looked over at Granny's chair, where Fluffy sat, mostly hidden under a pile of blankets. That cat was such a weirdo. "Granny's out playing poker. She said something about Swedish tourists. I don't know. I think she's getting rich."

"Oh I get it," said Betsy. "You're feeling lost and confused. Although you're so often a beacon of hope in the lives of others, you don't know where to go with your murder investigation, and you're feeling hopeless. To top it off you're probably sitting on Facebook, wallowing in self-pity about your mudslide of a love life."

I laughed. "OK. You might be close."

"Slam the laptop closed and get over here. No open-toed shoes. I'm a stomper."

I reached out and grabbed the lid of the laptop. One more glance at the photo and then the laptop was closed.

Nineteen minutes later, I knocked on the door to Betsy's tiny home. She opened it with a smile, wearing a silver sequined dress and hiking boots. "Welcome to the fiesta, Amy." Betsy grabbed her phone, pressed play and a disco song started.

"Love the dress, Betsy. Lot of different vibes going on here."

Betsy winked. Or at least I think it was a wink. One of her eyes spasmed. "And I love your black sweatshirt covered in Fluffy hair. Get in here."

I stepped inside. Betsy closed the door behind me and

then paused the music. "Don't worry. We're not going to be dancing to music that's playing off of a phone. Adam's coming over with speakers or something soon."

"I wasn't worried, Betsy. I'm not convinced anything could put me in a disco-fiesta-clogging mood."

Betsy flopped onto the couch and gave me a serious look. "What's wrong? Is your brain still in Facebook territory? Open up your account and let me see those pictures right now."

I sat next to Betsy. She grabbed a bag of potato chips from the floor and handed it to me. I grabbed a handful without thinking and popped them in my mouth. "I think I'm getting a little freaked out about this investigation. I know that's not like me. Usually I have such confidence. And I know, deep down, we're going to solve this thing. But I'm not sure what to do next."

"Let's talk it out before Adam gets here," Betsy said. "Spill."

I ate another handful of chips then unloaded all the details of the case onto Betsy. Betsy listened with a furrowed brow. Then, once she was all caught up, she stood and paced. "So Kitty Kat claimed Sandra knew all about Gerard and Lovey. But when you confronted Sandra about the affair she seemed surprised. Is it possible Kitty Kat is throwing you off a scent somehow? Could she be the murderer?"

I shook my head. "No. Although I suppose it is possible Kitty Kat gave us bad information. I've only met her a couple of times but I can tell she loves gossip, and she's probably not that concerned with its veracity. Plus, she's a hairdresser, so she probably gets all the juicy details about every single woman in town, true or invented. Maybe she got some of those details confused."

Betsy poured herself a glass of ginger ale and chugged it.

"It sounds to me like you think Sandra's surprise was genuine. It seems like your gut is telling you Sandra is not a good suspect in this murder."

"You're right, that is what my gut is telling me. And I suppose that's why Granny and I aren't pursuing her."

"Good. So we can cross Sandra off the list. Are you starting to feel better?"

"I am, thank you," I said.

Betsy jumped off the couch, did three big twirls and then gave me a strange curtsy. "At your service, boss." Betsy flopped back onto the couch to catch her breath from the twirls. "Now you need to start thinking straight again because if you don't figure this thing out you could end up in jail. Maybe not for murder, if the cops aren't treating this as a homicide, but for snooping. Who knows what the sentence is for unlawful snooping these days? Could be years! Jail's not a good place for a woman who just started a business. The bills are going to pile up. Before long, you'll be buried in debt, your credit will be ruined, and then you won't know where to turn. Six years from now, you'll be living off the grid in the desert, eating lizards and telling yourself they taste like candy. Lizards are not candy, Amy. That's disgusting."

Suddenly, a loud power ballad started playing from somewhere in front of Betsy's house. The volume was so high I could feel it rattling my rib cage. Betsy skipped to the front door and flung it open. I joined her at the front door to find Adam, the guy who loved Betsy, standing on the lawn holding an enormous boombox above his head.

"This incredibly loud love song is a symbol of my devotion to you, Betsy."

Betsy winced. "Turn it off. You're going to freak out the neighbors."

"Oh thank goodness." Adam lowered the boombox with great effort, placed it down, and turned it off. "That thing is so heavy I think my arms were about to fall off."

Betsy turned to me. "He doesn't have good upper body strength."

"But what I lack in biceps I make up for with emotional intelligence," said Adam, smiling.

It was clear the two of them expected a reply from me. But my attention was focused on the boombox Adam had just lowered. Watching him place the boombox down reminded me of Gerard Crimper's death. He had been bashed in the head with a speaker. For the whole investigation we had somehow overlooked that fact.

But in that moment I was convinced the boombox was going to lead us straight to the killer. And I knew exactly what to do.

51

FLUFFY'S TAIL, PART SIX

*I*t's hard to watch the woman who loves you spend all night clicking through Facebook, eyes welling with tears, shoulders slumped. For one thing, you're powerless to help her feel better. Sure, you can sit on her lap or rub up against her leg. I did those things. But she barely noticed. Nor did she notice when I climbed under my blanket fort and did my best to look cute.

Yes, it was frustrating watching Amy click from one picture, to another, to another. I was also frustrated because she was sitting right in the kitchen and I knew my adversary, the mouse, wouldn't come out unless Amy left. I was on pins and needles when Betsy called, urging Amy to go over to Betsy's place for a dance party. Yes, I thought. Go dance. It will make you feel better and it will get you out of the house to clear the way for my stakeout.

If I could have crossed the toes on my paws I would have. But all I could do was wait and urge Amy to leave with the power of my mind.

When she finally left, locking the door behind her, I jumped up to the windowsill to make sure she wasn't coming back. Then, after a few moments, I sat in silence and waited for the mouse to make a move, either for a cookie or for my tuna. It didn't take long. After less than ten minutes, I heard that all-too-familiar rustling in the cookie cabinet and I knew the tiny little burglar was hard at work.

To catch her, I would need to jump from the refrigerator to the top of the cabinet. It was a great distance, longer than any I had jumped in the past, but I had no choice except to try.

I jumped from the floor, to the counter, to the coffee machine, to the top of the refrigerator. Then I set my sights on the top of the cabinet. The distance had once seemed impossible to me, but desperation makes all things feel possible.

Once, when living with Gerard Crimper, I'd heard him talking about the magic of mental visualization as it applies to enhancing one's skills at a musical instrument. Gerard claimed that he could improve his understanding of the guitar and his ability to play challenging solos by thinking through the solos while he was driving or at the supermarket. At first, I hadn't believed him. The solos featured in the songs of *Liquid Staple* were little more than noise to me and they all sounded so simplistic I doubted they required any advanced visualization techniques. But then Gerard's abilities improved, often after he had spent the day out and about.

And I realized maybe there was some truth to his claims about the powers of visualization.

I felt a little silly, but I closed my eyes and visualized myself jumping from the refrigerator to the top of the cabinet. In my mind's eye, I saw my body flying through the air like a bird. I saw myself landing on all four feet, unbothered by my journey through the sky. And I felt the thrill of victory coursing through my veins. When I opened my eyes, I backed up a few steps, preparing for launch. Jump for justice, I thought. Jump to keep this home safe from intruders.

I got a running start and leapt. As I soared through the air I felt that time froze all around me. Somehow I could see myself almost from above. I could feel the weight of the air beneath me, propping me up and supporting my journey. Confidence surged from my paws through my back and tail.

Then, as if waking from a dream, I was on top of the cabinet. I listened. The sound of my landing must have scared the mouse because I didn't hear any rustling for almost a full minute. I stayed still as I listened, hoping that my stillness would lull the mouse into a false sense of security.

It worked.

Eventually, the sound of the rustling resumed. Once again, I made use of Gerard's visualization techniques. That time, I imagined myself dropping into the cabinet and catching the mouse in the act of eating the cookie. I visualized the look of shock on the face of the mouse and I felt anticipation jolt through my limbs.

The time is now, I thought. Assert yourself. Protect your kingdom. Live like a leader.

I glanced over at the puppy, wondering if he was watching, curious if he had any idea the act of service I was about to perform for him. Of course, the dog was aggressively playing with a ball like it was the greatest thing on earth.

I shook my head, turned back to the cabinet, and nudged it open with my paw. The rustling sounds did not stop. I continued to nudge the cabinet door open half an inch at a time until there was enough space for me to slip through and drop into the cabinet.

Once again, it was as if waking from a dream that I found myself suddenly in the cabinet. And there, less than ten inches away from me, was a pudgy little gray mouse nibbling a chocolate chip cookie. The mouse had enormous brown eyes and a white stomach and a little tail that moved a bit while she ate. The mouse froze in horror when she saw me but when her eyes met mine, all my contempt turned into something awful. Something like...affection.

The mouse was adorable, OK? She was so cute, she deserved all the cookies in the world. I felt silly for wasting my time pursuing such an adorable creature like she was a villain. This little mouse was just trying to eat like all of us. She didn't need to be set free, she needed to be welcomed into the home.

I extended my right paw toward the mouse. The mouse took a few cautious steps toward me, her nose twitching with fearful curiosity. She had the cutest little ears and a friendly, open face.

"Go on, little mouse," I said. "Don't be scared. I want to be your friend." What was I saying? This was heresy, I knew, but I couldn't help it. I spoke the truth.

The mouse rubbed her head on my paw. I'm not a cat prone to surges of emotion, or really anything bordering on the maudlin. But, my whiskers, when that mouse nudged her tiny face into the pink pads of my paw, I think I melted. Just a tiny bit! And I refroze immediately. But for a second there, that mouse had me in her miniature, painfully cute clutches.

Suddenly, Puppy barked at the top of his shrill, awful lungs. The sound of the bark scared the mouse and before I knew it, the creature had disappeared from the cabinet. I heard her scurrying in the ceiling above me and within seconds, the sounds were gone.

The disappearance of the mouse left me feeling an unfamiliar way, perhaps...something like what humans call loneliness. Yet I knew deep down, the rodent and I would meet again. Ours would be a lasting friendship.

As long as that stupid puppy didn't get in the way.

52

ALL BETS ARE OFF

"*A*re you sure you want to call that bet, Dirk? I'm not bluffing." Granny placed her cards face down on the table.

Dirk bit his bottom lip. He looked at the spectators gathered around the poker table at the *Commerce Casino*. Everyone waited with baited breath. "Yes, I'm sure. I'm a principled man and I'm going to stick with my convictions. I don't care what happens, as long as—"

Granny turned up her cards to reveal she had a pair of aces. Dirk slammed his cards on the table, pushed his chair back with a squeak, and hurried away. "I need to go to the restroom. I'm not going to cry so nobody start any rumors."

Granny shook her head as she raked the heaping pile of chips toward her seat. "I told him not to call. You all heard it."

I cleared my throat. "Granny."

Granny turned back and smiled when she saw me. "Oh hey, kid. You here for a little taste of the fast life? Take a seat in Dirk's spot. Something tells me he won't be back for a while. The guy cries slower than molasses."

I leaned down and whispered in Granny's ear. "I need to talk to you about the case. I've had a breakthrough."

Granny gave me a quick nod and then addressed the fellow players at the table. "OK, everyone. I'm getting a little tired of winning so I'm going to stretch my legs with my granddaughter. No one steal my chips while I'm gone. I counted them."

Granny walked over to an ancient, dusty vending machine along a far wall. I followed her. "Alright what do you need to tell me?" Granny said. "I don't trust those people around my money. I need to get back to the table."

"Right, sorry," I said. "I think I had a realization. See, I was just over at Betsy's place and this guy Adam came over and he was carrying this huge speaker and—"

"Get to the realization." Granny shoved a few quarters into the vending machine and out popped a Dr. Pepper. She took a big sip. "Oh how I'm pleased by the Pepper. This stuff is so good."

"Gerard was killed by someone who bashed a speaker on his head," I said. "I think the speaker is more than the murder weapon. I think it's also linked to the motivation of the killer and it's a clue to their identity. Do you want to guess or do you want me to come out with my accusation?"

Granny took another sip of her Dr Pepper. "Hold on I'm thinking. I'm letting the Dr. Pepper soak into my brain to give me ideas. Let's see... You think the fact that Gerard Crimper was killed by a speaker indicates who the killer was and what their motivation was." Granny grabbed a couple of folding chairs off the wall, opened them up and took a seat on one. I sat next to her. Then she snapped her fingers and looked right at me. "My good old friend Eleanor. She told us herself she hated the sound of Gerard's guitars and all the loud music he always played. You think she finally snapped when he wouldn't turn it down and bashed him with the speaker?"

I nodded. "Yep. I think Eleanor spent years and years begging Gerard to turn his music down. Gerard refused so then Eleanor began bashing the ceiling of the bakeshop with her broom. She created her own noise hoping he may turn the music down. That's how the ceiling got damaged. There's no plumbing problem there and there's no other evidence of water damage in the bakeshop. She was having those guys repair the crack in the ceiling that she caused herself. I'm sure she figures she might as well fix the ceiling now that Gerard is dead. She won't have any need to bang on it anymore."

Granny took another big sip of Dr. Pepper. "It's a strong theory, Amy. But I'm not sure I'm convinced. Eleanor is so nice. I've known the woman for quite awhile and I've never seen her seek out confrontation. She's not the type to bang on the ceiling and she's certainly not the type to murder. I mean, I guess any of us can be pushed past our limits to do something that's objectively wrong... And maybe I shouldn't tease Dirk so much at the poker table... But I just don't know. Besides, Eleanor is a little old lady. You said the speaker was heavy. I don't think she's strong enough to lift up one of those things, let alone kill someone with it."

I shrugged. "People are capable of incredible strength when they're angry or otherwise filled with adrenaline. And it's possible she knocked the speaker off the shelf and it killed Gerard unintentionally."

"I guess that makes sense," said Granny. "So what now?"

I stood. "Now we need to go find Eleanor."

Granny put her hand on my arm. "Amy. We don't need to go find Eleanor. She wanted more of a social life, remember? I invited her to poker. She's on her way here."

53

POKE HER FACE

I paced back and forth outside the recreation center, smartphone to my ear, waiting for someone at the Toluca Lake Police Department to pick up.

"Just hang up already," said Granny. "Samuel's probably asleep at his desk. Rotund, I'm sure is buried in a pile of French fries. And who knows where Officer Handsome is. Probably spellchecking a love note he wrote to you. No offense, but the kid isn't the brightest bulb in the box. I'm sure there are plenty of errors for him to catch. And more than a few that he'll miss."

I hung up the phone. "This is so annoying. Just when we finally have a real suspect the cops are unreachable? Officer Handsome, I mean Mike, has been around every corner since Gerard turned up dead. And now I can't find him anywhere? Ridiculous."

"I agree." Granny crushed her soda can with her foot, picked it up and tossed it in the recycling bin. "That's the whole reason we took on this case in the beginning. The police in Toluca Lake are well-meaning but inept. So this town needs amateur sleuths like me and you and I guess Betsy to keep things on the straight and narrow."

A squeaky old Buick sedan cruised toward the casino at about two miles per hour and parked in a nearby handicapped spot. "That must be her," I said.

Granny shrugged. "I guess. But we don't get a lot of speeding drivers attending these poker games, if you know what I mean. Could be anyone."

I shushed Granny as the Buick door opened and Eleanor emerged. The little woman took a moment to straighten her clothes and grabbed her handbag. Then she pulled a cane out of the car and hobbled toward the casino entrance.

"OK, Granny. Here comes a big showdown. Our number one suspect is coming toward us. She might be a dangerous woman. That cane might be a shotgun in disguise."

"You sound crazy, Amy. All we need to do is accuse her and she'll start blubbering and spill the whole thing." Granny waved to Eleanor. "Hey, Ellie. Over here."

Eleanor spotted us and gave us a big smile and a wave. "Girls! It's such a beautiful night tonight. It's so rare to see stars like this near Los Angeles. Not movie stars, the kind in the sky. Back in the day you could see the Big Dipper every night, before light pollution."

"I bet that was also before Toluca Lake had become such a dangerous place," I said. "Long before people like Gerard Crimper, innocent enough, turned up dead in their apartments...bashed by a speaker."

Eleanor furrowed her brow. "You sound upset, Amy. Your voice is so much less pretty when you're upset. What happened? Did you get your heart broken again?"

"No, I did not get my heart broken again. I don't just run around letting every man I meet devastate me."

"You kind of do, though," said Granny. "A little bit. I'm just saying, you don't pick them well."

"Thanks, Granny." I took a step toward Eleanor and crossed my arms. "I sound upset because I think you hurt Gerard Crimper."

Eleanor stopped walking. "You — you do?"

I read somewhere that silence is the most important tool in an interrogation situations. So I didn't speak.

"You do understand, I'd been patient with the man for so long," said Eleanor. "It's not easy having a neighbor like that. *Liquid Staple* isn't a good musical group. Mind you, I'm not against heavy metal as a genre just because I'm an older woman. I think *Metallica* has quite a few tasteful tunes and I enjoy a nice double bass drum. But I'm trying to run a business out of that building!"

"She has a point," said Granny.

"So what did you do to him?" I said. "Just come out with it."

"For so long, I did nothing. My mother taught me to be kind, always. She lived by the Golden Rule and so did I. Until..." Eleanor's chin quivered. She clutched the handle of her cane so tight her knuckles almost vanished into the white handle. "A few months back, I started banging on the ceiling to quiet him. Every time I heard the music I took my broom and I jabbed at the ceiling so loud and so hard. The first few times, it worked. He would turn off the music and he would keep it off all day. No one likes an angry lady banging on the ceiling. But after Sandra left him, the man was incorrigible. I would bang on the ceiling and he would turn the music down. But then after five minutes the music would be back at top volume. It was ruining my business."

I swallowed. "So you killed him?"

Eleanor's jaw dropped. "What?! No! I didn't kill Gerard Crimper. He was my neighbor. What kind of Golden Rule would that be?"

I scratched my head. Looked over at Granny. She shrugged. "So what did you do?" I said.

"That day, the day Gerard died...I marched right up those steps and I yelled at him. I want to say I gave him a good piece of my mind but I gave him the bad piece. I used a four letter word, Petunia. I'm not proud to admit it. But I was at the very end of my rope. The music was loud, as always. But I also discovered that he had written a terrible review of the bakeshop online and dozens of people had liked it. He said I was an inhospitable and angry woman and that I was incapable of baking with love. Can you believe that? Love is my number one ingredient!"

Dirk approached with his hands clasped. "Petunia. We're thinking about switching over to Omaha high/low split. Does that work for you?"

"Yeah, sure," said Granny. "Go back to the table. I'll be there soon."

Eleanor hung her head. "Gerard died before I had a chance to apologize for my tirade. I wish I could have talked to him before he passed so I could have told him I was sorry. And, maybe, I could have convinced him to take down that horrible review. Now that he's dead, his words will live forever."

"Don't worry too much, Eleanor," I said. "I'm sorry I suspected you like that. And I'm going to have to take Granny on a little mission right now so she's not going to be able to play with you tonight. I'm sorry about that too."

I hurried toward the *Creature Comforts* van in the parking lot. Granny followed behind me. "Where are we going? This better be good if I'm missing the switch to Omaha!"

I called back. "It is. Trust me!"

54

BUNCH A HUNCH

"*W*hat is going on, kid? You're scaring me."

"You'll see in a second." I climbed inside the van. Seconds later, Granny got into her seat and I locked the doors.

"Now can you tell me what's up please," said Granny. "Poor Eleanor. Usually I'm not one for sympathy, but we got that girl all upset and then we ran away like she was the devil or something. Look at her out there."

I looked back toward the building. Eleanor was standing where we had left her, looking around in confusion. I felt bad but I didn't have time to explain anything to Eleanor. My hunch was too big and nagging to ignore. I pulled out my smartphone and opened to the review site. Granny leaned over to look at what I was doing. "Are you reviewing something right now? I'm so lost."

I didn't look up from my phone. "I'm pretty sure this whole thing comes back to reviews."

"But what do you mean?" Granny asked with insistence in her voice.

"Hold on, I'm searching." I pulled up the page for the *Big*

Baby Diner. "Look here. The *Big Baby* has 453 good reviews and only three bad reviews. Gerard left one of those bad reviews, we already know that."

Granny gasped. "Don't tell me... You think Lovey left one of the other bad reviews for the diner? You think Apollo is going around killing anybody who talks trash about his restaurant online?"

"There's only one way to tell." I hovered my finger over the button for the three bad reviews and then pressed it. The page went blank and then a little spinning wheel popped up to indicate that the bad reviews were loading. Granny tapped her knee with quick motions as if that might hurry things along.

"Come on, come on," said Granny.

At last, the three bad reviews populated. "Here they are," I said, scrolling through the page. "The first review is from Gerard Crimper. He had a lot of horrible things to say about the diner. The second bad review is from Tommy Flynn. Apparently he goes there every day to pick up food for voters and sometimes the burgers are so greasy the grease rips the bag. He also seems to think the food takes too long."

"I believe that," said Granny. "What about the last review? Is it from—"

"Lovey Kirsch." I put my hand to my heart. "Yes. The third review is from Lovey." I'm not sure why the tears welled in my eyes. Could Lovey and Gerard really have been killed over a couple of bad online reviews? That felt so wrong it hurt.

"Read it," said Granny. "What did Lovey write?"

I swallowed and blinked back the tears, then began reading:

"Are you looking for a rundown diner experience that's sure to disappoint? The *Big Baby* will deliver that and more.

When I was a kid, this place was a shimmering, clean establishment with delicious food and great hospitality. The first French fry I ever tasted came from the *Big Baby Diner*. That fry was crisp, hot, and perfectly salted. I'll never forget it. But I came here to eat yesterday and the French fries were soggy.

I told my waiter about the problem and asked if he could make some new fries. Then the owner of the place, Apollo, came over and yelled at me. He was stern and gruff and he made me feel stupid. I'm sorry, is it wrong for me to expect crispy French fries in keeping with the *Big Baby* tradition?

Whatever. Ultimately the guy said he'd make me new fries, so I decided I'd wait for them. I had already come a long way, I didn't want to leave hungry! Well, let me tell you, the second batch of fries took forever. The fries took so long, in fact, I needed to visit the restroom before the food arrived. That's when the real problem started.

Let me tell you something, if you own a restaurant, one of the most important things is a clean bathroom. If your bathroom isn't clean, I'm sure your kitchen is filthy and that means your food is probably poisonous. There were flies in the bathroom at this place. The faucet was crusted with moldy junk. It was an abomination. Look, I get it, it's hard to keep a place in perfect condition all the time. I don't blame the staff for this. I blame that guy Apollo. Maybe he's too busy yelling at customers to make sure the bathrooms stay clean. I'll tell you what, I had lunch at *Mel's Diner* in Hollywood last week and their bathrooms were spotless. Plus, their French fries were crisp and delicious. Just saying. Whatever. I would write more but I've already given too much of myself to this place. I'm never going back to the *Big Baby Diner* and neither should you. One star because there's a nice, big parking lot."

Granny covered her mouth. "That's one of the worst

reviews I've ever heard in my life and I've lived a little while now. The *Big Baby* never seems that bad to me."

I shook my head. "No. Every time I've been in there the bathrooms are clean. Maybe she really was there on an off day or something."

"Maybe she was sabotaging the business with malice," said Granny. "Hey, I don't know, it's possible."

"So this means…"

Granny nodded. "Apollo is our killer. And if history is any indication, he's going after Mayor Tommy Flynn next."

55

DRIVING MISS PETUNIA

*U*nder normal circumstances I'm a very safe driver. But my driving had been erratic, at best, since arriving back in Toluca Lake. And that night as we searched for Tommy, I went so fast in the van I was afraid Granny's dentures would fall out of her mouth.

My first stop was the mayor's official residence, a stately brick home just a block from Town Hall. The residence was an uncommon perk for small-town mayors but that had been written into the town constitution many years ago. Although townspeople had often rallied for the town to sell the mayoral residence as a way to save money or cut taxes, the motions never passed. Although if any mayor was going to be enough of a push over to give up the big house near town, it would have to be Tommy Flynn...that is, if he was still alive.

We pulled up to the front of the house and I slammed on the brakes. "I'm going to see if he's home."

Granny nodded. "Run. You're faster than me."

"You think?" I jumped out of the van, darted up the front steps two at a time, and knocked on the front door. No one answered. I rang the bell but still got no reply. Running as fast as I could, I scurried around the back and looked up at the home. Every single light in the house was off. "Where are you Tommy?" I said to no one. "Are you in there?"

"I don't think we have time to break in and find out," said Granny, approaching from the side yard.

"I thought you were waiting in the car."

"I got bored and you're taking forever. Maybe the kid is still at work. Let's check at town hall."

Less than five minutes later, I pulled up to Town Hall, my brakes again screeching as I stopped. "You want to come with me this time?" I said.

"No. I'm a little tired from chasing you around that big house back there. You go ahead."

"What if it's not safe out here?" I asked. "Maybe you should come with me."

"If anyone wanted me dead, I'd be dead already, sweetheart."

Town Hall, like the mayor's residence, was pitch black. Nonetheless, I tried the front door. It was locked. Then I ran around the side of the building to get a look at the parking lot. There wasn't a single car there.

"He must not be here, either," said Granny, approaching from behind me.

I shrieked and jumped back. "Quit doing that. If you're going to come with me to investigate you need to come from the beginning. You're going to give me a heart attack."

"You keep taking too long. If I knew this was going to be a big snooze fest I would've brought a poker book."

"This isn't a snooze fest, Granny. We're literally hot on the heels of the Bad Review Killer."

"Oooh. Nice nickname."

"Thank you," I said.

"Maybe we should have looked more at the house," said Granny. "What if Apollo has Tommy in the basement? He could be torturing the poor kid. I don't want Tommy to die. I heard he might run for president next cycle. Sure, tradition says you need to be thirty-five, but the American people have never been brought a sandwich by someone quite like him."

"No more jokes," I said, running back toward the car. "I have an idea."

The next place we visited was Apollo's place of business, the *Big Baby Diner*. The diner was a 24-hour restaurant but all the lights were off, so I knew something was wrong as soon as we arrived.

Granny scratched her cheek. "The *Big Baby* is closed. I don't like that. I mean, this place hasn't been closed since the time of the dinosaurs."

I took a deep breath and let it out. "Let's go try to find out why."

We stepped out of the *Creature Comforts* van and onto the sidewalk. Granny blazed a path straight toward the front entrance but I caught her arm to stop her. "Hold on a second. I know we're amateur sleuths and we're fearless and all that. But I think it would be irresponsible if we didn't at least try to call the cops right now."

Granny buried her head in her hands. "Fine. Call them again. I'm sure it's just going to ring a hundred times."

I put the phone on speaker and Chief Samuel picked up after one ring.

I explained the situation, speaking as quick as I could. There were fifteen seconds of silence, then Samuel responded in a slow croak, "I'll send someone to check it out as soon as I get a second."

"No. You don't understand. You have to send someone—"

Samuel hung up. Granny looked at me as if to say, what did you expect?

"OK, you're right about the police. But I don't think we have time to wait for them. We need to find out what's up at the diner."

The front and side doors were locked. Then I led Granny around back and noticed that the kitchen door was cracked open just a fraction of an inch. I pointed toward the door. "Let's go in that way. Be quiet."

"You be quiet," said Granny. "I'm always quiet."

I shushed Granny and then crept toward the door. When I got close enough I reached out and opened it a couple of feet, then Granny and I slipped inside. We had entered into some kind of storage area. Metal shelves were lined with cooking oils and potatoes. And there were cleaning supplies stacked in the corner across the room. Granny pointed out the cleaning supplies. "Oh look, a mop and a broom. Maybe Apollo wouldn't be in this situation if he and his staff had learned to use those things."

The sound of talking emanated from deep within the kitchen. I turned back to Granny and whispered. "Do you hear that?"

She nodded.

I took another step toward the main part of the kitchen and heard what can only be described as evil laughter along with the sound of muffled straining and gagging. I took another step, then peered around the shelf to get a look inside the kitchen.

Mayor Tommy Flynn was tied up on a stool near the stove and Apollo was force-feeding him an enormous cheeseburger. "Tell me the cheeseburger's greasy now, Tommy. Oh wait, you can't. You're suffocating."

I took a big step into the room. "Drop the burger and step away from the mayor!"

Apollo spun and looked at me. "You... What... What are you doing here?"

"Better question," said Granny, "is what are you doing here?"

"Nothing."

"You're force-feeding our baby mayor cheeseburgers, man" said Granny. "We just saw it happen."

Tommy groaned and nodded his head in agreement.

"OK fine." Apollo's demeanor darkened and turned angry. "You got me. I'm force-feeding the mayor cheeseburgers. But that's not all I've force-fed him tonight! He's also eaten all the other foods he criticized at my diner. Banana cream pie. Chocolate covered donut. Milkshake. Chicken fingers. Omelettes. Plus I made him drink a whole pot of quote unquote 'burned' coffee." Apollo threw back his head and laughed.

Tommy strained at his bindings. He tried to speak but his mouth was full of cheeseburger. I took a step toward Apollo, then another. He grabbed a butcher knife off the counter and walked toward me. As he approached, I thought back to all the survival skills I'd learned from my father in the wilderness. Make loud noises. Attack the throat. Stay low. Don't let them see your fear.

"Careful, Amy," Granny said.

Apollo laughed. "There's no use being careful. She's going to die just like the others. All three of you are."

Apollo lunged at me. I sidestepped the blade of the knife, then grabbed two pans from a hanging rack and banged them together. Apollo stumbled back, confused. "What are you doing?"

I tossed one of the pans at Apollo. He dropped the knife to catch the pan and I seized the moment, rushing toward him. Before Apollo had a chance to use the pan I had thrown, I hit him over the head with my pan and he fell to the ground.

I walked toward Apollo and knelt on his back to try to keep him down.

"Amy, catch!" Granny tossed me a spool of kitchen twine. I caught the twine and used it to tie Apollo's hands behind his back. I used the Palomar knot, which my dad had taught me when I was a kid. The Palomar is impossible to slip, and I also use it on leashes. But never until that moment did I think I'd use it on a killer! After I tied Apollo's hands, I tied up his feet, then I stood and looked over at Granny.

When I stood, Granny had already freed Mayor Tommy from his bindings and he had managed to spit out the cheeseburger. "Amy," he said. "Thank you. I think I'm gonna..."

Tommy rushed over to the sink and vomited. Granny clapped him on the back. "Poor kid's never gonna eat a cheeseburger again."

Tommy looked back at Granny. "Or drink coffee."

Granny chuckled. "You're too young for coffee anyway."

Suddenly the lights flipped on and a voice boomed from near the back door. "Hands up! Everyone put your hands up."

I turned to find Mike and Detective Rotund brandishing their weapons and stepping into the kitchen.

Granny gave them a casual wave. "Hey, guys. You're a little late."

56

SLEEPING LIKE BIG BABIES

I slept well that night and I had a hunch Granny and Betsy did, too.

There was something about having the mystery solved and behind us that comforted me. I suppose that's obvious. It's stressful when there's a killer running around your small town murdering people. But for me, the sense of relief went deeper than that.

Until we caught Apollo, I had been questioning my decision to move back to Toluca Lake to open *Creature Comforts*. Wrapped up in that doubt was my sense of self and my confidence, two aspects of my personality that had never been shaken so hard in the past.

But can you blame me? I had chosen the catastrophically wrong guy not once, but twice. I had moved all the way across the country and then back again. And as soon as I arrived in Toluca Lake I got caught up in a big murder investigation. I think I felt that if I didn't solve the murder, my business would go under. The things weren't necessarily connected in real life, but they were in my heart. And I wasn't sure what I would have done in that scenario.

Apollo's arrest lifted so much weight off my shoulders I felt like I had gotten a gastric bypass, and it felt so good to watch Mike shove the murderous restauranter into a squad car.

Anyway, I woke the next morning feeling fresh, bright, and light as air. But when I breezed into the kitchen, I found Granny examining what appeared to be a piece of mail with a concerned look on her face. "What you looking at?" I said.

Granny pushed the paper my way. It was a pink piece of construction paper with black writing that said "*Eleanor's Bakeshop*: 5 PM. Be there."

I swallowed. My stomach gurgled with dread. "What is this? Is the killer still out there? Is this a threat?"

Granny shrugged. "I guess we'll wait until 5 PM and see."

I grabbed my smartphone. "I'm not waiting until 5 o'clock to find out if the murderer is still out there. I'm calling Eleanor. Maybe—"

Granny smiled and snatched the phone for my hand. "It's not a trap, crazy! It's a surprise. Just be patient."

"But—"

"Patience, Amy!"

I sighed. "OK fine."

Granny and I spent the day grooming pets. My favorite was a wee little spaniel who kept chasing her tail while I tried to spray her down. We locked up a little before five and headed over to *Eleanor's Bakeshop.* As we got close, I noticed a crowd of people eating, talking, and laughing under a tent out on the street in front of the bakeshop.

"What are all those people doing here?"

Granny gave me a little grin. "Maybe they want to

welcome you to town? Or thank you and your heroic Granny for saving the day..."

I looked out over the crowd again and a smile spread across my face. All those people were there...for me? "Wait...what?"

After a few seconds, Eleanor pushed her way through the partiers and hurried toward me and Granny. "Girls! You're finally here! I'm so glad my guests of honor could make it. So sorry about the crude invitation. I've run out of my custom stationery and I had to make do with what I had. Plus, there was a line at the shop so I didn't have time for my calligraphy."

"Eleanor," I said. "You didn't have to do this. Thank you so much! I mean, we were barging in and out of your place for days, acting suspicious and sneaking around. I wouldn't be surprised if you were mad at us."

"You solved Gerard's murder," said Eleanor. "How could that anger me? The guy was a grouch, but he was my neighbor grouch. He deserved justice and you gave it to him. So now I'm giving you this party. Go grab a finger sandwich or a muffin. Everything is made from scratch, as always."

"Finger sandwiches always make me think there's going to be literal fingers between the slices of bread," said Granny. "I'll stick with the muffins."

Granny trudged away. Eleanor followed behind, going on about the origin of finger sandwiches and how she would never include human body parts in her food. And I hung back for a second, taking in the scene.

It was so nice to see new friends, old friends, and neighbors gathered together, celebrating. Jackie Love, Gerard's estranged son, complained loudly to a stranger about his desperate need for new teeth. My sister, Megan, led Mr. Buttons through the crowd, parading him about like the prince he was. I'm pleased to say Mr. Buttons' hairstyle had grown in nicely and he looked quite dapper that afternoon. And Mike Fine lingered by the muffins, looking at them curiously, like deciding which muffin to eat was the biggest choice he'd ever make in his life.

I smiled and approached Mike. "Picking the right muffin can be tough."

Mike looked serious. "You're right about that, Ames. But it's not as hard as catching a killer."

I pointed to a muffin in the center of the platter. "I like that one because it has a lot of muffin top, which is the most delicious part."

Mike grabbed the muffin. "I'm sold. Oh, hey, I owe you some gratitude, by the way."

"You mean because I did your job for you?" I said with a smirk.

"Hey now." Mike unwrapped the muffin with care. "I still cuffed the guy. Drove him to the station. I handled the paperwork. Paperwork is tough for me. I hate reading anything that's not wizard-based."

"I understand. It's hard to do paperwork when you could be at Hogwarts, caught up in the adventure of a lifetime."

Mike let out a nervous laugh. "Right. Hey, so, I got a promotion?"

"Are you asking me or telling me?"

"I'm telling you. And, uh, thanking you. Yeah. That's why I wanted to thank you. Samuel was so happy the murderer got locked up, he promoted both me and Rotund. So I'm a Detective now."

"Congrats," I said. "But Rotund was already a detective. What's his new title?"

Mike shrugged. "Super Detective, I guess."

"Wow," I said. "Maybe next time you guys can actually

catch the killer and the chief will step down and let you and Rotund share his job."

Mike winced. "Burn. Ouch."

"Yeah. Sorry. That was harsh. And uh... Let's both hope there is no next time."

"Deal," said Mike. "This big promotion comes with a raise, by the by. So as a token of my gratitude... maybe I can take you to some snobby restaurant in downtown LA for something? We could eat snails or whatever snobby people eat. Man, I take that back. I can't believe anyone eats snails, even French people. I mean, snails are the boogers of the earth."

My eyes widened. Mike was asking me out and I wasn't sure if it was as friends or potential... something else. But my heartbreak still felt fresh and I wasn't sure I was ready for a new romance.

Thankfully, Betsy barged her way into the conversation before I had time to answer.

She slapped both me and Mike on the back and gave us a huge smile. "Hey, team. Oh man, that was a tough one. I did a lot, I was integral in the investigation, I know. But you two are the true heroes. And Granny, where is that tough old oak tree of a woman?"

"I'm not sure where she is." Mike pointed toward the other side of the crowd. "But look over there."

I looked over where Mike was pointing to find Tommy Flynn kissing an older woman with passion. I squinted to get a better look. "Whoa. Who is the mayor kissing?"

"I can't believe anyone would kiss Tommy," said Betsy. "Don't get me wrong, the guy is nice, but I could never kiss the man who brings me my sandwiches."

Tommy and the woman separated. I glimpsed her face and my jaw hit the floor. "Oh my goodness. Tommy is kissing Sandra Crimper! I bet you anything Sandra was with Tommy the night Gerard died! That's why she had no alibi. She was ashamed to be having an affair with her 20-year-old, sandwich-toting mayor."

"Makes sense to me." Betsy groaned as the couple kissed again. "But I can't watch this public affection any longer. I need a muffin to wash the taste out."

Mike broke a piece off his muffin. "You should let Amy help you pick. She's got great taste in muffins."

"I think I can handle it myself," said Betsy. "Although, Amy, I'm curious which one looks good to you..."

I laughed and selected a plump strawberry muffin for Betsy. Then I wandered into the crowd and chatted with the people of Toluca Lake. The party carried on for hours. It was a lot of fun. And I only thought about Mike's dinner invitation a few hundred times, which I think was good.

Later that night, after Granny and I helped Eleanor clean up the party, the two of us strolled through the back roads, taking the long way back to Granny's apartment at *Toluca Gardens*. About halfway between town and Granny's place I spotted a cute little two-bedroom house for rent. My eyes lit up and I grabbed my phone and called the number. It rang twice and then a man picked up on the other end. "Hello?"

I took a deep breath and smiled. "Hi. I'm calling about the house for rent on Magnolia Street. Is that still available?"

Turns out, the house was furnished, affordable and move-in ready. I told the guy I'd take it and that I was ready for anything.

But nothing could have prepared me for all the adventure that was yet to come...

57

FLUFFY'S TAIL, EPILOGUE

I don't want to get all mushy or anything, but that evening while the girls were at the bakeshop party, I had a nice time hanging out with my new friend, Mouse.

It turned out she and I had lots in common. We both like to nap, for instance. And we both like to get up to mischief when Amy and Petunia leave the house. That particular night, we played a fun little game of cops and robbers or, as you might call it, cat and mouse.

The way it worked was, Mouse would grab a little chunk of tuna from my bowl and scurry away. I would give her a five or ten second head start, then I would chase after her and try to catch her before she disappeared. The girl was fast and I never managed to catch her, but after each round of the game, she came back out and we played again.

After awhile, the two of us were tuckered out. I jumped up on the armchair and rested my head on the pillow. Mouse hopped up on the pillow beside me and also napped. I looked over at Puppy and for the first time, he too seemed sleepy. I realized perhaps maybe one day he would get off the drugs, and maybe then he would be a friend as well. All in due time, I thought to myself as I drifted to sleep.

All in due time.

I'm not sure how long I slumbered but it was long enough so that when I woke up, the sun had disappeared and night had fallen. Mouse still slept beside me. Puppy was asleep in his pen. Everything should have felt peaceful. Happy, even. But my whiskers tingled and the fur on my neck stood at attention. I jumped off the couch, trotted across the room and hopped up on the windowsill. It was raining outside and thunder clapped overhead. I looked through the biggest raindrop on the windowpane, out onto sidewalk. The raindrop distorted the image, expanding it and shrinking it at once. As I sat there, I searched my soul for the source of my unease.

It didn't take long to find what was bothering me... Somewhere, deep down, I had the feeling that we would see more murders in Toluca Lake.

I'm not sure how I knew, but within a matter of months, I would be proven right. Another body showed up in Toluca Lake before Crimper's carcass was cold.

The girls would be in danger once again. And it would be up to them to keep the town safe.

The End

Dear Reader,

Thank you for reading *A New Leash On Life*, the first book in the Dog Groomer Mysteries.

My husband Matt and I spent almost ten years living just a few minutes from Toluca Lake, so we loved writing this story and we hope you liked reading it. Amy and Petunia were such fun characters in Pine Grove, but they're even more fun in their natural SoCal environment!

As Fluffy mentions at the end of this book, there will soon be another murder in Toluca Lake. But will the ladies solve the murder before they meet their own untimely demise?

I think you'll love book two in this series because everyone loves cozy mysteries with cute, tiny animals and lots of laughs.

Click here to order now.

- Chelsea

P.S. Reading on paperback? Search "Ruff and Tumble by Chelsea Thomas" on Amazon to grab your copy of book two today!